WITHDRAWN

D1637656

CHAPTER ONE
RACHEL COAST

A bell rang as I opened the shop door. The sound of its chimes startled me and broke my concentration and I looked up, searching for its source. My eyes quickly found it: an old brass bell was swinging merrily back and forth at the top of the door. With its chimes still ringing in my ears, I straightened my suit, pushed my hair back and announced myself.

'Hello, I'm Rachel Coast, the new area sales representative from Chandler's Photographic Supplies.'

This must have been the tenth time I'd introduced myself today, and by now I was sure I was relaying the words in the style of a well-trained parrot.

This was my first full-time job, and it had absolutely nothing to do with the art degree I had just obtained from three long years in university. I had, in short, made the very quick transition from 'Rachel Elizabeth Coast: Art graduate', to 'Rachel Elizabeth Coast: Area Sales Representative'.

I had had to take this job — I'd really had no choice. My rent was due and my fridge and bank account empty. My student loan days were well and truly over and, one way or another, I had to pay my way.

The alternative was too awful to even think about.

If I couldn't support myself I'd have to move in with my parents. They were great parents, don't get me wrong, but they had recently retired to a quiet rural village in Wales. Just the thought of having to live that dull existence horrified me. I *had* to stay in London and to do this I needed a job, any job, and working as area sales representative for Chandler's would have to do ... at least for now.

Today marked the end of my first week as the new area

sales representative and it had, in short, been a nightmare.

After attending a short product and sales training course, I met my boss who turned out to be a very serious and stuffy man called Mr Kenneth Turnbull. He'd handed me a very long list of potential customers to visit and sent me on my way without so much as a 'how-do-you-do'.

The shop I had just walked into was the last name on the list and I couldn't wait to get the meeting over with.

As I closed the singing door behind me a loud voice resonated from a large elderly man standing with his back to me.

'Hello, Rachel Coast. I'm Mr Jacobs.'

As he turned around, his face broke into a broad, avuncular smile. I smiled back at him, walked towards him and handed him Chandler's catalogue.

Before I had a chance to utter another word, the old brass bell on the shop door rang again. A sudden downpour of rain came through the open doorway and as I turned around I saw a guy rushing in, his shoulders and back bent over, his jacket pulled right over his head in a vain attempt to protect him from the summer rain.

'Don't you just love our British summers?' he joked.

I nodded as he pulled his jacket back on to his shoulders, stood up and straightened himself.

As soon as I saw his face I felt my nerves constrict and my cheeks redden. He looked about the same age as me, and his arrival was having a totally unexpected effect on me. I found myself unable to control my body's involuntary reactions; I could feel my cheeks reddening further and desperately hoped he hadn't noticed.

He closed the door behind him and shook his head slightly to shake off the excess rain. His dark wavy hair was wet and a drop of rain that had been clinging to it suddenly landed on my cheek. I flinched as its sharp coldness startled my hot, blushing skin. I reached up nervously and quickly wiped it away.

Mr Jacobs' voice cut through the air. 'Where the heck have you been, Austin? You know how much work there is to do!'

This guy – Austin – didn't seem bothered by Mr Jacobs' stern tone. He just looked up at him and smiled.

'Please, Dad, calm down. You know you're not supposed to get worked up. I'm sorry I'm late but it was unavoidable, there were delays on the District line. I know there's a lot to do, I'll get to work straight away.'

Mr Jacobs glared at him from under his furrowed brow. Then his face suddenly softened and in a more pleading tone he asked, 'Any news today, Austin? You know how anxious I get.' Mr Jacobs looked searchingly at his son as he waited for his reply.

'No, Dad ... I'm sorry, there's no news.'

Mr Jacobs' arms fell limply to his sides, a deflated look upon his face. 'Okay, Son. Well go and dry yourself off before you start clearing up, you don't want to catch a cold.'

'Yes, Dad. I'll get to it right away.'

As Austin walked away, he smiled at me before disappearing through the door at the back of the shop.

I turned back to look at Mr Jacobs. His head was bent and his eyes were scanning the floor. I could see that his mood had changed dramatically.

'I'm sorry, Rachel, I really can't focus on this at the moment. Could you come back another time?'

His voice was quiet, despondent.

'Of course, Mr Jacobs, no problem at all. It was a pleasure to meet you. I'll call back next week.'

Mr Jacobs' reaction was confusingly intense and totally unexpected. As I walked out of the door to the sound of the singing bell, my thoughts were tumbling in chaotic confusion. Relief was the first discernible feeling that swept over me.

This guy, this Austin Jacobs, had just reduced me to a virtual blubbering mess, and all he had to do to achieve this was to stand in the same room as me. It was ridiculous; nothing like this had ever happened to me before. The relief I felt to be out in the open air and out of this compromising situation was incomparable.

I was a curious soul at the best of times, and on this occasion even more so.

What news was Mr Jacobs hoping for, and why was he so severely disappointed when there was none?

As I walked to my car, my out of control nerves began to

settle. By the time I opened the door and turned the key in the ignition, it was safe to say that I was completely intrigued by my encounter with both Austin and Mr Jacobs.

***

Later that evening, as I sat waiting for my boyfriend, Julian, to pick me up, I found that I still couldn't stop thinking about my last call of the day. The image of Austin Jacobs striding through the singing door kept flashing through my mind. What was the content of the mysterious news — or rather, lack thereof — which had affected Mr Jacobs so badly?

Julian was sweet, tolerant and very lovely. He had persistently asked me to go out with him throughout the whole of my last year in university, and I had persistently turned him down. I had promised myself that I would avoid any distractions from my studies, and boyfriends fell into this category. Eventually, he accepted this as the status quo and waited patiently for me to finish my final exams. Tonight was our sixth date. Yet somehow, I couldn't stop thinking of Austin Jacobs and his mysterious news.

Throughout the whole evening I kept inadvertently touching my cheek where the raindrop from Austin Jacobs' hair had landed. I replayed that moment over and over again, and every time I did, my stomach flipped over.

As the evening progressed, an anxious ball of energy began to grow wildly in my stomach. The way I had reacted to Austin Jacobs today and the fact that I couldn't stop thinking about him was beginning to get the better of me. Even though I knew I hadn't actually done anything wrong, I was plagued by my conscience and I began to feel incredibly guilty. Here I was, sitting next to Julian, holding his hand whilst thinking of someone else. These uncontrollable thoughts were completely distracting me from him, and the film we'd gone to see.

By the time Julian drove me home, a quick embrace in the car was as much affection as I could muster towards him. Desperately needing time alone, I made my very apologetic excuses and hotfooted my way to my bedsit. Julian looked surprised and hurt that I was leaving him so suddenly, but he said nothing, and neither did I.

As soon as I got in, I flopped on to my three-quarter length bed. Its familiar comfort was exactly what I needed. I clutched my pillow tightly and wrapped my guilt-ridden and confused state into the reassuring comfort of my feather duvet.

The weekend passed slowly. I was supposed to meet up with Julian again but I really didn't want to, so I feigned illness and cancelled our plans. Two lazy duvet days in a row ensued, and by the time Monday morning arrived I found myself consumed by an absurd urgency to get to work. This wasn't because I had suddenly developed a keen interest in my new job; on the contrary, my motivation was seated in another place entirely. I would be visiting Jacobs' Photographic later that day and not only had I thought of very little else over the weekend, I had also managed to successfully work myself up into a little bit of a tizzy about the possibility of seeing Austin again.

Throughout the morning my excitement grew and multiplied. The time was passing quickly and by the time I arrived at Jacobs' later that day my tizziness was hitting its peak.

It was a strange feeling of relief mixed with disappointment when I realised my anxiety was totally unfounded. Austin didn't make an appearance throughout the whole meeting. Mr Jacobs didn't even mention him.

It was, however, a very successful meeting in a business capacity. Mr Jacobs had agreed to use Chandler's as their new supplier and I was delighted. Not because it meant extra business for Chandler's of course, but because it meant that I would now be in with a very good chance of seeing Austin again.

Before leaving we arranged our next appointment and I booked it in my diary. I had two whole weeks to wait; I had never wanted time to pass more quickly.

***

Eventually, after a painstakingly slow fortnight filled with work and dodging Julian's phone calls – pass, it did.

Here I was again, staring at Jacobs' Photographic singing

shop door and, despite the fact that my priority was to garner as much business from them as I could, this was not the first thing on my mind. *Will Austin be there? If he is there, will he cause me to blush uncontrollably again? Will I be able to control my reactions a little better this time?* Listen to me! Who was I kidding? 'A little better this time?' I was totally out of control the first time I saw him – there was no better about it. The real question was: would I be able to control my reactions *at all?*

No matter how hard I tried to dismiss these invasive thoughts, they kept hijacking all others that entered my head.

My pulse was racing as I made my way towards the shop – the nearer I got, the louder it thudded in my ears. I was ridiculously nervous and no amount of self-preaching could calm me. This was it. My last deep breath of anticipation had been taken and as I reached for the handle; the door suddenly opened.

A customer was just leaving. He smiled and held the door open for me. There was no more time to think or evaluate the situation; I walked through the door into the shop.

My lungs took a sharp gasp of air.

Austin!

He was there ... standing at the back of the shop. My wonderings of what effect he may have on me were wonderings no more: my temperature began to rise and I could feel my face begin to redden. Thankfully, he was standing with his back to me and I was relieved that he hadn't witnessed my reaction to his presence. He was so busy serving a woman that he hadn't even noticed me arrive.

'Hello, Rachel Coast!' boomed Mr Jacobs, his voice as large as his stature.

Austin and the woman turned around and looked at me. I could feel my cheeks heating up. The woman merely glanced at me, but Austin stopped for a brief second and gave me a small nod of acknowledgement before continuing to serve her.

I prayed that my voice would not falter as I responded to Mr Jacobs' greeting.

'Hello, Mr Jacobs. How are you today?'

'Yes, Rachel, I'm pretty good. Happy to see the sunshine.'

I immediately agreed with him. It had been a pretty lousy

but typical British summer.'

'Me too, Mr Jacobs.'

He stopped and sat on the stool behind the counter before continuing. 'We lived in California for a while,' he mused. 'We had a good little business there. The sun would shine for months on end but, I've got to be honest, it started to get on my damn nerves.'

I was now engaged in idle pre-sales chitchat and, in an attempt to feign interest, I responded to his statement questioningly.

'Really, Mr Jacobs, you surprise me?'

'Well you see, Rachel, it's like this: I like British weather. I like seasons, I like to see the rain, but we've had a bit too much of it lately. It's really good to see the sun today ... and you too, Miss Coast.'

His face now widened under the enthusiasm of that broad avuncular smile of his.

I was finding it hard to concentrate — really hard. I have to admit, I was only half listening to Mr Jacobs throughout our whole conversation. My eyes were firmly fixed on him but my ears kept trying to tune in to Austin's conversation with his customer.

I felt so self-conscious knowing he was behind me. My mouth kept drying up and my palms had begun to perspire.

As soon as Austin's customer left, Mr Jacobs looked up from the catalogue I had given him.

'Rachel, have I introduced you to my son?'

My pulse began to thud loudly in my ears again. I could feel a surge of blood rushing through my veins. Then a lump the size of a golf ball suddenly appeared in my throat. For a moment I didn't think I was going to get my words out.

Clearing my throat with the most subtle cough I could muster, I replied. 'No, Mr Jacobs, I don't think you have.'

'Austin, come over here and meet Rachel Coast from Chandler's Photographic suppliers.'

Oh no! He was walking towards me. As he neared, I could feel my resolve starting to crumble even further.

'Hi, Rachel, I'm Austin. Pleased to meet you.'

I took a deep breath. 'Hello, Austin. Pleased to meet you

too.' I smiled at him as I tried to keep myself together.

'Dad, Rachel, please excuse me. I'm going to carry on getting the studio ready. Nice to meet you, Rachel – later, Dad!'

As he walked towards the door at the back of the shop and disappeared from my view I could feel my heartbeat beginning to slow.

When I turned back to look at Mr Jacobs he was standing in front of me, shaking his head despairingly and muttering, 'Studio, indeed.'

I was a little confused by his reaction. 'I'm sorry, Mr Jacobs?'

He looked up at me and smiled. 'Sorry, Rachel, please excuse me. That son of mine is trying to turn the junk room out back into a photographic studio. He reckons it'll bring in more money for the business. The only trouble is, we're going to have to spend money to get it up and running – money we don't have. Don't get me wrong, Rachel, Austin definitely has a talent as a photographer, but it's such a competitive business ... but that's not your worry, my dear.'

Suddenly, my sales representative training kicked in and I responded automatically. 'Well, if you do decide to go ahead with the studio, Mr Jacobs, please give me a call. I'll look for the best deals Chandler's can offer. You've got my business card, just ring me, I'd be more than happy to help out with anything. Oh, and by the way, we also offer a very good credit facility, should you need it.'

Mr Jacobs smiled at me again. 'Why thank you, Rachel. I'll be sure to bear that in mind, now where were we ... ah yes.'

Mr Jacobs placed a small order and when the meeting was over I found myself exiting the shop with an extra spring in my step. Being formerly introduced to Austin was nerve racking for sure, but it was also the exact thing I had hoped for.

From the very first time I'd set eyes on him, he had completely infected my thoughts. I hadn't been able to stop myself thinking about him. I knew deep down that this was all quite crazy, and a part of me worried that it was also a little over the top and a bit obsessive. After all, I didn't know a thing about him! I'd only spent a matter of minutes with him.

He could be really weird or a psychotic mass murderer for all I knew. However, irrational though all of this seemed, the one thing I knew for sure was that Austin Jacobs had become the focus of my thoughts, and I had two long weeks ahead of me before my next scheduled appointment with his father.

CHAPTER TWO
RACHEL COAST

Surprise is not a descriptive enough word to explain how I felt when, barely two days later, I received a phone call from *him*.

'Hi, is that Rachel Coast?'

'Yes,' I replied. 'This is Rachel Coast.'

'Oh! Hi, Rachel, it's Austin Jacobs here, from Jacobs' Photographic. We met briefly the other day.'

My heartbeat pounded erratically, like it could be on the verge of arrest.

'My father said you could help us set up the studio.'

'Yes, that's correct,' I replied weakly.

'I wondered if you could come to see us on Monday?'

Monday? I quickly checked my diary. Damn! Monday was crazy! I really didn't have the time to fit him in, but how could I say no? I would just have to rearrange or even cancel other appointments. One way or another I was going to make it to Jacobs' Photographic on Monday!

'Yes that's no problem at all, I'll call in on Monday.'

***

After what seemed like the longest week in the history of the world, Monday finally arrived. As I walked through the door of Jacobs' Photographic, the bell began to sing its tune and my senses overloaded with excitement as each chime serenaded me.

'Hello, Mr Jacobs,' I said brightly.

'Hi, Rachel, you're here! Austin is out back in the junk room.'

Austin's voice echoed as it neared its way to the front of the shop. 'I heard that, Dad, how many times, it's not the junk room ... it's the studio!'

Austin had just appeared in the doorway at the back of the shop. His blue jeans hung off his hips and his black shirtsleeves were rolled up to his elbows. Flustered by his presence, I found myself babbling nervously to Mr Jacobs as Austin approached me.

'Hi, Rachel,' Austin said softly. 'Thank you for coming today. If you'd like to follow me this way.'

Mr Jacobs smiled and gestured me towards Austin. I followed his direction, my legs hardly holding my weight. This was the first time I would spend more than a few moments with him. The brief encounters on two previous occasions were so fleeting. Today was different, very different.

I followed him through the door into a square hallway beyond. Old wooden stairs on the left stretched up to the first floor. I noticed that a large pile of unopened bills sat wantonly on the bottom stair.

Austin opened a large set of double doors just to the right of us. 'After you, Rachel.'

The room that lay beyond them was huge and completely empty. I was quite taken aback! I had imagined it to look so different. When Mr Jacobs had shaken his head disapprovingly and described it as a junk room, I thought it would be exactly that: a room full to the brim with junk.

Austin bent over in front of me, picked up a copy of Chandler's catalogue from the floor, and handed it to me. 'I've marked some of the equipment I'm interested in, but I really need your input.'

It was down to business straight away. I drew on every little bit of composure in me to deliver professional and informative responses to all of his questions about the pros, cons and prices of every item.

My nerves were still on high alert, and I daren't look straight at him for fear of having a sensory meltdown, so I concentrated on the items in the catalogue and focused on his questions.

By the end of the meeting I felt no more relaxed in his company than I had at the start. He was so out of my league; I was out of my comfort zone. Even though for weeks I had wanted nothing more than to see him again, I was relieved when this meeting came to an end.

Just as I was about to leave, he turned to me. 'Thank you for coming today, Rachel, it has been really helpful. Thanks to you, I know exactly what equipment I want to order.'

I smiled politely. 'No problem at all, Austin, it was a pleasure.' I was so keen to get out of the door I'd forgotten all about the business aspect of this meeting. My sales training soon came back to me. 'I'm sorry, Austin, I should have asked sooner. Do you want to order it all today?'

He glanced around at the stained walls before answering me. 'Well I'm not quite ready for that yet. I need to get this room painted first, and it's going to take me a while. It's quite a big job on my own.' He turned to look at me — a cheeky smile flashed across his face. 'So I was wondering, Rachel, in the interest of speeding up the order, are you any good with a paint brush?'

He was teasing me and it felt wonderful. My nerves took a small step back, allowing me enough time to muster up the courage to seize the moment. And seize it I did.

'As a matter of fact, I am. If you really need help, Austin, I'm more than happy to offer my services.'

He smiled playfully. 'I was only joking, Rachel. I'm sure you have far better things to do than help me.'

I was determined to not miss this opportunity so I repeatedly insisted that I really didn't, and that I really enjoyed decorating.

After he had repeated, 'Are you sure you don't mind?' several times, he eventually accepted my offer.

The very next evening I was standing there in white overalls, paint roller in one hand, brush in the other.

CHAPTER THREE
RACHEL COAST

The next two weeks were glorious, and I longed for my working days to end and my painting nights with Austin to begin.

The affect he had on me was addictive and it was in no way weakened by our growing familiarity. Every time he came within a few feet of me my pulse would race, and my heart would threaten to fail me.

Many moments were spent stealing glances at him when he wasn't looking. His dark wavy hair speckled with paint, his perfect skin, his deep amber eyes ... He really was quite beautiful, and I was definitely punching above my weight.

This was without a doubt an obsessively acute crush. I was bonkers about this guy; I had been from the first moment I saw him. Was this what was meant by 'Love at first sight?' This was all so confusing and completely alien to me. I was caught in his spell and happy to be so.

My mother told me on many occasions that I shouldn't just base my choices of boyfriend on looks alone. They were not ornaments. You couldn't just put them in the corner and look at them. Austin would have made the perfect ornament by anyone's standards, but it was more than that. The more time we spent together, the stronger my feelings became.

How Austin Jacobs felt about me, however, was a complete mystery. A friendship was definitely blossoming but I hoped for more, so much more. Austin seemed to be oblivious to the affect he had on me. He didn't notice my dilated pupils, my overzealous laugh, or my blush-ridden cheeks every time he stood within two feet of me.

After almost two weeks of nightly painting sessions the job was almost finished, and I had learned many things about my captivating painting partner.

One thing that surprised me was that he didn't have any close friends. He had explained that this was because he and his father had moved around a lot. He had never stayed anywhere long enough to form any long-term friendships with anyone. He had gotten so used to this that he didn't miss having friends. He was, by his own admission, quite content to be a lone wolf.

I had also learned that his father wasn't in the greatest of health. He'd suffered a stroke two years previously. His heart was weak, and he'd been told by the doctor to avoid stressful situations. Mr Jacobs was a sweetie and always made me feel so welcome — I was saddened to hear that underneath his lovely jolly exterior his health was suffering.

It turned out that Austin had attended university here in London. He explained that he had nursed ambitions of one day becoming an international fashion photographer, but unfortunately his dreams had been temporarily put on hold. He had only managed to complete the first two years of his photographic degree, as his father had been taken ill just before he was about to begin his final year. Mr Jacobs now needed constant care. It made me even more attracted to Austin when I learned that he put his father's welfare and health before his own needs.

Though he had the looks to be one of those arrogant guys (you know the type: they look like angels but they have the morals of an alley cat, and the manners of a pig), it seemed Austin wasn't like that at all. He really didn't seem to know how attractive he was, or at least he didn't choose to abuse it. Everything I'd learned about him so far led me to believe that he was a sweet, loving, compassionate guy and a devoted son.

On one occasion in between brushstroke chit-chat, I'd asked him about his mother. He hesitated before answering me, and when he eventually replied he just said that it was a very long story. I gauged by his tone that this was not something he wanted to discuss any further, so I changed the subject and told him a few things about me.

He soon learned that I had just graduated from university, and taken the position at Chandler's as a temporary job to enable me to stay in London. I confessed that one day I hoped to exhibit and sell my paintings instead of lenses, cameras and film. I also told him that my mother and father had me later on in life, and that they had recently retired to a small village in Wales.

I also managed to slip into the conversation that, up until recently, I had been dating a boy named Julian. I didn't divulge the real reasons why I had ended this relationship to him.

The truth of the matter was my conscience had got the better of me. I had become so besotted with Austin that it just wasn't fair to carry on dating Julian. I knew from the very first time I set eyes on Austin that my relationship with Julian was never going to go anywhere. Julian was lovely, but he just wasn't Austin. I was relieved that he took our break up better than I expected. I think he knew that I wasn't trying to hurt him. We ended up parting on pretty good terms and I was overjoyed. Firstly because he seemed to be okay about it, and secondly because I had freed myself from my guilt ridden conscience.

After almost two weeks of chatting over brushstrokes and tins of white emulsion, Austin and I stood back and looked at this huge, white, glowing space.

'Rachel,' he said with excitement, 'you have been an absolute life saver. I can't thank you enough. Come on, let me take you for a celebratory drink, there's a great little pub just around the corner from here.'

This was another new step with Austin. Sitting in a pub just him and me, no paint or brushes to distract us from each other.

Austin and his father lived in the flat above the shop so we cleared up quickly, and before leaving Austin shouted up the stairs.

'Dad, Rachel and I are popping out. We're going to the pub around the corner.'

'Okay, Son, see you later. See you soon, Rachel.'

'Goodnight, Mr Jacobs,' I yelled. 'See you soon.'

It was a short walk to the pub and when we arrived Austin spotted a small round table in the corner and made a beeline for it.

'So, Rachel, what would you like?'

Sitting there with my auburn hair splattered with paint and scraped back in to a ponytail, it suddenly dawned on me that I must look a mess.

'Just an orange juice, please.'

As he stood by the bar ordering our drinks, the awful thought that this would probably be the last time we'd spend any real time together washed over me. Seeing him nearly every day had been amazing, how could I go back to seeing him once every few weeks?

He returned with our drinks and I posed a question.

'So, Austin, now that the studio's painted I guess it's time to get the equipment ordered. I told your father that I'd look for the best deals Chandler's had to offer. We also offer a credit facility, if that helps.'

He looked quite serious and leaned towards me. 'Yes, you're right, that would be the next thing to do, but I have a bit of a problem. It's something I've been meaning to talk to you about.'

I waited patiently whilst he fidgeted in his seat before continuing.

'We're definitely going to need to apply for credit, Rachel, but I'm worried that Dad won't pass the credit checks. The shop hasn't been doing so well of late and he's missed a lot of payments. There are unopened bills stacking up everywhere. I wondered if we could apply for the credit in my name instead. I may stand a better chance of getting it ...' He leaned in closer to me. 'I wondered if you could possibly put a good word in for me?'

There really was a lot of unopened mail on the stairs at the back of the shop, and I knew how important it was that Mr Jacobs remained as stress-free as possible.

Austin's concern and anxiety about this situation were obvious, and in that moment, I was compelled to reassure him that we'd work something out; I told him that I'd speak to my boss on Monday and vouch for him.

As I turned to pick up my drink his phone rang. It was his father.

'Okay, Dad, I'll be there now.' His face changed. 'I'm so sorry Rachel. I have to go.'

'Is everything alright?'

'Yes, it'll be fine, but I've got to go. Dad's got himself stuck in the bath again and he needs my help to get him out of it ... I'd better go before he turns into a giant prune.'

The serious tone that had been occupying his voice turned in to a comical laugh and I laughed too.

'I'm really sorry I have to leave, Rachel. Thank you for everything. Hope you have a good weekend! I'll speak to you on Monday.'

That weekend all I thought about was the fact that the fate of his photographic studio was in my hands. One way or another, I had to secure credit for him.

First thing on Monday morning I met with my boss, the very serious and humourless Mr Turnbull. He was short, round and very bald. I was convinced that his seriousness seemed to somehow make him look rounder and balder than he actually was.

With my well-prepared speech formulated and rehearsed, I began my plea.

Mr Turnbull sat and listened intently as I stated the case for Jacobs' Photographic. To my shock and delight he responded very favourably.

'Okay Rachel, I'll make a call and we'll see what we can do.'

He ushered me out of his office, and I took my seat at my desk.

After a while, Mr Turnbull called me back in.

'Rachel please sit down ... I'm afraid to say that Austin Jacobs has failed the normal credit checks.'

My heart dived into my stomach. Damn, this was not what I wanted to hear!

'However, Conik Penster Dewe will sometimes pass high-risk credit applications. In the case of the young Mr Jacobs, it seems that he is prepared to consider giving him a loan. This is a very favourable outcome Rachel. Now go and fill out this application form and bring it back to me.'

My heart resurfaced and my spirit lifted.

'Thank you, Mr Turnbull. Thank you!' I gushed.

Conik Penster Dewe was the big, big boss. Not only did he own Chandler's Photographic, he also owned hundreds of other companies in all sorts of fields. He was a recluse and never attended any public events, but his name was synonymous with wealth and power. Whenever he was mentioned, I couldn't help but imagine him as a modern day Howard Hughes.

About an hour after we'd faxed the application through to Conik Penster Dewe's office, Mr Turnbull called me back in and announced that Austin had amazingly been cleared for a loan. An hour after that a courier arrived with the credit agreement. All Austin had to do was sign it and return it.

Bursting with triumph, I almost danced out of his office. The agreement was firmly in my grip and I couldn't wait to take it to Austin.

***

Ding-dong! The sound of the beautiful antique bell on the shop door sang its merry tune. To me, every little thing about Jacobs' Photographic was wonderful and exciting. The endearing Mr Jacobs was sitting behind the counter in his usual spot, and as soon as he saw me he smiled. My voice was singing like the bell as I greeted him.

'Good afternoon, Mr Jacobs. How are you?'

'I'm fine, Rachel, and you?'

'Yes, I'm great.'

I leaned towards him and whispered, 'Is Austin here? I have some good news about the credit application.'

He smiled as he whispered back. 'That's wonderful Rachel, he's in the studio go on through.'

I skirted by him towards the back door and walked straight through into the studio. Austin was sitting crossed-legged in the middle of the floor. His black jeans and black t-shirt were a stark contrast to the bare brilliance of this large white space. His hands were cupped and his face was buried in them.

'Hi Austin ... are you okay?'

'Yes, I mean hi. I mean yes I'm fine. Sorry, Rachel, I was daydreaming, you surprised me.'

I walked towards him, bursting to tell him the news. 'Would you like another surprise?'

He leaned on his hands to pull himself up.

'No Austin! Don't get up, not yet.' I reached into my briefcase and pulled out the paperwork. My face now bursting with excitement, I waved the agreement in the air. 'You can have your equipment, your credit has been approved!'

As the words raced out of my mouth, Austin leapt off the floor, put his arms around my waist, picked me up and span me around. The paperwork flew out of my hands and on our second revolution he tripped and fell, and we both ended up on the floor in a heap.

His cheek was pressed awkwardly against mine — I could feel the warmth of his skin. My heart stopped and my breathing ceased. His arm was still wrapped around my waist and we lay there, quite still, silent. Then he turned his head to look at me, his lips now only an inch away from mine. He pulled back just enough to look into my eyes and we held each other in a silent stare, just for a moment.

'Rachel! Are you okay? I'm so sorry.'

Still holding my breath, I nodded.

'Rachel Coast, you are the most brilliant woman I have ever known.'

Then he kissed me very quickly on the lips — so quickly I had no time to respond.

He bounced up onto his feet and offered me his hand. The touch of his skin and this unexpected kiss had reduced my entire body to a jelly-like state and I was worried that my legs wouldn't hold me up. I took hold of his hand and, as he pulled me up, my heart started to beat again and my lungs filled with air.

I straightened my suit jacket and brushed myself down in a desperate attempt to compose myself. This sudden display of affection had flanked me from all sides — I didn't know what to do. Looking for a distraction to ease my tethered nerves, I remembered the paperwork. I quickly started to gather it up from the floor. Austin kept apologising for making me drop it and started to help me.

'I'm sorry, it's my fault, let me pick it up. I was so excited ... I still am! I'm sorry, I hope I haven't offended you, please let me take you for a drink tonight. We have to celebrate.'

'Yeah!' I blurted out, not thinking. 'Yes, that would be great,' I added, my voice more composed now. 'And don't be silly, of course you haven't offended me.'

Austin's broad, enthusiastic smile beamed across his face. 'Good, shall we say 7.30pm? There's a really nice wine bar about a mile away, The Decanter. I'll meet you there.'

Relieved, I turned to leave; the paperwork was still in my hand. In all the excitement I almost forgot to give it to him to read and sign.

'The agreement, Austin, I almost forgot — here it is. When you've read it and signed it you can give it back to me. When I take it back to the office it will be official.'

'Well, in that case I'll sign it here and now. Have you got a pen?'

'Yes I think so. But don't you want to read through it first?'

'No I'm sure it's all in order and above board.' He winked at me. 'Anyway, I trust you.'

As he finished signing the agreement we heard the shop bell ring. I carefully folded the document and popped it into my briefcase.

'See you later.'

'Yes, Miss Coast, you certainly will,' he replied.

As I left, I motioned a silent wave goodbye to Mr Jacobs: I didn't like to disturb him. He was talking to a very official looking man in a long black coat.

I found myself staring at him as I walked passed, I couldn't help it. The strange colouring of his hair had caught my attention.

It was predominantly black, but for a man of his age you'd expect to see a peppering of grey running through it. His hair however, was streaked with thick, random golden stripes.

CHAPTER FOUR
CONIK PENSTER DEWE'S OFFICE

The only warmth in Conik Penster Dewe's cold bleak office came from the crackle and spit of an open fire.

A leather armchair dominated the space in front of it, and sitting in its comfort was the elusive international business magnet and owner of Chandler's Photographic, Conik Penster Dewe.

He drummed his long, thin index finger against his strong, square chin as he stared purposefully into the flames.

His surroundings were authentically antiquated. Fifteen-foot high ceilings boasted their height above him. Walls clad in dark oak panels surrounded him. Various oil paintings and tapestries clung to the walls. Its authenticity was, however, flawed.

Directly to his right stood a huge wall made up of black opaque glass that stretched from the floor to the ceiling. An awkward-looking large wooden desk strewn with paperwork stood right in front of it.

A double knock on the intricately carved twelve-foot wooden doors suddenly broke Conik Penster Dewe's meditative concentration.

With no visible effort, his deep calm voice projected towards them. 'Come in, Underling.'

A middle-aged man wearing a long black coat entered the room.

His clothes made him look quite affluent and distinguished, but his complexion told another story. It was as white as snow and riddled with time. The enormous doors closed behind him and he announced his presence. 'Sire ... The application from the final one has arrived.'

He spoke with a nervously humble and respectful tone as he stood there silently and obediently holding Austin Jacobs' credit application form delicately in his hand.

'Bring it here, Underling.'

Underling was braced as always, ready to respond to Conik Penster Dewe's every command. With the paperwork tightly in his grip, he moved silently across the hard black marble floor and handed it to Conik Penster Dewe. As soon as it left his hand he quickly retreated and left the room.

Conik Penster Dewe stared at the application. At first he just looked at it, smiling quietly and contentedly to himself. Then he leapt out of his chair and began muttering manically.

A look of twisted jubilation occupied his face as he made his way across the room and opened the top right-hand draw of the large wooden desk. He reached inside it and pulled out some dust-covered paperwork. This paperwork was more important than its innocuous appearance suggested: it was a contract that had been prepared for Austin Jacobs almost twenty-two years ago, and it had been sitting patiently in this drawer waiting for this day to arrive.

After several more moments of wallowing in his manic episode of elation, he returned to his leather armchair and called Underling back into the room.

Underling quickly entered.

'Here, Underling!' said Conik Penster Dewe, as he thrust the agreement towards him. 'Send it to Chandler's immediately. I want young Austin Jacobs' signature on it by the end of the day.' He turned to the large painting of a woman that hung on the wall above the fire and smiled. 'You see, my dear Catriona, it begins.' He turned back to Underling. 'You know what to do next, Underling'

'Yes, sire. I must be at Jacobs' Photographic at the very moment Austin Jacobs signs the agreement.'

'Yes, Underling you must; this is imperative. His success must begin the moment his signature is secured. I want him to have a taste of getting exactly what he wants, and I want him to like it.'

'Yes, sire.'

Underling scuttled out of the room and the enormous

carved oak doors closed silently and majestically behind him.

Conik Penster Dewe sighed with delight as he sat back in his armchair. With no more than a flick of his wrist, the red velvet drapes that hung above the painting of the woman unhooked themselves and swung shut.

Lost in his silent reverie, Conik Penster Dewe sat staring into the flames.

Several hours passed before another double knock landed on the twelve foot carved doors. It was Underling, he had returned.

The signed agreement that Conik Penster Dewe had so eagerly awaited for had finally arrived.

With one swift movement, his long thin arm reached into the air. The paperwork flew swiftly out of Underling's hand and shot across the room. Conik Penster Dewe grabbed it out of the air and quickly flicked through it to the last page that held both his and Austin's signatures.

He placed the agreement inside his coat and let out a long satisfied groan that reached around the room. After a long pause, he spoke in a low whisper.

'The meeting with Austin Jacobs went well I presume, Underling?'

'Y-yes sire, very well.'

'And all is as it should be?'

'Yes, sire, everything is just as you planned it.'

'Good. You are dismissed.'

Underling retreated out of the room in his usual subservient manner, and as soon as the large oak doors shut behind him, Conik Penster Dewe bolted out of his armchair and stared into the roaring flames. He stretched out his arm and submerged it into their depths. The flames retreated immediately, and as he pushed his arm deeper into the heart of the fire they began to lap gently. When his arm was elbow deep in soft flames he stopped, reached around and smiled before pulling his arm out of the fire again. Firmly gripped in his hand was a large silver key. He held it up to his mouth and pressed it against his pursed lips. A look of much-awaited satisfaction filled his eyes.

He glided across the room and stopped in front of a

wooden panel on the wall. With the silver key in one hand, and the signed agreement in the other, he stood in front of it and knocked it gently. '*Aperire*,' he whispered. The moment the last vowel exited his mouth the wooden panel began to dissolve away until it had vanished completely.

Behind it stood a large metal door. He stroked it with fondness as he took the silver key and pushed it firmly into the lock. Three times he turned it: the first turn was in a clockwise direction, and the others anticlockwise.

A loud clicking and clattering of metal on metal filled the room as the door's intricate locking system clanked opened.

Conik Penster Dewe stood back and stared with pride at what lay behind it.

Thousands of scrolled documents sat neatly on small individual shelves. Every shelf was occupied except for one. He stared at the dust that had gathered on it before running his fingers along it and brushing it clean. He rolled Austin's agreement into a scroll and placed it on the empty shelf.

The sound of the locks turning and grinding as they clattered shut filled the room again and the wooden panel began to reform as soon as they silenced.

Conik Penster Dewe returned to his leather chair, sat back, closed his eyes and tossed the silver key back into the depths of the fire's flames.

CHAPTER FIVE
RACHEL COAST

I arrived at the wine bar to find Austin bursting with excitement.

'Rachel, sit down. You're not going to believe what happened after you left the studio today.'

I sat down opposite him. He wore the most elated expression, and his words flurried excitedly out of his mouth.

'Well I didn't think the day could get any better, and then ... Sorry, Rachel, I'm running away with myself. Let me get you a drink.'

'No, it's fine, I'll wait. Just tell me what happened.'

'No, I insist,' he replied. 'What would you like?'

'Really, Austin, I'll wait.' After several more exchanges of a similar nature I finally gave in to his insistence. 'I'll have a small glass of red wine, please.'

I'd travelled by tube tonight. Austin had insisted that I have at least one alcoholic drink so I'd left my car at home.

'No problem, I'll be straight back.' He was back in record time. 'Here you go, Rachel, a glass of wine. Let's toast to health success and happiness.' Our glasses clinked together. He was almost jumping up and down in his seat as he said, 'Did you see the man my father was talking to when you left?'

I knew exactly whom he was talking about; no one could have failed to notice such a striking looking man. 'The man in the long black coat with the strange-coloured hair?'

'Yes that's the one. Well, that was Mr Underling. He's an agent and he finds photographers for a variety of clients all over the world. He said he'd seen some of my work displayed in an exhibition at the university some time ago. He was very impressed with it, and he tracked me down. Rachel, he wants to hire me! He has so much work that he wants to book me for the next year. He's booked me for a shoot this Friday. Can you believe it Rachel ... everything's working out brilliantly?'

This was indeed excellent news, it was actually quite amazing, and the timing was absolutely incredible.

'Austin that's amazing! Brilliant!' I held up my glass for another toast.

'Rachel, I couldn't have done this without you. To Rachel!' he toasted.

'We haven't toasted to you yet, Mr Hotshot Photographer ... to Austin!'

'Yes, to me,' he said jokingly, in a terribly posh voice. He sounded so funny. We both laughed loudly as we downed our drinks.

During the course of the evening I was more than overjoyed that Austin had asked me to help him get the studio ready for his first shoot on Friday. Any excuse to spend more time with him was fine by me.

The wine bar eventually closed and it was time to go home.

'Austin I've had a wonderful time, thank you.'

'Me too! Rachel, please allow me take you home. I'd like to make sure you get there safely, I feel awful about leaving you alone in the pub the other night. It was very rude of me, I could have at least walked you to your car. Please allow me to accompany you home. It's the very least I can do.'

Delighted by his offer, I answered him imitating the same posh voice he had used earlier in the evening. 'Thank you, kind sir, I would like that very much.'

He laughed. 'After you, my fair lady.'

As we walked out of the wine bar I turned to him and smiled. 'It's about forty-five minutes by tube to my stop from here. You'll be really late getting home. Are you sure you're okay with this?'

'Rachel, I insist on seeing you home safely. It's late for you to be travelling alone.'

'Okay, well in that case, thank you.'

It was only a short walk to the tube station and we were soon on the train sitting quietly, 'people watching'. It was me who instigated the 'guess their occupation game' as the commuters left the carriage. It was a pointless game but lots of fun. You would never know if your guesses were right or wrong, but that really wasn't the point of it.

A man in a grey suit carrying a briefcase was our first victim and we both concluded that he was probably a lawyer or a barrister. As more passengers left the train we found that we'd quickly made our way through a selection of occupations. There were doctors, accountants, builders, stockbrokers, etc. Austin was in such high spirits that he soon moved on to more fantastical and incredulous careers. Vampire-slayers, snake-milkers and wrinkle-chasers were a few that made the list.

When we got to my stop I was faced with a dilemma: should I invite Austin in for the clichéd cup of coffee? And if I did, would he say yes or no?

We arrived outside my door and my mind was made up. 'Austin, would you like to come in for a coffee?'

He stood back and bowed his head, then he looked straight at me.

'I'd love to, Rachel, thank you, but I should get back to my father ... another time maybe.'

'Yes, of course another time,' I replied. I felt like such an idiot.

'I'll see you tomorrow though,' he said, his smile broad and sincere. 'You did agree to help me, Miss Coast. The rest of the studio needs sorting out, I can't believe that I need to have it up and running by Friday. I'll never get it ready in time without you.'

Before I knew what was happening he wrapped his arms around me. My chest tightened.

'Sleep tight, Rachel Coast, see you tomorrow.'

He pulled himself back and looked straight at me. Then he leaned forwards and kissed me quickly, just as he had earlier in the studio.

'Got to go ... Dad will be waiting up for me. See you tomorrow.'

He turned on his heels and ran off, blowing enthusiastic kisses to me as he left.

***

The next day couldn't pass quickly enough. I arrived in the shop and the song of that beautiful singing bell flooded my senses again.

Mr Jacobs was again sitting in his usual spot, and I greeted him with my usual opener.

'Hi, Mr Jacobs, how are you?'

'Great, Rachel, it's so good to see you.' He winked at me. 'He's out back – just go on through.'

Austin was busily unpacking the equipment and my arrival startled him.

'I see you've made a start, then,' I said.

'Oh, Rachel, I didn't hear you coming in – I was miles away.'

'Somewhere nice, I hope?'

He smiled and laughed without answering me and we set to work immediately.

It seemed to take forever to unpack everything and check it was all there. Empty boxes, packing foam, and bubble wrap lay all over the floor. We stood looking at the carnage we had just created.

'I don't know about you, Rachel, but I'm exhausted,' he said as he proceeded to fall awkwardly on to a pile of boxes and bubble wrap.

I laughed at his comical fall and he looked up at me as he wriggled himself into a foetal position.

'You may laugh, Miss Coast, but this is a lot more comfortable than it looks. Come here. Try it for yourself.'

I looked at him dubiously but I decided to join him anyway. 'Okay I will.' It really was comfortable. I wriggled myself in between two large pieces of packing foam and lay back. 'Good call, Mr Jacobs, you're right, it is more comfortable than it looks.'

He smiled across to me. 'I tell you what I could do with now …'

'What?' I asked

'A steaming mug of hot chocolate. Do you fancy one?'

I never could refuse anything that had the word chocolate attached to it, so I responded enthusiastically. 'Absolutely, I'd love one.'

He came back with two mugs of hot chocolate and a plateful of chocolate biscuits. This was pure bliss; a double dose of chocolate and Austin in one beautiful combination. We sipped our drinks and munched the biscuits before lying back contentedly and staring at the ceiling.

We were more exhausted than either of us realised and it was hours later that I awoke. Slightly dazed and a little confused by my surroundings, it took me a few seconds to take in that I was still in the studio and that Austin was fast asleep next to me.

His leg was leaning on mine and it was as much as I could do to fight the urge to snuggle up to him. He looked so peaceful and so perfect. He stirred and rubbed his forehead with his hand.

'We'll find her, Dad, don't worry.'

I didn't have the heart to wake him so I lay still, just listening to his mumblings and looking at him. After a few minutes, he held his arms up to his eyes and squinted through them, looking up at me.

'Rachel? Sorry … I'm so sorry … I fell asleep didn't I? I wasn't snoring, was I?'

'No, Austin you weren't snoring … but you were mumbling.'

He suddenly looked a little concerned.

'Don't worry, Austin, I fell asleep too. I only woke a little while before you. We must have needed it. That's what my dad always says. He constantly falls asleep in the chair and snores like a bear.'

Babbling away about my father and his rhymes and reasons for why things happen, I must have sounded like a complete idiot. He suddenly stopped me babbling midsentence.

'Rachel, what was I saying?'

'You said something like … "we'll find her, Dad, don't worry".'

'Oh, I see.'

His response sounded knowing and deflated so I enquired further.

'I'm guessing this makes perfect sense to you.'

He sat up and looked at me. 'Yes, Rachel, it does. I'll tell you all about it another time but not tonight. Please let me walk you to your car ... it's late and I've kept you here long enough.'

By the tone of his voice I didn't like to push the point any further so I kept my curiosity in check and grabbed my handbag and coat.

As we walked to my car I couldn't help wonder: what exactly had he been dreaming about? Who was it that he was reassuring his dad they would find? For whatever reason, he wasn't prepared to talk about it tonight and I got the feeling that any further questions would not be welcomed.

As we walked closer to my car, my thoughts switched and I wondered if I'd receive another quick kiss. This time I was prepared and waiting; I would be ready to kiss him back.

We walked in perfect silence. It was the click of my car door opening that broke it. He reached out grabbed the handle and opened the door for me.

'Rachel, thank you again for coming over. I'm so sorry I fell asleep.' His voice was genuine but slightly preoccupied.

'No need to apologise, Austin ... remember, I fell asleep too.'

Suddenly, a broad teasing smile flashed across his face. 'Yes, Miss Coast... that is true, how rude of you.'

There was a moment of silence then we both burst out laughing. I felt a sudden relief as his seriousness dissolved into playful banter.

This was it, this was the last chance he had to kiss me before I got into my car and drove away. I braced myself; every fiber of my being was on high alert as I waited in eager anticipation for him to make his swift and sudden move.

The quick sudden kiss that I was expecting didn't come. Instead he took my hand and held it gently.

'Rachel, I love spending time with you.'

As I began to attempt to formulate a response to this unexpected proclamation, he took my other hand and pulled me gently towards him. I could feel his body pressing gently against me and I closed my eyes.

At that very moment the world around me suddenly stopped turning. His lips had found mine, their touch was soft and temperate and, as he pressed them against mine, my body began to shake.

All of my senses, every particle of me, every ounce of life that occupied me reverberated. I could feel our energy flowing back and forth between us as he continued to brush his lips gently against mine. It was intoxicating and debilitating as every concentrated blast forged its way through every particle in me.

My body quivered with excitement as he slowly pulled his lips away. Then he wrapped his arms around me and squeezed me tightly. Speechless and immortalised by the perfection of the moment, I clung to his embrace.

We held each other tightly and silently until eventually, he pulled away from me.

'I'd better let you go,' he said in a quiet low whisper. 'I really don't want to, I've waited so long to hold you like this, but it's late and we've both got to be up in the morning.'

I nodded in agreement and got into my car. I was so blown away I was unable to utter a single word.

From there on I floated my way home; my car was a cloud, the road the sky. I touched my lips, constantly reliving every beautiful moment. My body felt weightless, my heart was full and bursting to the brim. I wanted to fast-forward to tomorrow night, eliminate the next however many hours it was before I would be back with Austin once again.

CHAPTER SIX
RACHEL COAST

The next day passed so slowly I thought it would never end. It did, of course, and I was back in my favourite place in the world.

I said a quick hello to Mr Jacobs and made my way to the back of the shop. Just as I was about to open the studio doors, Austin burst through them to greet me. He bowed and kissed my hand.

'Rachel, I've missed you so much today.'

I took his hand and pressed it against my face. 'I've missed you too.'

Mr Jacobs popped his head around the door and smiled at us. 'I'm off upstairs. See you later, kids.'

He winked at me in his usual avuncular way as he climbed the old wooden stairs in the hallway.

Our romantic moment was just that: a fleeting moment. With no time to waste we set to work immediately, moving the equipment around the studio. We had so much to do and we started by setting up the rigging for the lights, and clearing away our makeshift beds from the night before.

By the time we finished I have to say it looked amazing and it was as state of the art as it came. Everything had a place and everything was in its place. Finally, after we'd set everything else up, we positioned the two large, black leather sofas that had been delivered that day. Austin let out a huge sigh of relief and fell back onto one.

'I think we deserve to sit down after all that hard work, Miss Coast. What do you think?'

I fell back onto the other sofa, mimicking his heartfelt sigh and floppy fall. 'Yes, Mr Jacobs, I think we do.'

He sat up and looked straight at me. 'Rachel on a more serious note, I have to say again that I really can't thank you enough.' He moved further forwards and leaned towards me and, in a tone that was almost confessional, his thanks continued. 'You know, Rachel, this is the happiest I have ever been, and it's all down to you. Ever since you came into my life it just seems to have got better and better.'

His compliments and gratitude made me blush. I wanted to tell him that I felt exactly the same about him, but before I had the chance his tone suddenly changed and he looked quite sad and serious.

'Do you remember last night, when you heard me talking in my sleep? I told you that I'd tell you what it was all about another time.'

'Yes, Austin.'

'Rachel, before I say anything I want you to know how much I care about you ... I want you to know everything about me.' He shifted himself forwards and perched himself on the end of the sofa. 'Rachel, for as long as I can remember, I have been on one long road trip. Constantly moving from one place to another. We've moved so many times I've almost lost count.'

I nodded. His voice was quiet and contemplative.

'I only found out why we needed to live this itinerant lifestyle the day after my thirteenth birthday.'

I sat quietly, waiting for him to continue. I wondered where exactly this was going. He looked so serious.

'We were living in California at the time. My father and I had been on a fishing trip to Castaic Lake, just outside Los Angeles, to celebrate my birthday. We'd spent the whole weekend there, and we'd had a great time. We were packing up to go home when he sat me down on the quiet riverbank. We began to throw small stones into the water, watching the ripples widen and disappear. I loved spending time with him like that. He was usually so busy running the business; these times alone with him were rare and treasured ... As we sat quietly, drinking in the view, he became quite serious. He said he needed to talk to me.'

Austin paused for a second before continuing.

'For a while my father spoke to me about how I'd soon

be a man, and that I'd be old enough to help him. He kept apologising for dragging me around the world and he kept telling me how much he loved me. He was becoming quite distraught by the time he got round to telling me what he really needed to talk to me about.'

Austin paused again, then looked straight at me. 'You see, Rachel, up until that day all I had of my mother were memories of asking my father about her … and just as many memories of him telling me that he'd tell me all about her when I was old enough to understand. I knew what she looked like only too well. He kept a wedding photograph of them at the side of his bed. Hours of my childhood had been spent staring at it. I'd lie back on Dad's bed and hold it above me, trying to imagine how different our lives would have been if she had been here with us.' He stopped and stood up. 'Rachel, I'll be back in a second.'

He left the studio and ran upstairs to the flat. Within five minutes he had returned and clutched to his chest was a silver framed photograph.

'Here.' He handed it to me. The frame was beautifully engraved and Austin's mother and Mr Jacobs looked so happy and so young. Austin's mother was very pretty. I could see whom Austin had inherited his amber eyes from. As I studied the photograph it dawned on me that even though I didn't really look like his mother, our colouring was very similar. She had auburn hair and a pale complexion like me, except my eyes were blue.

'So you have no memories of her at all?' I asked.

'No, Rachel, not one; I knew very little about her until that day at the lake. I still remember sitting there on the riverbank waiting and watching my father intently. He kept wringing his hat with his hands and looking down at his feet. His voice was so quiet and serious. He eventually explained everything. You see, the reason we kept moving from place to place was because he'd been trying to find my mother. He'd been looking for her for exactly thirteen years to that day.'

This wasn't making any sense. Why did Austin and his father need to look for her? Had she ran away from them, and if she had, why?

'Looking back, I can understand how difficult this

conversation was for my father,' Austin continued. 'He kept fidgeting and adjusting his shirt collar as if to delay what he was about to tell me. There was so much he'd kept from me, so much I didn't know. I remember feeling shell-shocked when he explained that I wasn't their first child. They had a son before me called James. I remember how his head bent forwards with such sadness as he struggled to say James' name ... I remember the look of concern that flashed across his face when he saw that I was excited by the news of a sibling. I had always longed for a brother or a sister. His eyes had begun to well up and I watched as the tears rolled slowly down his face, gracefully tracking their way to the corners of his mouth. I had never seen him look so lost. I pleaded with him not to cry.'

Austin looked so sad as he recalled this day. This was obviously sensitive family history. I placed my hand on his knee and he placed his hand on top of mine.

'Rachel ... James died when he was a baby. He was just two days old.'

'I'm so sorry, Austin, that's awful.'

Austin squeezed my hand gently, silently acknowledging my sentiment. 'Rachel, I don't know if this makes any sense to you. Even though my father had only just told me about James' existence, when he went on to tell me that he'd died, I felt an incredible sense of grief and loss.'

I squeezed his hand and nodded. 'How did it happen?' I whispered. 'Why did he die?'

Austin took a breath before answering. 'My father said that he'd caught a virus in the hospital and that his heart wasn't strong enough to fight it. It broke my heart to see my father so broken. He was always such a strong man but on that day he looked crumpled.'

'That must have been so hard for you, Austin. You were so young.'

'It was a bit of a crazy day, I have to say. He kept repeating how tiny James was and that he could still see his tiny little hand clutching my mother's little finger as he fought to hold on to his life. Apparently she wouldn't believe the doctors when they said that he was going to die. She was convinced that he would pull through and be okay.'

I held Austin tightly as he continued.

'I remember my father sounding almost angry at one point. He said that he'd never felt so useless in his entire life. He said the grief was unbearable, the most crippling and desperate emotion that he had ever known. After that, they were too scared to try for another child – neither of them could cope with that kind of loss and grief again. Six years passed before they discovered that my mother was pregnant with me. They were both really scared that something awful would happen again ... and then it did, it was like history repeating itself.'

What did he mean, 'something awful happened'?

I squeezed his hand. 'But you're here, Austin, you're okay ... you are okay aren't you?'

'Yes, I'm absolutely fine, but when I was first born I wasn't. I was six weeks premature and there were complications. The doctors once again broke the news that I would die like my brother had. My mother was inconsolable and sobbed uncontrollably. She was torn apart, she just couldn't bear the pain. She ran screaming out of the room. Dad said that she locked herself in the bathroom and refused to come out. She screamed at him to leave her alone. He did as she asked and left her alone to deal with her grief. That was the last time he saw her. When he went back to check on her she had disappeared from the hospital. It was as if she had vanished into thin air. My father is convinced that she suffered some kind of mental breakdown caused by the trauma of the news. She already blamed herself for James' death. My father believes that she blamed herself for mine too. He whole-heartedly believes that she is still out there somewhere, suffering needlessly, completely ignorant of the fact that I lived.'

He looked up at me, emotion etched upon his face.

'So you see, Rachel, the other night when I was talking in my sleep, I was talking about my mother.'

My heart welled with sympathy; I had become very fond of Mr Jacobs, he was a real sweetie and my feelings for Austin were boundless. For Mr Jacobs to lose the woman he loved under such awful circumstances was beyond tragic. I wanted to run upstairs to console him, and tell him how sorry I was. Then I remembered my first visit to Jacobs' Photographic when

Mr Jacobs had asked Austin if he had any news. I had longed to know what that conversation was about and now seemed like the perfect time to ask.

'Austin you know the first time I came to the shop, your dad asked you if you had any news. Was that about your mother?'

He looked at me. 'Yes, it was. I'd been out all day looking for her.'

'So you think she's in London at the moment?'

'Yes, Uncle Trevor is certain of it.'

'Uncle Trevor? Sorry, who's Uncle Trevor?' I'd never heard him speak of any relatives before.

'Uncle Trevor works for Interpol and has done for the last thirty years. After the local police gave up looking for her a few weeks after she disappeared, Uncle Trevor opened a missing person file on her. He's an old school friend of Dad's and as a favour to him he's made sure that the file has been kept open and active since then. He lets us know when there are possible sightings of her.'

I took Austin's hand. 'Austin, if there's anything I can do to help.'

He reached out, put his arm around me and pulled me towards him. 'Thank you Rachel, you've already helped me more than you know.'

He snuggled up to me and rubbed his cheek against my hair. He reached up with his hand and touched my face gently as he turned my head to face him. He kissed me gently on the side of my mouth and my stomach flipped, and then he moved to my cheek, it flipped again and then he whispered in my ear. 'Rachel, you mean everything to me.'

My body crumpled under the intensity of the moment, and my heart raced as our intimacy deepened.

From that night on we became closer and closer.

CHAPTER SEVEN
RACHEL COAST

The studio was thriving thanks to Mr Underling, who kept booking in fashion shoot after fashion shoot.

Two gloriously blissful months had passed by and we were now officially together as boyfriend and girlfriend – I'd never been happier. Every spare moment we had was spent building, securing and furthering our relationship. Boat rides in Hyde Park and picnics on Wimbledon common ensued, as well as glorious visits to museums and visits to the cinema to see the latest blockbuster films.

My daily conversations with Mum and Dad became shorter as I spent every free moment I had with Austin. I'd almost forgotten about my own plans and ambitions. I was far too busy having an amazing time with Austin and helping him realise his.

It was Monday morning when Mr Turnbull called me into his office.

'Sit down, Rachel. Did you have a good weekend?'

Small talk and pleasantries were not one of Mr Turnbull's strong points, and I was surprised that he even bothered to enquire about my leisure time.

'Yes, thank you, Mr Turnbull. I had a very nice weekend.'

Austin and I had spent the whole weekend together. The Tate Gallery on Saturday followed by a romantic walk along the Thames. On Sunday we had visited Camden market, followed by Sunday lunch in what I called an oldie worldly pub. It was "The Dog and Duck", unchanged by time and doused in the decor of a bygone era.

'Good, Rachel. Now, regarding the credit agreement for Jacobs' Photographic ...'

My concentration was back in the room. 'Yes, Mr Turnbull?'

'The first payment is due tomorrow.'

I'd forgotten all about it. Desperately trying to sound professional in an emphatic tone I replied, 'Yes, Mr Turnbull, that's right.'

'Well, there's been a development.' He paused, stood up and walked towards the window before continuing. 'Yes, Rachel, it seems that Conik Penster Dewe has decided to defer the monthly payments and in their place he would like you to write a monthly report on Austin Jacobs' business activities accompanied by a photograph of Austin. He has taken a keen interest in this client and he is looking at him and his business as a possible long-term investment.'

I couldn't believe what I was hearing. 'Really Mr Turnbull?' I exclaimed excitedly.

'Yes, really,' he said in an exasperated tone.

'It seems Conik Penster Dewe sees Mr Jacobs and his studio as a potentially excellent investment opportunity and he would therefore like to keep a close eye on progress.'

Conik Penster Dewe had his fingers in every business you could imagine. If he was championing Austin then surely the skies were the limit.

'These are Mr Dewe's instructions, Rachel, and they must be carried out to the letter. Please have the first report ready by the end of play tomorrow.'

Things were getting even better for Austin and I knew he would be completely bowled over by this news.

'Yes, Mr Turnbull, no problem. I'll inform Mr Jacobs and I'll begin writing the report straight away.'

He handed me an old "point and shoot" camera.

'Could you take just the one photograph with this, please? It will not be necessary for you to develop it — just hand in the camera with the report.'

'Yes, sir, no problem.'

'That will be all, Rachel.' He sat back down and picked the phone up, before gesturing me to leave his office.

I couldn't wait to see Austin and tell him this incredible news. Grabbing my briefcase and keys, I sped my way to Jacobs' Photographic.

CHAPTER EIGHT
CONIK PENSTER DEWE

Underling was busily attending the fireplace whilst Conik Penster Dewe sat riffling through a pile of paperwork on his desk. The phone rang loudly.

'Underling, answer that, will you?'

Underling stopped immediately and scuttled over to the old black telephone on Conik Penster Dewe's desk. 'Hello, Conik Penster Dewe's office ... Ah! Mr Turnbull, good to hear from you again.'

Underling was Conik Penster Dewe's contact with the outside world and dealt with all and any communications and correspondence.

Mr Turnbull had been making regular calls to Conik Penster Dewe's office since before Rachel got the job as sales representative. Mr Turnbull was under strict instructions to keep Underling fully informed of Rachel's progress with Jacobs' Photographic. He had been told that it was imperative that she win their business and build a trusting rapport with Edward and Austin Jacobs.

Underling put the phone down and turned to Conik Penster Dewe.

'Sire, Mr Turnbull has just informed me that he has given the sales representative Rachel Coast her instructions regarding the preparation of the monthly report.'

'And the camera? She has that too?'

'Yes, sire, Mr Turnbull has given her the camera. She has just left the office and is on her way to see Austin Jacobs. The report and the first photograph will be here tomorrow.'

'Excellent, Underling! Excellent!'

CHAPTER NINE
RACHEL COAST

As I arrived at Jacobs' studio, two gorgeous models were walking out from the back room, closely followed by Austin. His eyes lit up when he saw me.

'Rachel, you timed that perfectly!' He turned to the models. 'Bye, girls, take care – great work today.' As soon as they left he ran over picked me up and swung me around. 'Rachel, do you know how long I've waited to see you today?'

'No, Austin – how long?' I giggled.

'Too long, far too long!'

I couldn't wait to tell him the news. Giggling and smiling, I waited until we came to a standstill. 'Austin we need to go and sit down, I've so much to tell you and you're not going to believe it.'

He looked at me quizzically. 'Good news or bad news? By the look on your face I'm guessing good ... I hope it's good?'

I kissed him enthusiastically and flurried my response. 'Oh it's good, it's really good. In fact this could be the beginning of something truly great – no, not great that's not enough, magnificent yes, it could be magnificent.'

He looked at me with a bemused expression as we sat down on the leather sofas in the studio. I hurriedly explained the content of my conversation with Mr Turnbull.

Austin sat and listened and as the information spilled out of me a flabbergasted and stunned look began to occupy his face. When I'd finished he sat quietly for a moment before questioning me.

'Rachel ... You are absolutely sure that that is what he said?'

'Yes, Austin, I'm absolutely positive. Conik Penster Dewe is very influential, and if he's singled you out as a good business investment then the skies are the limit.'

'Okay,' he said in an only half-convinced tone. 'Well in that case I guess we need to get the report started. What do you need to know?'

After a few hours of going through figures and compiling charts we had finished it.

'Okay, what else do you need, a photograph wasn't it?'

I reached into my briefcase. Damn – it wasn't there. I ran out of the office so quickly I was sure I'd put it in there. I must have left it on my desk.

'Austin, I can't believe it, I've left the camera on my desk. I'll have to call in tomorrow.'

'It's okay, use one of the cameras here,' he said.

'I don't think I can, Austin, the instructions were so specific. I have to use the camera Mr Turnbull gave me. I'm to take one photograph and then I'm supposed to hand the camera in with the report.'

'Oh okay, well no problem call in tomorrow. I'm booked up for most of the day but if you can call in at about twelve, that would be great.'

'Twelve it is.'

Wrapped in hopeful thoughts of success, clearing debts and a stress-free future for Mr Jacobs, we curled up on the sofa and talked of all the amazing possibilities Conik Penster Dewe's backing could bring.

***

Twelve o'clock the next day I arrived at the shop and when I walked into the studio, three six-foot models were poised and posed in front of Austin. They moved like liquid around each other. They were so beautiful, but as gorgeous as they were, Austin, to my delight, was not taking that kind of notice of them. He looked up and saw me.

'Rachel! You're here.' He ran over to me and hugged and kissed me quickly. He then explained that he was running really late and that he had less time than he had hoped to finish this current shoot. The models were waiting and he couldn't stop for long.

I told him that I didn't want to hinder him and that he

should carry on working. I'd take a picture as he worked. He began shooting the models in various positions, working his way around their profiles. He was amazing to watch; I'd never seen him in professional photographer mode before. He looked like he really knew what he was doing.

Totally distracted from the purpose of my visit, I stood back and watched him. After about half an hour he turned to me and smiled. 'I thought you were going to take the photograph.'

I reached into my bag for the "point and shoot" camera. 'Yes – just about to do it now.'

He chuckled to himself before turning his attention back to the models.

I held up the camera and caught him in its lens. Click! I took the photograph.

Just as the shutter of the camera closed, he fell to the ground. I gasped and ran to him.

'Austin! Are you okay?'

He looked completely shocked and bewildered and a little bit embarrassed too. He shook his head and slowly stood up.

'Yes, Rachel, I'm fine. I'm not quite sure what happened ...' He shook his head again.

I wasn't convinced he was fine at all. 'Austin, are you sure you're okay?'

'Yes, Rachel, honestly I'm fine. I just felt a bit ... well, faint, I guess.' He looked at me imploringly. 'Honestly, Rachel, I'm okay. You get back to work, you need to hand that camera in with the report. I'll finish this shoot and I'll see you tonight.' He hugged me tightly and whispered in my ear, 'I'll be counting the minutes.'

CHAPTER TEN
CONIK PENSTER DEWE'S OFFICE, LATER THAT DAY

Underling knocked twice on the large oak doors and waited to hear the summoning voice of Conik Penster Dewe before entering.

'Come in, Underling.'

Underling entered and the fireplace roared like a lioness protecting her pride. Conik Penster Dewe sat in his leather chair staring into the maternal flames.

'Underling! Do you have the report?'

'Yes, sire. It is here.'

'And the photograph?'

'The photograph too, sire, developed in your dark room as per your request.'

'Good! Excellent! Bring them to me.'

Underling moved towards the chair in his usual subservient manner, bowing continuously as he went. He handed over the report and retreated.

Conik Penster Dewe leaned forward and threw Rachel's written report into the fire with distain. The flames lapped at it, devouring it like kindling. All that remained was the precious photograph of Austin Jacobs.

He held the photograph up to the large painting of the woman above the fireplace and began taunting her with it, laughing.

'Would you like to see what I have here, my dear Catriona? You would?' His tone was both rhetorical and sinister. 'Now let me see, will she see? Won't she see?'

He continued to taunt her. The image of the woman

remained still and unmoved by his provocative display.

'My dear, the time is nearly here. At last it is the beginning of the end. You, my dear ... will soon be free – and so will I!'

He placed the photograph inside his coat pocket and glided towards the large oak doors. Without so much as reaching for the large brass handle in front of him, the oak doors hurriedly flew open as if they dare not stand in his way.

A long, dimly lit hallway spanned in front of him, and with lightning speed he glided towards the open elevator that stood at the end of it. Black birdcage wrought iron doors concealed the elevators entrance, and just as he was about to reach them, Underling appeared and opened the doors in perfect time for Conik Penster Dewe to sail through them.

Once inside the elevator Conik Penster Dewe's hand reached towards what looked like an ordinary panel within the elevator's walls. He pressed his hand firmly on top of it and whispered the words '*Toneme alli.*' The panel slid open revealing a large black button. He placed one hand on top of his coat just above the inside pocket where Austin's photograph was, and the other on the button inside the concealed compartment. He breathed deeply and pressed the button firmly.

The elevator responded immediately and began to move, shaking and rattling as it made its downward journey. Eventually it came to a screeching stop.

The elevator doors creaked slowly open and another long, narrow hallway stretched out in front of him. He had arrived at the floor he called "The Hallway of Torches".

The walls either side of it were as black as night. Seven beautifully crafted ornate silver candleholders adorned them, but only one of them bore a lit flame.

Two hooded figures stood like centurions in front of two golden doors at the end of this dimly lit hallway. Conik Penster Dewe calmly made his way towards them and as he approached the hooded figures, they moved silently out of his way.

Beyond the gold ornate doors lay another elevator. Conik Penster Dewe entered and the hooded figures closed the doors behind him and returned to their positions. He closed his eyes and whispered two words: '*Camera Cella.*'

As the last vowel exited his mouth the elevator began to shudder violently. He stretched his arms out and placed his palms firmly on the elevator walls either side of him. Totally unfazed by the chronic vibrations, he held his position with ease as the elevator continued to shake and vibrate.

Finally after several moments it stilled, and the doors flew open.

A gust of cold damp air flew in as it rushed to escape from the vast cavernous room that lay beyond it. Only a small dim light glimmering in the distance broke the blackness that spanned in front of him.

Conick Penster Dewe shot swiftly out of the elevator, tearing his way into the black abyss. The small, dim light grew brighter as he made his way into the darkness. Its source was now becoming clear. In the middle of the room stood an old antique lamp. It bore an antique tapestry shade decorated with scarlet fringes. The fringes began to swing from side to side, moved by the fleeting touch of Conik Penster Dewe's coat, as he tore past it. An old leather armchair just like the chair that lived in front of the fireplace in his office, stood proudly next to it.

He suddenly ground to a stop, throwing his head back and closing his eyes. '*Denique Unus.*'

With a sudden surge, he leapt into the air. His body began hurtling upwards, flying through the cold, damp air above him. He continued to soar until he was hundreds of feet above the ground. Only then did he stop.

He was now hovering in the air in front of a cold metal wall that seemed to never end. A large metal door suddenly opened in the wall in front of him, and he glided forwards into the room that lay beyond it.

Conik Penster Dewe had just entered a dark, silent vault. The floor and walls were clad with black marble; rich gold veins ran sporadically through it, breaking its darkness. In the centre of the room stood a huge crystal pedestal; its circular base spanned at least twelve feet across, and its structure tapered sharply upwards into a twelve-foot narrow column.

On top of this spectacular plinth stood a beautiful glass crystal box.

Conik Penster Dewe stood a few feet away from it and reached inside his long black coat. He pulled out the photograph of Austin and held it tightly in his hand. He took one more look at it before thrusting his arm into the air with the photograph still firmly in his grip.

'Cantartis awaken!' he cried.

The glass box reacted immediately to his words and it began to rock slowly from corner to corner on top of the pedestal. The rocking motion became faster, until it was now spinning on its axis. It suddenly hit a speed that caused it to look like a blur, and it was at that point it became air born.

It rose off the pedestal, climbing higher and higher into the air. Then it began floating towards him. As it got closer it began to lose its solid form, soon transforming into a gaseous state. Silver-white smoke billowed and swirled around the photograph of Austin, twisting, grabbing and wrapping itself around it until the photograph disappeared into its wispy core.

Conik Penster Dewe stood silently, watching it as it shot into the air above him. It twisted and swirled in loops before gliding back through the air towards its pedestal, slowly regaining its solid state as it travelled.

The Cantartis was now back in its resting place, and it stood silently and inanimately on top of the crystal pedestal. It was no longer an empty glass box — it now had a very small but brilliant light shining inside it.

Conik Penster Dewe stared at the small light that glowed so brightly, both admiring and despising its illumination. His eyes narrowed and he smiled deeply, then turned swiftly to face the door.

He shot out of the marble clad vault, charging downwards towards the ground until he landed calmly and seamlessly in the large leather armchair that stood next to the old lamp.

Looking straight ahead of him, he clasped both arms of the old leather chair; sat forward, and with a shrill cry he bellowed, 'Release your locks!'

As the last echo of his bellowing voice drifted away, the searing sound of metal grinding on metal began to fill the silence that surrounded him.

In one unified motion, thousands of metal doors flew open

simultaneously in the metal wall in front of him. Each one revealed a light that shone as bright as a newborn star. Each beam of light bounced and danced from one surface to another, refracting recklessly and brilliantly around the room.

The darkness that had surrounded him was now flooded with their brilliant light. The extent of the dark room he had entered from the elevator could now be clearly seen.

Thousands of metal doors were housed in a never-ending metal wall that stretched up into the darkness above. A highly polished black and gold marble floor shone like the water of a millpond. Two rows of enormous black and gold marble pillars lined the room for as far as the eye could see. From the centre of the metal wall shone a small dim light that had been almost silenced by the brilliance that surrounded it; the light that Conik Penster Dewe had observed so closely only moments earlier.

CHAPTER ELEVEN
AUSTIN JACOBS

It was nearly seven o'clock and I was struggling to get myself ready. Rachel would be here any minute. Today's photo shoot had taken a lot longer than I had anticipated, and I was battling against time.

On top of this challenge to beat the clock, I felt absolutely awful. My head was hot and I kept experiencing sudden cramping pains in my stomach. This was so unlike me, I was never ill. I had a heavy schedule in front of me, and the sudden interest that Conik Penster Dewe had taken in me meant that I couldn't afford to be out of action for any amount of time.

I continued to battle on as I got myself ready for Rachel's arrival. By the time she got here I was beginning to wish that she wasn't coming. Not because I didn't want to see her, on the contrary — I adored her, I'd never felt like this about anyone. I was besotted with her and spending time with her was my favourite thing to do. But I felt so ill, all I wanted to do was crawl into my bed and curl up into a ball. The shop bell rang ... that would be her. She was always so punctual and tonight was no exception.

'Austin ... hi, it's me, I'm here,' she called, her voice ringing through the shop.

The pitter-patter of her feet, a sound that I usually loved to hear, thumped like tiny hammers pounding in my head. She walked into the studio, took one look at me, and her demeanor changed from bright and cheerful, to worry and concern.

'Austin, you look awful. Are you all right?'

I was sitting on one of the black leather sofas, and as she finished speaking, a wave of nausea swept over me. My throat tightened and my stomach turned. I closed my eyes and began taking deep breaths as I sat back, trying to rid myself of this god damn awful feeling. I didn't even want to move off the sofa, let alone go out to a fancy restaurant.

'Rachel, I'm so sorry, I really don't feel well.' It was a struggle to get my words out.

A frown broke across her brow. 'You don't look too good,' she said anxiously.

I managed to muster a weak smile. 'I'm sure it's not that serious.'

I didn't want to concern her, but I really did feel terrible. All I wanted to do was lie down.

'I'm so sorry, Rachel. We're booked into that fancy restaurant tonight. I know you've been looking forward to it. I'm sorry, I really don't feel up to going, but I promise I'll make it up to you.'

Her frown softened. 'Austin, I really don't care about fancy restaurants. I just want you to be okay. You should know by now that I don't care where we go or what we do. I just love being with you. I could sit in an empty room watching paint dry as long as I was with you ... Oh, wait a minute, I've already done that.'

She smiled and waited for my usual jovial response. Sadly I disappointed her. My sense of humour had suffered a total bypass. I really wasn't well!

'Austin,' she began in a serious tone, 'I'm really worried about you.' She leaned forward and felt my brow. 'You feel quite hot; your temperature is definitely up a little. Come on let's get you upstairs.'

Too weak to argue, I agreed to her offer and she helped me up the stairs. I could hear Dad snoring in the living room as we stood in the small hallway. I gave her a quick hug and apologised once more.

She hugged me back. 'Are you sure you're going to be okay? I can stay for a while if you want me to,' she whispered.

As much as I loved her and loved being with her I didn't want her to stay. Not when I felt like this. I just wanted to sleep and deal with this awful feeling on my own. The last thing I wanted to do was upset her, but despite my heartfelt apologies, I could see that I had. I hit her with another wave of apologies, and promised her that I'd be fine and that I just needed to sleep. She eventually left, looking a little bit happier, and insisting that I ring her later to let her know how I was.

With Rachel gone and Dad fast asleep in the living room, I pushed open my bedroom door. My head was thumping and my stomach was churning. I had never suffered from anything like this before. All I wanted to do was lie down in a quiet, dark room and soak in its silence.

The streetlights were shining in through my window. They darted around the room; their brightness was too much to bear. I yanked at my blackout curtains and they closed in a desperate flurry.

I climbed into the sanctuary of my double bed and gently wriggled my body into it until I was bedded down in the mattress. Grabbing a pillow and pulling it close to me, I wrapped my arms tightly around it. After a while, the silence and softness that it offered slowly began to soothe away the loud pulse that had been hammering away inside my temple.

My turbulent stomach began to feel calmer. I was at last beginning to feel some relief from the unbearable discomfort that had been haunting me for the last few hours. Whatever it was, a virus or stomach bug or whatever, I prayed that it would desert my system by the morning. I had another long day ahead of me tomorrow and a lot to do. I couldn't cancel my photo shoot. I had to prove to Conik Penster Dewe that I was an excellent investment. I also had some making up to do to Rachel. I pulled the pillow closer to me and clung to its comfort before drifting off to sleep.

***

My eyes flew open. I was wide-awake and soaked in perspiration. It was still night-time and I'd just had the strangest dream ... I'd been standing in the middle of a black marble room bathed in the glow of a warm bright light travelling towards me. My mother and father had been standing in front of me, looking like they were screaming at me — but their screams were silent. Not a sound had come out of their mouths. Rachel was there too, but she looked different, almost unrecognisable. She was standing next to a woman and two men whose arms were outstretched. Their eyes were all focused on me. Then everyone disappeared. A deep darkness fell all around me. Then a small, dim light broke the darkness and began to twist its way around me. As it twisted and spun faster a loud, sinister, spine-chilling laugh powered its way through the blackness – it was then I woke up.

Whatever this was, it was playing absolute havoc with me. I sat up and wiped the perspiration off my face. My digital alarm clock was glaring at me; it was four o'clock in the morning.

I needed the bathroom. As I walked in and turned on the tap I caught sight of myself in the mirror. My eyes were glassy and shining brightly. I stared at their unfamiliarity and looked at my pale complexion. Dad's voice shouted from the living room. 'Austin, is that you?'

I stared back at myself once more before answering. 'Yes, Dad, don't worry it's me.'

'Oh! Okay, Son. Just checking.'

I washed my hands, splashed my face, brushed my teeth and stared at my reflection again. I definitely needed more sleep. Before going back to bed I popped my head in to check on Dad. He was half-snoozing comfortably in the living room chair. He often slept in it all night. He had a quilt tucked neatly behind it so that he could just grab it and easily settle himself there for the night. His back wasn't too good and he swore the chair was better for it than his bed.

'Hello, Son? Are you all right?' he mumbled.

I wasn't all right, but I was definitely better than I had been. 'Yes, Dad, I'm fine.'

'What time is it?'

'It's four in the morning.'

'Okay, go and get some rest, Son. I'm going to get a few more hours myself. Love you, see you in the morning.'

'Goodnight, Dad, love you too! See you in the morning.'

A tiny chink of light beamed its way through a small opening in the shut curtains. I lay there and stared at the caught dust particles dancing frantically in its beam. It was mesmerisingly quiet and peaceful – until my alarm went off.

It was 7am, time to get up.

My eyes were open and I stretched my arms towards the headboard and tensed my legs. So far so good: my head didn't ache any more. I stretched again. My stomach to all intents and purposes felt like it was back to normal. Whatever it was that had disabled me last night seemed to have left my system.

As soon as I was up and on my feet my first thought was Rachel. I reached for my phone. I'd promised to ring her last night but then I'd fallen asleep.

'Rachel! Hi it's me I'm so sorry about last night. I know I should have rang and I would have, but I fell asleep. Thank you so much for looking after me.'

'Austin, I've been so worried about you. Are you feeling better?' Her voice sounded concerned and caring.

'You know what, Rachel? I feel great. Whatever it was that got a hold of me yesterday has gone completely. How about you? Are you okay? I hope you haven't picked anything up from me?'

'No, I seem to be fine.'

I had to make it up to her; I felt so bad about letting her down last night.

'Good!' I said. 'That's really good! I'm going to contact the restaurant I was going to take you to last night and I'm going to book us a table for tonight. I can't wait to see you later.'

'Can't wait to see you either,' she replied.

After breakfast I went downstairs to the studio and began preparing for the long day ahead. The crew began to arrive, and in no time, the entire studio was alive with makeup artists, models and stylists. I was ready to start the shoot.

The first three models walked out wearing sheer, floor length black designer dresses, and very little else. I had photographed models over the last two months in the most scantily clad garments; capturing them with my lens, always looking for the best angle or the right expression to sell the product.

Today something was different. As the models walked in I found an aberration in my behaviour. I suddenly and very unexpectedly found myself looking at them in a very different – and, frankly, unprofessional – way. Something was off; they had never had this effect on me before.

I quickly readjusted my train of thought and tried to focus on my job. Just as I was feeling confident that I was back on track, a voice in my head began whispering ... *look at those long, beautiful legs.* I tried my best to ignore it. *Austin, it whispered again, imagine what it would feel like to touch those smooth long legs. It could be so easy for you. You're so handsome. With just one click of your fingers you could have any woman you wanted.*

This whispering voice and the thoughts and feelings that were bombarding me were completely unnerving me. Though I continued to battle against them, they refused to go away, and they stayed with me all day. One minute I was in control and winning. The next I was experiencing thoughts and feelings like never before.

My mind kept wandering, imagining myself in seriously intimate situations with all of these beautiful creatures. It was as though my perspective and moral standing had suddenly been inexplicably altered.

Don't get me wrong, I had always admired beauty. I was as warm-blooded as any man, but to me physical intimacy had always meant so much more than just a lustful animalistic sexual act. It was just the way I was. Physical intimacy was a sacred and shared connection between two people deeply in love. Lust for lust's sake had never been an option or a consideration in my life. This just wasn't the way I was wired.

After several more hours the shoot was over and everyone had left. I let out an audible sigh of relief.

As I made my way upstairs to get ready to go out with Rachel, Dad was standing there waiting for me.

'Austin, come into the kitchen and sit down. I want to talk to you.' His voice was serious.

'Is everything ok, Dad? Are you okay?'

'Yes, I'm fine, Austin, take a seat.' He looked up at me and a frown began to appear in his brow. 'Austin, since the studio has taken off, you have been busy. I know it's great for business and it's really taken the pressure of me, and I'm delighted about this, but since its success you've hardly had time for anything else.'

I knew where this was going. It had been weeks since I'd

had the chance to go looking for my mother. What with the studio and my relationship with Rachel, he was right – I'd had no time for anything else. The last time I'd gone looking for her was about two months ago, just after I'd told Rachel about her.

'Austin, it's almost like you've forgotten that she is the reason why we're here in London ...'

It was true, looking for my mother had always been the priority no matter where we were, or how well or badly our business was doing. Rachel, the studio, my career, making money to keep us afloat ... they were all taking up my time up, vacuuming up my days.

'I'm sorry, Dad. I know you're right. I promise I'll make time soon.'

With that, Rachel beeped the horn outside; I looked out of the window and waved to her.

'Dad, we'll talk about it later. Rachel's here I've got to go. See you later. Ring me if you need anything.'

'Okay, Son. Give my love to Rachel and have a nice time in that fancy restaurant.'

***

The restaurant was incredible and very exclusive. Rachel looked stunning with her auburn hair hanging loosely around her shoulders. As we began our starter, Freda, one of the models from today's shoot, walked in. She didn't notice me at first. A man who was years older than her accompanied her. All five feet and eleven inches of her glided into the restaurant. She had curves in all the right places and her chiffon dress scooped dramatically, revealing the whole of her beautiful back. As her long, smooth legs glided past me, I couldn't stop my eyes from following them.

What the hell was wrong with me? I was like a dog on heat.

My attentions had suddenly turned from Rachel, the woman I cared for so deeply, to this model who I hardly knew at all. I had to get a grip and block this madness out.

After a few moments Freda saw me and smiled, then blew me a kiss. I nodded in response. Rachel was looking at the menu and didn't see our quick exchange. A voice began to whisper and echo in my head once more. *You could have her; you could have Freda, just click your fingers. Just try it, just one click and she's yours.*

I shook my head in an attempt to block out the whispering. What was happening to me? What was wrong with me? Maybe I wasn't completely over this sickness, or virus, or whatever it was that was affecting me.

I hurried through the main course and rushed through the dessert. All I knew at this point was that I was desperate to get out of there. After making my lame excuses, we left the restaurant and Rachel graciously drove me home.

CHAPTER TWELVE
RACHEL COAST

The knot in my stomach was growing and twisting as I gripped the steering wheel tightly. A heady mix of anger, jealousy and disappointment fuelled me as I drove Austin home.

The closer we got to Jacobs' Photographic, the emptier and more rejected I began to feel. Austin had hardly said a word to me throughout the whole journey.

I loosened my grip on the wheel. We had finally arrived back at Jacobs' Photographic. Austin apologised for cutting our evening short, then he kissed me quickly on the lips and left. He turned to look at me and waved as he disappeared into the shop. I managed a limp wave back to him.

As I drove home the confusion and hurt that had just walloped me was becoming unbearable. My journey home was longer, sadder and lonelier than I could have believed. By the time I arrived at my bedsit, the pent-up tears I'd been holding back were streaming uncontrollably down my face.

This evening had been absolutely awful and had left me feeling totally undesirable and thoroughly unattractive. My buried self-doubts and insecurities had exhumed themselves with vigor during the first course of dinner.

A tall girl with the longest legs I had ever seen had walked in. She was with a man many years older than her, and as she gracefully glided past us Austin tried, but failed, to hide the fact that he couldn't take his eyes off her. From that moment on Austin's eyes kept wandering towards the beautiful girl with the long legs.

I wasn't used to seeing him distracted like this, and it was enough to really pull my trigger. My mood took a drastic change. I didn't like it, not one bit. I was usually the focus of his attention, and that was how I liked it. It was how it was supposed to be.

As the evening progressed I began to hate and envy this long-legged beauty with a passion. How I wished that I had been born with legs that long; wished that I had been bestowed with her immaculate beauty. Most of all, I wished that it had been *me* that had stolen Austin's attention tonight – not her.

As the evening went on the situation did not improve, and my cynical paranoia was running amuck. It intensified to the point that I was even beginning to wonder if Austin had just used me to get his studio up and running.

Perhaps now, it was only a matter of time before he would cast me to one side for someone like this long-legged beauty that he couldn't keep his eyes off.

Battling through this myriad of consuming emotions, I kept trying to tell myself that I was just having a silly green-eyed moment and that my paranoia was hysterical and unfounded.

I kept reminding myself that Austin had told me on many occasions how he felt about me, but words are, they say, cheap, and his actions tonight were definitely in direct conflict with them. I kept questioning and justifying my reactions to the situation, and I kept coming back to the same conclusion. How else was I supposed to react?

I thought every guy knew that eyeing up another girl in front of his girlfriend was totally, irrevocably and universally understood to be completely wrong and unacceptable.

The evening didn't improve. Austin rushed his way through the main course. Then he announced that he really needed to go home, that he didn't feel very well, that he didn't think that he had quite got over whatever it was that had made him feel so ill yesterday.

This was not the evening I had hoped for – it was a total disaster and by the time I arrived back at my bedsit I was a blubbering mess. I threw myself on my bed and cried myself to sleep.

I awoke early the next morning still fully-clothed with my bed half-made. I stared at myself in the mirror. My face was tracked with black streaks of mascara, my eyes were puffy and red and my hair looked like I'd been dragged through a hedge backwards.

As I sat on the edge of the bed, sipping my tea, the phone rang. It was Austin apologising profusely for his behaviour last night.

His apology sounded incredibly sincere, and the hurt that I had been feeling began to slowly wane — at least it did until he announced that it was probably best that we cancel all of our plans for the coming week.

Despite his sincere apologies, disappointment and a gnawing sickening concern for the future of our relationship began to consume me as every day of the coming week passed by. I was finding it really hard to remember what exactly it was that I did with my evenings before meeting Austin.

With so much free time on my hands, I began to over think everything and beating away my skepticism about him was becoming harder to keep under control.

Perpetual justifications from me were followed by perpetual excuses from him, until eventually he ended up putting off seeing me for three whole weeks.

By this time I was absolutely convinced that our relationship was coming to an end. I kept thinking about the last time I saw him on our date in the restaurant. Bearing witness to his obvious attraction for the beautiful tall girl had been horrible. After three weeks of not seeing him, I had successfully convinced myself that the reason he didn't want to see me was not because he was ill, but because he was spending his time with one of these beautiful girls instead of me.

Enough was enough; I couldn't take any more excuses from him. This state of limbo that I've found myself in was driving me crazy. If Austin didn't want to be with me, why not tell me straight that it was over? Why play spurious games with me like this? This was cruel and hurtful, and I was at the end of my rope.

Throughout my teens I had been plagued with my fair share of insecurities, and I had worked really hard to deal with them. Eventually, by the time I started university, I was finally coming to terms with myself. I looked how I looked. Mildly attractive — I think — but definitely not a knockout. I was never going to have legs up to my armpits; I was only five foot two so it was a distinct and definite impossibility. I was never going to grace the cover of a magazine or win a Miss World contest.

All of this I knew very well.

I had worked really hard to try and accept and like who I was. I was just beginning to feel secure with the knowledge that there was only ever going to be one of me, and that this alone was something to claim, own and be proud of. I was unique! I had accepted my physical limitations. I was never going to be a supermodel and, though popular society places incredible importance on appearance, I believed that this was not the only thing to define me, or dictate the extent or degree of fulfillment and contentment I could achieve in my life.

My mother had helped my confidence so much with her wonderful words of wisdom. She would say things like, 'Being incredibly beautiful or having fame and fortune is no guarantee of happiness darling. Life just isn't like that.' Her tone was always emphatic and matter of factual. It was as if she was quoting a great philosopher or divulging knowledge that had been written and immortalised somewhere in sandstone.

These philosophical words of wisdom had recklessly abandoned me over the last three weeks, and I kept looking at myself in the mirror and pulling myself apart, piece by piece. I hated my shoulder length auburn hair, my pale complexion was such a disappointment and the fact that I just about made five foot six in my tallest heels just capped it all.

The last three weeks had passed painfully slowly in this agonisingly self-deprecating and morose way. Even though I had graciously accepted his eternal excuses, inside I was seething with anger, hurt and confusion.

Tomorrow was my chance to confront him. The next monthly report was due and he couldn't put off seeing me any longer: ill or not.

***

The bell on the shop door rang as I walked in.

How I'd missed its sweet song and, as its chimes rang out, I remembered the very first time I saw Austin. My cheek recalled the feeling of the raindrop from his hair landing on it.

My stomach flipped as a nervous anxious excitement tore right through me.

Mr Jacobs was standing right in the middle of the shop and his face lit up when he saw me.

'Rachel, my dear, where have you been? It's been so long!'

He was right, it *had* been a long time. I passed off his question with a suitably benign response.

'Oh, busy, Mr Jacobs. My work load is hectic at the moment.'

Mr Jacobs obviously didn't have a clue that Austin had been putting off seeing me. He could see me looking anxiously towards the door at the back of the shop. 'Austin's in the studio, Rachel, go on through.'

I walked towards the back door of the shop and stood quietly outside it.

These three weeks apart had managed to put so much distance between us. Despite all the time we'd spent together, and how close we had become, I was now back in the same nervous state I was in the very first time I set eyes on him; my anger wasn't enough to stop these feelings. I found myself unable to control my physical responses, which had completely taken over; my hands began perspiring and the thud of my pulse in my ears was deafening me.

I stood there in front of the door, breathing deeply, trying to prepare myself. It was hopeless, I was in such a state I was unable to formulate one lucid thought.

I took a breath as if I were about to dive into a deep ocean and opened the studio door. Austin was standing there, large as life, joking and laughing with two gorgeous models. They looked directly at me as I walked through the door. He turned sharply following their gaze.

'Rachel, you're here!' he said in a surprised tone. Then his usual enthusiastic smile dared to beam its way to me.

'Yes,' I said curtly, 'I'm here.'

Seeing him like this helped to turn my nerves to anger. What was going on? He looked fine ... in fact he looked amazing. He walked over to me and flung his arms around me – it was at this point that I began to lose my resolve. As much as I wanted to reject him and pull away from him, I just couldn't.

'It's so good to see you,' he said, hugging me tightly.

I wasn't convinced that he meant this, but I was buckling under the weight of his charm. Really! Was it? Was he pleased to see me? I had to admit that he did seem genuine, but I still wasn't completely convinced of his sincerity.

'I'm just about to start another roll of film, Rachel. Are you ready, girls?'

He turned to the models and they giggled annoyingly amongst themselves. As he worked his way around them I took out the camera and waited for the right shot.

He turned to face me and winked just before he turned back to carry on shooting the models. Click! I took the photograph of him.

He tripped suddenly over a lighting cable and he fell to the floor, holding his head.

'Damn these blasted cables,' he cursed.

I ran over to him; he looked really pale, the colour had completely drained from his face.

'Are you all right, Austin?'

'I don't know,' he said, as he rubbed his head.

I helped him up and sat him down on one of the black leather sofas. He looked awful. All of my angst towards him had disappeared and the only emotion I felt at that moment was genuine concern.

'I'll be okay, Rachel, I just need five minutes.' He sat back and closed his eyes.

'But you haven't been right for weeks, Austin.'

'I'll be fine, just give me a minute. I've got to get through the rest of this shoot and I'm already running late.'

He opened his eyes, sat up and smiled at me.

'I'm starting to feel better already, Rachel, honestly I'll be fine.'

He leaned towards me and put his arms around me before kissing me gently on the forehead. The tiny little part of me that was still feeling angry towards him made me want to pull away from him, but I just couldn't.

'I've missed you so much, Rachel,' he whispered gently into my ear. 'I'm so sorry it's been so long since we've seen each other. I should be finished here by about five-thirty. I'll ring you at six.

I have to see you tonight.'

His breath was warm and intoxicating and made the fine hairs on the back of my neck tingle.

By the time I left Jacobs' photographic I was more confused than when I'd arrived. My intentions of confronting him about the state of our relationship had completely gone out of the window. I had melted under the weight of his bloody charm. My worries about our relationship were somewhat eased; he did seem genuinely sorry, and he wanted to see me later, but, on the other hand, my concerns about the state of his health were reignited.

My afternoon appointments dragged on as I willed the hours away. At last my working day was finally over.

Six o'clock came and went.

I came to the conclusion that Austin's shoot must have run late, so I sat tight and waited patiently for his call. An hour of twiddling my thumbs and pacing around my bedsit passed by, it was now seven o'clock and still no phone call. By the time the clock struck eight, the hurt and anger that had been temporarily dispelled began to well up inside me again. What would his excuse be this time?

Regardless of the outcome, one way or another I had to know where I stood.

I picked up the phone; I was finally going to confront him. His father answered.

'Oh, Mr Jacobs! Is Austin there?'

'Yes, Rachel, but he's in bed,' he whispered. 'He came up from the studio earlier, said he felt really tired. He didn't look too good, Rachel.'

On hearing Mr Jacobs' words a sense of guilt, relief, concern and hope washed over me simultaneously: Austin was ill that was why he hadn't rang me.

'Oh I see, Mr Jacobs. Well I hope he's feeling better soon. Will you tell him I called?'

'Yes, of course, Rachel. I'm going to check on him in a bit. Make sure he's all right.'

'Thank you, Mr Jacobs, see you soon.'

'You too, Rachel. Take care.'

I put down the phone, my hopes of seeing Austin tonight squashed. It seemed that he really was ill and I just didn't know what to think anymore.

The next morning my alarm buzzed loudly in my ear and my neck ached as I reached out to stop it. I'd fallen asleep watching TV and I was still sitting bolt upright on my little sofa.

Before doing anything else I picked up the phone and rang Jacobs' Photographic. I had to know if Austin was okay.

Austin answered.

'Austin, it's you.'

'Yes,' he said slowly, 'Who were you expecting it to be?'

'Sorry, Austin, I was expecting your Dad to answer. He said you were in bed and that you were ill again. Are you feeling okay?'

'Yes I'm fine, never felt better. I'm so sorry to cut you short, Rachel, but can I ring you later? I'm right in the middle of a shoot. Thanks – bye.'

He put the phone down on me before I had a chance to say any more.

He was so blunt and curt. He didn't even make time to apologise for not calling me last night. I burst into a flood of tears; this was all becoming too much to cope with.

By the time I'd finished my first cup of tea of the day and dressed for work I had just about managed to pull myself together.

My enthusiasm for my job was dubious at the best of times and today mustering up any kind of conviction was virtually impossible.

Austin eventually rang me back at 5pm, just as I was leaving the office.

'Rachel! Please accept my apologies. I'm so sorry I cut you short when you rang this morning and I'm sorry I didn't ring you last night, please forgive me. I was really ill again. I wondered if you were free tonight? Please say yes. I'm really sorry that I haven't spent a lot of time with you lately. I really want to see you, Rachel. Please say yes. I've missed you so much.'

In truth I was desperate to see him too. In spite of everything, what I really wanted more than anything was for things between us to be back to normal again.

I accepted his apology and we arranged to meet at the studio at seven.

Chapter Thirteen
Conik Penster Dewe

Awash with hubris and self-satisfaction, Conik Penster Dewe glided silently across the floor towards the elevator.

He had just offered the second photograph of Austin to the Cantartis, and he was smugly making his way out of the cold, dark, cavernous vault room.

He took one last look at the vast metal wall behind him, and the thousands of doors held in it before entering the elevator to leave.

Once inside, he steadied himself against its walls. The elevator began to move and it was soon travelling violently upwards. The Hallway of Torches was its destination and its mechanics screamed as it took him there.

A sudden and violent stop signaled the end of its journey and Conik Penster Dewe stood tall in front of the two ornate golden doors in front of him.

Within seconds the doors were open and the two hooded figures that stood on guard silently moved out of his way.

The Hallway of Torches spanned in front of him and he glided down its narrow darkness towards another elevator at its end. A large, heavy metal door concealed the entrance and he yanked hard on its crude metal handle before gliding into the elevator beyond.

Once inside, he reached out and pressed the large black button in the concealed compartment, and within moments he had returned to the floor above.

Underling was waiting for him. His timing, as always, was perfect and, as he yanked back the birdcage doors, Conik Penster Dewe flew swiftly out of them.

A gust of air fierce enough to blow Underling's hair out of

place followed Conik Penster Dewe out of the elevator as he swept down the corridor, gliding through the oak doors into his office with his coat tails flapping behind him.

He turned and smiled at the woman in the painting above the fireplace, tipped his head and addressed her.

'Good evening, Catriona.'

He walked over to the large blackened windows to the right of him and stood silently in front of them, smiling to himself as he drummed his chin with his fingers.

Then came the double knock on the door.

Conik Penster Dewe's voice bellowed loudly and effortlessly.

'Enter, Underling.'

As Underling entered the room, Conik Penster Dewe continued to look straight ahead through the blackened windows in front of him as if he were able to observe the world through them quite clearly.

'Sit, Underling.' Underling did as he was told and took a seat in front of Conik Penster Dewe's desk. His master didn't move. 'How is young Austin responding to the extraction ritual, Underling?'

Underling shifted nervously in his seat before responding. 'He is losing a little of his reserve, Sire, he is beginning to change.'

Conik Penster Dewe span around and stared at him intently with narrowed eyes. 'Really, Underling? Then why do I detect a concerned tone in your voice?'

Underling paused before taking a deep breath. 'Sire, he seems different to the others, he seems to have more resistance than them ... more reserve.'

Conik Penster Dewe smiled contentedly to himself. 'Ah, is that all? He is the last of the Crystal Bloodline, Underling. His contention was always going to be far more potent than the others. Time will change this. As each month passes and the rest of the seven extractions are taken ... then so it will be. His resolve will weaken and his bloodline's influence will decrease to nothing. He will soon be like the others.'

Underling nodded. 'Yes, sire.'

Conik Penster Dewe stared at Underling again. 'This is not

all that troubles you, is it, Underling? There is something else.'

Underling was slow to come forward with any further information, and Conik Penster Dewe's face twisted itself into a silent but explosive expression.

'DO NOT TRY MY PATIENCE, UNDERLING. TELL ME!' he screamed, his acrid breath wafting into Underlings terrified face.

Underling's legs buckled and he hit the floor. He lay there on his side with his arms over his head and his knees drawn up to his chest. His state of terror caused him to hurriedly stutter out his words.

'Yes, sire. I'm sorry sire — it is the girl, sire, the girl, Rachel Coast. Austin Jacobs has feelings for her, and her for him. I believe that this may be affecting the extraction.'

Conik Penster Dewe growled loudly; and suddenly doubled in size. He turned and slammed his hands on the desk in front of him.

'Get up, Underling! This is NOT acceptable — she was supposed to win their trust and their business, nothing more! These sentimental feelings will not get in my way. I want these romantic ties severed as soon as possible.'

Conik Penster Dewe had spent many years observing and studying mankind's psyche. He knew only too well that love was a powerful and unpredictable emotion and to simply wipe Rachel off the face of the earth, which he was more than capable of doing, would not help his cause. Making her disappear without a trace would only empower her hold on Austin's heart and reserve. It wasn't Rachel that he needed to get rid of. It was Austin's love for her that needed to be destroyed.

'Out, Underling! Get out! I need time to think.'

Underling scrambled his way up from the floor and swiftly left the room. Conik Penster Dewe took a seat in his leather armchair. He looked fleetingly at the picture of the woman above the fireplace and then into the flames of the fire.

A complication he had not foreseen now savaged his thoughts. His plan so far had been executed perfectly. He would not allow this love that Austin had developed for Rachel Coast to get in the way.

Austin was the last heir of the Crystal Bloodline, and even

from before Austin's birth, Conik Penster Dewe knew that Austin would probably be the most difficult extraction of all.

The Crystal Bloodline's virtues were intrinsically ingrained in Austin. Every molecule every atom that occupied him was saturated with temperance, charity, chastity, diligence, kindness, patience and humility. He was untouched by greed, envy, anger, lust, gluttony, sloth or pride.

Conik Penster Dewe had already had to implement unorthodox and deceptive methods to get his signature on the agreement. He still needed to corrupt and seduce him to the point that, of his own free will, he would relinquish his virtues before he could extract the final piece of him. This situation that had developed between Austin and Rachel had to be destroyed, one way or another.

The Crystal Bloodline would meet its demise and nothing and nobody was going to get in his way.

He sat quietly drumming his finger against his chin as he deliberated over this infuriating situation that had presented itself.

After several hours of silent contemplation he called Underling back into his office.

'Underling, I need you to organise a few things. We need to put some distance between Austin and Rachel. I want you to send Austin to Paris on a photo shoot. Let Monsieur Medone knows that he will be coming. Inform him that he needs to arrange a fashion campaign *tout suite*. Tell him to pull out all the stops so that Austin is kept as busy as possible. Oh, and most importantly tell him that I want his special girls on the case working their charms. Austin will be paid an extortionate amount of money for the job, and his father can go with him too. Book them into the Imperial Suite at the Hotel Ritz. Give them an open-ended expense account. Keep him there until the next report is due; I want him showered with decadence.' He paused for a second. 'Oh, and Underling, one more thing. I want you to send him the Lamborghini Diablo as a gift from me. Get Sophia to deliver it ... that will be all.'

CHAPTER FOURTEEN
RACHEL COAST

When I pulled up outside Jacobs' Photographic there was a very expensive cherry-red sports car parked right outside. Austin was inside, staring at it through the window. He only broke away from his trance when I walked in.

'Rachel!' His voice was overly enthusiastic, and despite my concerns I was pleased that he was so delighted to see me. He walked me out of the shop and stood at the side of the car. 'Rachel, look at this car, isn't she a beauty?' He waved his arm across the bonnet. 'Say hello to the Lamborghini Diablo!' He held up a set of keys and shook them in the air. 'Get in, go on. Sit in it. Let's take her for a ride.'

I stepped into the car, wondering what was going on.

'This car is a gift from Conik Penster Dewe. Apparently he's been looking at your reports and he's really impressed. So much so that he's given me this car as a gift. How amazing is that?'

This was *more* than amazing, it was unbelievable ... Mr Turnbull certainly hadn't mentioned a thing to me – perhaps he didn't even know about this gift. Perhaps now that Conik Penster Dewe had taken an interest in Austin only certain things were passed through Chandler's. Either way, it was becoming quite clear that the enthusiasm I witnessed when I arrived was not because of me; tonight it seems I was to share his attention with this metal box on wheels.

'Come on, Rachel,' he said. 'You've driven me around enough. Tonight it's my turn to drive you around.'

The engine roared and his eyes glistened as his foot gently pumped the throttle.

'So what do you think of her, she's a beauty isn't she?' he asked rhetorically.

I agreed with him, though personally I wouldn't have cared if we were sitting in a go-cart.

As we drove down the road the smell from the leather seats began to overwhelm me. He put the sound system on and a song I hadn't heard before came blasting out at me. He accelerated a little more and in seconds we were zooming down the high-street.

I sat there, stunned by Conik Penster Dewe's generosity and Austin's excitement. He had never expressed a love for cars. My mother's words of wisdom began to ring loudly in my head. She would often say that the only difference between men and boys was the price of their toys. This car was a very expensive and extravagant toy and Austin obviously loved it.

Still ... I was here sitting in it with him and we were together again for the first time in weeks.

As the evening progressed my hopes for its success began to dwindle. The Lamborghini was the main recipient of Austin's attentions tonight. We drove up west and around the city. Passersby were staring at this cherry-red vision flashing past them; it was a car that could not be ignored, if only because of the sound of its engine roaring loudly as it accelerated.

Austin was determined to tell me the whole story of its arrival at the shop today, and its history and spec. After driving around for hours listening to every laborious detail, we eventually started to make our way back to the studio and Austin finally stopped talking about the damn car.

'Rachel,' he said, 'tonight has been amazing. I'm so sorry that I haven't spent a lot of time with you lately but I really haven't felt very well at all. I've missed you so much.'

It was at this point that I had to say something. Not wanting to be direct about my frustrations, in a teasing tongue in cheek manner I breached the subject.

'I'm glad to hear that, Austin. I thought that you were trying to get rid of me.'

My tone had obviously not been as teasing as I had hoped for, and he stopped the car.

'Please don't say that, Rachel, not even for a second. This last month has been awful and I've wanted to see you more than anything but I really haven't been myself ... I'm still not feeling one hundred percent but I just had to see you tonight.' He hugged me tightly and kissed me reassuringly. Then he dropped the next bombshell. 'Rachel, I'm going away for three weeks. I leave tomorrow. Mr Underling has booked me for a fashion campaign in Paris. I'm going to be working for a very prestigious French client.'

My heart sank. 'Wow that's amazing, Austin.' I smiled as widely and as convincingly as I could.

One half of me was thrilled for him: Paris was one of the fashion capitals of the world, and I knew he dreamt of working there one day. The other half of me felt like I was losing Austin with every passing second. I'd hardly seen him over the last few weeks and it was only in the last few moments that I'd felt any reassurance at all about our relationship. Now he was telling me that he wasn't even going to be in the same country as me for almost a month.

Then I thought about Mr Jacobs. How would he cope without Austin there to keep an eye on him?

'What about your Dad, will he be okay on his own? I can pop over to see him and help to make sure he's okay if you like?'

'Rachel, thank you but there's no need ... Dad's going to come with me. I'll be back in London three weeks tomorrow ... I'll ring you every single day, I promise.' He held me tightly in his arms and whispered in my ear, 'I'm going to miss you so much, Rachel. When I get back we'll spend so much time together you'll be sick of the sight of me.'

CHAPTER FIFTEEN
AUSTIN JACOBS

Gatwick Airport was a hive of activity and we had arrived in good time. A short forty-five minute flight was all the time it would take to get to Charles de Gaulle airport.

I thought it quite absurd that we would have to spend more time waiting for our flight to Paris today than we would spend on the actual flight itself.

No expense had been spared for this trip, and we sailed past the economy class queues as we made our way to the first class lounge. Dad sat down on the first available soft furnishing he could find, and I wandered around checking out the free stuff that was on offer.

This was amazing! I was finally achieving what I had set out to do and more. Being able to take care of Dad and make sure that he didn't have any mental or physical stress had been my main goal. What had happened so far had completely surpassed these ambitions.

We could easily afford to shut the shop for three weeks. In fact, we could afford to shut the shop on a permanent basis with the kind of money I was making. On top of this I had paid off all of our debts, and for the first time in years we actually had some spare cash in the bank. With all of these worries now taken care of, I must admit I was feeling pretty pleased with myself.

Getting booked for this three-week fashion campaign in Paris was a huge cherry on top of a cake that was, as far as I was concerned, already smothered in cherries.

Unfortunately not everything in my life was going so well. Amongst all of this heady success there were two things that were suffering.

One was my relationship with Rachel ... and the other was my health. I didn't know what to do for the best regarding either of them. One way or another, I was determined to do the right thing by Rachel and recently I hadn't. I had to put things right between us; I couldn't bear to lose her.

As far as my health was concerned, I knew that something wasn't right, but it was all so confusing. I had suffered some very unpleasant physical symptoms on a couple of occasions over the last couple of months, but they really hadn't lasted that long. It was the change in my state of mind that seemed to be more permanent, and it was this that I was more concerned about.

A voice blared over the Tannoy system. They had just called our flight. It was time to leave the comfort of the first class lounge and make our way to the terminal.

We boarded the plane and took our places in the large leather seats in the first class cabin. Neither of us had ever travelled first class before and I marveled at the sheer size of the seats, compared to economy class.

'What do you think, Dad?'

He could see that I was really impressed.

'I think this is wonderful, Son,' he said in a slightly patronising tone, as he patted my hand and laid his head back on the headrest. 'It would be absolutely perfect if your mother was here too.'

I had been avoiding the subject of my mother recently. I had become so wrapped up with the success I was enjoying I hadn't had time to think about her or look for her, and I really didn't want to discuss this with Dad ... not now ... so I changed the subject quickly.

Mr Underling had explained that it would be an intensive three weeks in Paris and that I'd be working for pretty much all of the time, so Dad had decided to plan several sightseeing tours to occupy himself for the duration of our stay. He had it all worked out, and he knew exactly where he wanted to go and what he wanted to see.

'So, Dad, where do you plan to go first? I know you've made a list of places to visit.'

My distraction seemed to work.

'Thought I'd go to the Louvre first. See that enigmatic

Mona Lisa smile for myself,' he said, glancing at me sideways. I could tell by the look in his eyes that he knew I was trying to avoid the subject of my mother.

I continued with my obvious distraction. 'Rachel would love the Louvre, Dad ... Get someone to take a picture of you next to the Mona Lisa, she'd get a real kick out of that.'

'Austin, they don't officially let you take photographs of da Vinci's masterpiece. I may get thrown out if I tried and I doubt I'll be able to get that close to it. Speaking of Rachel, I noticed you haven't seen a lot of her lately. Everything all right with you two?'

My relationship with Rachel was another subject that I really didn't want to discuss with him.

'Yes, everything's fine. I've just been feeling a bit tired with all of the work I've been doing lately. I just haven't felt up to going out or seeing her. I've just wanted to rest up a bit. You know, take things easy and get plenty of rest. My workload has been wearing me out.'

He could tell by my verbose response that I was making excuses for my lack of contact with Rachel, but I couldn't tell my father what had really been going on. How could I explain it to him, when I couldn't even explain it to myself?

He nodded at my response and picked up a magazine.

I lay my head back as the plane took off and I began to think about how badly I had treated Rachel recently.

The excited feelings that had nestled in my stomach about this trip to Paris were now being pushed away and replaced by a dark and unforgiving feeling of guilt.

As I lay there with my eyes closed and the jet engines roaring in the background, my mind began to run over the events of the last few weeks. I thought about the fact that I had made up one excuse after another to not see Rachel for over three weeks. My head had been all over the place, especially since the sudden arrival of the voices whispering in my head. They had really shaken me up. They were clouding my judgment and causing me to constantly second-guess myself, and my loyalty to our relationship. I hadn't wanted to see her whilst I was battling against these kinds of demons.

I had hoped to be rid of them before seeing her again. I

wanted to be able to look her in the eyes with the love, honesty and integrity she deserved. Unfortunately, I hadn't got back to normal by the next time I saw her. The monthly report was due again and I'd run out of time to sort my head out.

My eyes flew open, the plane had rocked and shuddered very suddenly and abruptly: we'd hit some turbulence that thankfully only lasted for a few moments. Dad didn't even so much as stir. I fidgeted in my seat before lying back and closing my eyes again. I concentrated on the sound of the humming jet engines and tried to blot out the awful way I'd behaved.

It was of no use – my conscience was determined to plague and remind me, and the sound of the engines faded into the background as I recalled the look of hurt in her eyes the moment she'd walked into the studio that day to finalise the second report.

She hadn't been able to hide her feelings and I couldn't fail to notice them. Seeing her like that had made me feel sick to my stomach and I knew that the decision I'd made to not see her whilst I sorted my head out was wrong. I knew then that my heart was completely loyal and it belonged to her regardless of my state of mind.

I'd tried to start putting things right, there and then, by immediately arranging to ring her later that day with a view to seeing her that evening. These heartfelt plans had not panned out.

My attempt at making things up to her failed miserably. That night I had fallen ill again. As soon as I'd finished the shoot it was as much as I could do to crawl up the stairs and make it to my bed. I didn't even have the energy to ring her and cancel. This was really unforgiveable. Then, to make things even worse, by the time she rang me the next morning I had already started a shoot: I just couldn't talk to her, I didn't have time. I had very rudely cut her short and I didn't get a chance to call her and apologise until gone 5pm.

On top of that, Mr Underling had rung me that afternoon to tell me that I was booked for a three-week campaign in Paris and that I'd be leaving the next day.

This news was not good for our already distant relationship and although I was going to see her that night it would be the first time I'd seen her in three weeks, and the last time I'd see her for another three weeks. All I could do was hope and pray that she'd forgive me and wait for me to come back from Paris.

Looking back on it, the whole day was crazy. About an hour before Rachel was due to arrive the only thoughts or plans I had were of showering her with as much reassurance and attention as I possibly could. Then, lo and behold, a red Lamborghini Diablo in mint condition pulled up outside the shop. A beautiful woman stepped out of it in a figure-hugging red dress the exact colour of the car. I remember thinking how lucky this beautiful woman was to have a set of wheels like that. To my surprise, she walked through the shop door and marched straight towards me. She stopped, stretched her arm out in front of her and dangled a set of keys in front of me.

'Austin Jacobs?' she'd said in a warm and husky voice. My name had slipped off her tongue like velvet.

'Yes,' I'd replied, 'that's me.'

'A gift from Conik Penster Dewe. He is very pleased with your progress and wishes to reward you ... Enjoy!'

After that, she'd released her grip on the keys and they had fallen towards the floor in slow motion. My reflexes had been immediately triggered and I'd caught them just as she glided gracefully out through the door. A black limousine with blackened windows was waiting outside for her and I'd watched as the car door flew open for her to get in.

I remembered thinking that I really liked this Conik Penster Dewe fellow. He really knew how to incentivise someone. It was barely an hour after this that Rachel arrived; she definitely wasn't as excited as I was about this glorious car.

It was only then, sitting on the plane, that it dawned on me. This damn mechanical masterpiece had completely stolen the limelight from her. Before the car had arrived my only intention had been to shower her with affection and reassure her of my feelings for her, especially as I was just about to leave the country for three weeks. My attentions, however, had been completely redirected to an inanimate, unfeeling machine. With this realisation fresh in my mind, I began berating myself even harder. I opened my eyes, sat up and marveled at my gross stupidity – I was such an ass!

The captain's voice suddenly cut through the air. 'Ladies

and gentlemen, we will soon be arriving at Charles de Gaulle Airport. We hope you've enjoyed your flight.'

With my newly found and freshly brewed guilt to wrestle with we made our way through the airport. As soon as we went through passport checks an immaculately groomed chauffeur, complete with peaked cap, greeted us. He announced that his name was Philippe and that he would be our chauffeur for the duration of our stay. He took our luggage and we followed him to a black stretch limousine parked outside.

Chapter Sixteen
Austin Jacobs

Three weeks in Paris lay in front of us. A suite at the Hotel Ritz was ours for the duration of our stay and I had read up on the hotel; it was something I always did whenever Dad and I went anywhere and I just couldn't break the habit. As we made our way from the airport towards the centre of Paris I began to relay some facts I had learned about the Hotel Ritz to my dad.

For example, I had learned that a royal architect designed the façade by the name of Mansart in the late seventeenth century and the construction of the hotel had begun in 1705. Apparently every Royal Head of State had stayed there. I could just imagine those grand souls slumbering under the down quilts on the finest linen sheets under fifteen-foot-high ceilings.

The rooms apparently looked out over the elegant Place Vendome, and Coco Chanel herself lived in the hotel for so many years that they named a suite after her.

Yes ... this was without a doubt one of the best hotels in Europe and it was steeped with history. We were booked into its most expensive and famous suite of all: the Imperial Suite.

After almost an hour of making our way through Paris' hectic traffic, Philippe, our chauffeur, pulled up outside its grand entrance. It was a beautiful looking building and I marveled at its architecture. As we walked in, its opulence and history began screaming at us from all sides.

My father and I looked wide-eyed at each other. It was obvious that we were both feeling quite overwhelmed.

The manager greeted us and took us to our suite on the first floor. His English was impeccable, as were his manners.

My father kept looking up at the intricate ceiling and admiring the eighteenth century paneling. The large gold baroque mirror on the wall looked like something out of a grand and wondrous fairy tale.

Gold and red furnishings that looked too pristine to sit on surrounded us. We were both too scared to touch anything in case we broke it or dirtied it.

The entire suite was listed as a national monument of France. The eighteenth century paneling was protected under the suite's historic monument status. That alone was enough to intimidate us,

After our initial shock and awe subsided, we eventually began to explore our surroundings. We had our very own dining room just for us.

We opened another door and found that it led to the bathroom. I gasped when I saw it. The first thing I noticed were the huge gold swan-shaped taps, they were beautifully ornate and perfectly crafted. I stared in disbelief at the Jacuzzi and the steam bath shower. The towels and robes were a beautiful shade of peach. Amongst the information I had found on the hotel, I had read that the colour peach had been chosen over white because it was believed to be more flattering to a woman's complexion. It seemed that every detail had been carefully thought out and planned.

I glanced at my watch; unfortunately the time for exploring was over. I had to get ready for my meeting.

Dad finally sat down, still staring at the grandeur as if he were caught in a trance, so I shouted my goodbyes to him before making my way downstairs. Philippe was standing in the foyer waiting for me.

He was to drive me to my meeting at the office of Monsieur Medone, the client that I would be working for. Sitting back in the back of the stretch limo, I took out a camera and photographed my way along the journey.

Philippe suddenly spoke, breaking my concentration. 'Monsieur Awsteen, could you put your camera away pleese, we will soon be at ze offices of Monsieur Medone.'

I did as I was requested. We were approaching a tunnel and it was only as we entered it that I could see how incredibly long it was. The light at the end of it was no bigger than a pinprick.

It took about fifteen minutes to travel its length and exit its darkness. Mr Medone's office block stood tall and proud just beyond it. It was an extremely modern looking building: the bottom half was made up of large, blackened windows, whilst the windows in the top half were as clear as crystal. I had never seen a design quite like it before.

Philippe escorted me up the steps and into the foyer. He led me to the elevator and announced that Monsieur Medone's office was on the fourth floor. The doors closed and I pressed the button.

When the elevator doors opened again a beautifully dressed woman greeted me. She looked more like one of the models I photographed than a PA or secretary. She led me down a long hallway and into Monsieur Medone's office.

***

His office was dark and very warm. The walls were completely covered with old wood paneling and an old marble fireplace roared at the back of the room. It was a surprising contrast to the super modern look of the building, and not what I had expected at all. The windows inside the office were as black and opaque as they appeared from the outside.

Monsieur Medone was sitting in his office chair behind his desk. He span around and flashed a beaming white smile towards me. The contrast between his cream three-piece suit and his ebony skin was striking. His Afro hair was short and slick and his cheekbones stood high in his face. I wondered if he had been a model in his younger days as he stood up to greet me.

'Awsteen come in please sit down. Monsieur Underling has told me so much about your work. You come highly recommended.'

I took a seat and our meeting began.

After two long hours, the meeting with the very charming, chic and sleek Monsieur Medone was over and I now had an exact itinerary of where I would be, and what I would be doing for the next three weeks. Some of the locations he had chosen were outstandingly beautiful. I could see that one of my biggest challenges on this campaign would be making sure that the locations did not outshine the models and dominate the photographs.

I had arrived in Paris in a whirlwind and Mr Medone informed me that my first shoot would be tonight – or should I say, tomorrow morning, as I had to be at the location by 3am. My schedule was all over the place, 3am one day, 6pm another. These next three weeks were going to be a challenge. It was almost 7pm when I got back to the hotel and I needed to get some sleep.

Before taking to my bed, I rang Rachel to let her know we'd arrived safely. Hearing her sweet voice made me feel sad and guilty. I couldn't stop telling her how much I missed her.

***

My alarm rang. It was 1am already. I sprang out of bed and within half an hour I was washed, dressed, and ready to leave for the shoot. Philippe was already waiting for me in the foyer.

Everyone was already there when I arrived. Makeup artists rushed around, and the dressers and designers were busily chatting amongst themselves.

After some formal introductions and further preparations the shoot was under way. It was going brilliantly: I had my head in the game, and I was getting all the shots I wanted.

The crazy images and whispers I'd been experiencing over the last few weeks were not haunting me tonight, and I was relieved that my focus was intact. Just as the shoot was coming to an end the last two models walked out. They were wearing royal blue jewel-encrusted lace bikinis that only just covered their modesty.

Suddenly, intimate images of them began to flash through my mind. The whispers began to taunt me again and I couldn't get the image of the two models lying on my very expensive Imperial Suite bed out of my head.

I had managed to get through the whole shoot unscathed until now. The whispers in my head were getting louder and I was finding it harder to hold on to my composure. *Look at those smooth, long, silky legs*, they whispered. I tried to ignore them. *Austin*, they whispered again, *Imagine what it would feel like to touch those long beautiful legs. It's so easy, you're so handsome, just click your fingers and the girls are yours, do what you want with them.*

I kept trying to think of Rachel. I had to fight this. Pure lust was such a dangerous and empty emotion. It was as old as time and as savage as a beast. What I had with Rachel was not going to be ruined by some animalistic urge that had no content or meaning. These thoughts helped me to hold my composure and, at last, the shoot was over.

Exhausted from my early start and the internal conflict I was battling with, as soon as the last frame was in the can I asked Philippe to take me back to the hotel. I needed to get away from everyone; especially those models.

I sighed with relief as my head hit the down-filled pillow. My next shoot was scheduled for later that day at 6pm and I slept through until 3pm. When I got up I walked through to the dining room and on the table I found a note from Dad.

Hi Austin, hope your shoot went well last night. I've gone to see Mona, be back later.
Love, Dad
Xxx

Ah! He was already at the Louvre. He was really looking forward to seeing Leonardo's "Mona Lisa", this was his first point of call on his sightseeing trip. I, however, had two hours to bathe, eat and prepare myself before leaving for the next shoot.

***

For the whole three weeks of our stay, one day merged into another with no real distinction between them. On top of my crazy schedule I also had these recurring and unwanted images of models in compromising situations calling me to them. The whispers were running a-muck in my mind and fighting them was proving to be exhausting.

Dad on the other hand was having a very relaxed time

and he looked really well. This trip was certainly doing him the world of good.

I was missing Rachel like crazy, and I focused on my intense feelings for her every time I heard a whisper or saw an image.

Even though I'd managed to ring her at least once a day, I'd barely had any time to speak to her at length.

Due to my hectic schedule and time constrictions, the luxury of the hotel was also wasted on me. However, Dad was savouring every moment and he was eager to tell me all about the gourmet meals he was enjoying, and how swimming in the hotel's Roman bath inspired swimming pool was simply incredible.

He reckoned that they played soothing music under the water. I was amazed that he had actually gone and bought himself swimming trunks. I don't think he'd stepped foot in a pool for twenty years. It was good to see him having a well-deserved break like this.

We were due to fly back on the Sunday evening and Saturday had finally arrived. This was our last night at The Grand Ritz Hotel. This life of luxury was coming to an end, and we would soon be back in our very penurious little flat above our photographic shop. As shabby as our little flat was I actually missed it, no matter how basic it was, it was home.

All of the scheduled shoots were over and the proofs looked amazing, even if I say so myself. It really was some of my best work and I was delighted and relieved that it was finished and in the can.

Dad and I had arranged to have dinner in the main restaurant and I was really looking forward to it. Other than a few quick snacks together, we hadn't seen a lot of each other. It would be wonderful to spend a few hours in the hotel restaurant with him. No more models on shoots to distract me and spark off any whisperings, just me and Dad and lots of amazing food and drink.

The restaurant, like the rest of the hotel, was simply stunning, and boasted a tree bearing lilac flowers right in the middle of it. Our table was right beside it and the smell of its blossom was faint but distinct.

We had just ordered a bottle of wine when my dreams of

having a quiet dinner with Dad came to a sudden and abrupt end.

Monsieur Medone and the two models that had distracted me on my first shoot had just walked into the restaurant. Mr Medone caught my attention and he and the models made their way towards us.

'Awstin, hello. I hope you don't mind. I thought we could join you for dinner this evening. This must be your father.'

My heart sank but I remained polite and professional. 'Yes it is. Dad, this is Monsieur Medone.'

Mr Medone bowed and held his hand out. 'Hello, Mr Jacobs. I'm very pleased to meet you.'

Dad stood up and shook his hand. 'Pleasure to meet you too,' he said, looking quite at ease with the situation.

'Mia and Louise will be joining us. You remember them, Awstin, they were two of the models on your first shoot.'

Of course I remembered them, I had spent nearly three weeks trying to forget the effect they had had on me. This couldn't have been any worse. Having to sit through dinner with them was the last thing I wanted to do.

'Yes, of course. Hello Mia, hello Louise.'

Their response to my greeting was sophisticated and alluring. '*Enchanté*, Awstin et Monsieur Jacobs.'

Dad nodded and smiled at them both. His face reddened slightly as he tried to hide the fact that he was quite taken aback by their beauty.

Several waiters suddenly rushed around us and moved us all to the large empty table on our right.

How could I voice my disapproval of this situation? How could I say no to Mr Medone? This was the client who was paying me, and picking up the tab for our hotel and expenses. I wanted to have a quiet meal with Dad. I really didn't want to be sitting here with these two models, or Monsieur Medone, but one way or another I had to grin and bear it like a professional. This was going to be hard work and I was not looking forward to it.

Monsieur Medone was, in fairness, an extremely charming and gracious host and offered us helpful suggestions and recommendations from the various dishes on the menu.

As the evening progressed I desperately tried to avoid any eye contact with Mia and Louise and I successfully managed to focus my attentions towards Monsieur Medone and Dad.

As each new course arrived so did a different wine and by the third course I was starting to feel a bit tipsy. I wasn't used to drinking like this, but my nerves were getting the better of me and I gulped down one glass after another.

Just as I was about to take another swig a vivid image and loud whisper flashed through my head and stopped me in my tracks.

I could see Mia and Louise dancing together. It was a very seductive dance, I saw myself sandwiched in between them as they twisted their bodies around me.

I slammed my wine glass down on the table and everyone jumped.

'Awstin are you alright?' said Monsieur Medone

'Son?' Dad said, a worried look on his face.

I needed some space — I had to get out of there. 'I'm so sorry, I don't know what came over me. Please excuse me, I must use the bathroom.'

The restroom was just outside in the foyer, and my legs couldn't take me there quickly enough.

My head was spinning and my face was hot. I placed my hands flat on one of the marble vanity units attached to the bathroom wall. My breath was short and sharp, and I reached for the tap and splashed my face with cold water in an attempt to cool myself down and clear my head.

I hadn't noticed the attendant sitting behind the door until he said something to me in French. I answered him with my standard response.

'*Non parle vous Francais, Monsieur.*' The words spluttered out of my mouth in my terrible French accent.

'Can I get you anything, sir?' he replied in his terrible English accent.

'No, thank you, I'm fine,' I replied. I was far from fine, and I wasn't ready to go back to the restaurant. I locked myself in a cubicle and thrust my head into my hands.

Rachel! I had to think of Rachel and how much I loved her.

It was only a matter of hours before I'd be back in London. Tomorrow night all of this madness would be over.

My head was finally beginning to clear. Dad would start to

worry if I didn't return pretty soon. I knew I couldn't hold out here much longer.

I stood up and straightened myself before exiting the cubicle. The attendant smiled at me as I walked towards the marble sink. After washing my hands and making sure I was presentable, I left the rest room and returned to the table.

At first Dad smiled when he saw me, then that silent questioning look flashed across his face. I knew that look so well; he didn't have to say a word. He was worried and wanted to know if I was all right.

I smiled back and tipped my head slightly to let him know that there was no need to worry – I was fine.

Our silent communication ended when his smile returned, and I sat down next to him hoping that this dinner would end, too. Surely there couldn't be many more courses. We'd eaten so much already. Monsieur Medone had just ordered desserts as well as the appropriate wine to accompany each of them. My hopes lifted; this night would soon be over.

After what seemed like far too long a time to spend eating desserts, the evening was finally reaching a conclusion.

I could almost taste it, I was almost there – home free!

Just as I was about to attempt wrapping up the evening, Monsieur Medone announced that he wanted me to go to an end of campaign party, saying that it was in my best interests to attend it with him. He insisted that there would be lots of influential people there that I needed to meet. Apparently it was being held at the most exclusive and private venue in the whole of Paris. Only the wealthiest and elite Parisians even knew of its existence.

WHAT? This was all I needed. His invitation was fuelled with dichotomies and sent my evaluation of the situation into overdrive. On the one hand, I wanted to run a hundred miles away, ring Rachel and lounge on the bed until I fell asleep. On the other, I knew that attending this party would be an incredible career opportunity. Somehow, I had the distinct sense that it would be a really *bad* career move if I tried to get out of going.

Monsieur Medone thrust a drink into my hand. 'Come on, Awstin, drink up. We'll be going soon – lots of important people to meet.'

Running on nothing but the effects of adrenalin-fuelled confusion, before I knew it I was sitting in the back of a stretch limo with Monsieur Medone, Mia and Louise.

Dad had managed to excuse himself from this outing. He had been quite emphatic that it was not the place for him, arguing that it all sounded too loud and energetic for a man of his tender age. His refusal was expected and accepted, but I knew that mine wouldn't have been.

Monsieur Medone opened a small fridge in the back of the limo and pulled out a bottle of Bollinger.

'Time to celebrate!' he said. 'Mia, Louise ... hand me the glasses.'

A glass of champagne was thrust into my hand, and I was encouraged to drink it up as the limo snaked its way around the Parisian streets.

After two more glasses of champagne, we came to a stop in a dark, quiet lane. Plain red brick industrial-looking buildings stood either side of us. Philippe opened the door and Monsieur Medone slid off his seat and got out.

'Okay, everyone, if you could just wait 'ere for a momant.'

He walked towards a small black door just to the side of one of the plain brick buildings. Then he disappeared into the shadows across its threshold.

Seconds later he returned. 'Okay, everyone, it's time to party.'

I gestured to Mia and Louise to step out of the limo before me and we all followed Monsieur Medone towards the small black door hidden in the shadows.

As we reached it, it creaked open and I could hear muffled music pounding in the background. Two huge men were standing in the doorway, and they nodded at us as we walked passed them.

We had just entered a small wooden-clad lobby. Old tapestries adorned the walls and red drapes hung from the ceiling. The decor was dark and antiquated and it reminded me a little of Monsieur Medone's office. At the far end stood two beautifully carved wooden doors. The pounding, muffled music seemed to be coming from their direction and I stared as the two huge men walked towards them and pulled them open.

The muffled music was suddenly unleashed and we were blasted with its full volume. The scene before us was electric. Hundreds of beautiful people lost in this musical, tribal bliss. I stood there for a moment as I watched them. I could feel their reckless energy bounding towards us. The music was loud – really loud. The bass pounded its resonance through the floor into my system, coursing through every part of me with every beat. I felt an intoxication sweep over me as we walked into this wonderful, madding crowd. Just as I was falling into the freedom of it all, I stopped suddenly in my tracks.

Huge projections of the photographs I had taken for the campaign were dancing around the walls. They twisted and turned as they moved along the brickwork's uneven surface.

Monsieur Medone took my arm and began introducing me to one person after another; so many people's names flew into my head in such a short space of time, I couldn't possibly hope to remember them all.

We finally reached a private balcony that overlooked the whole room. Two beautiful girls stood tall, holding trays of drinks at the top of the stairs, and we all took a glass before making our way to the edge of the balcony. The music suddenly stopped and everyone looked up at us. A tall blonde girl wearing a white leather leotard, and a black sequined top hat handed Monsieur Medone a diamond-studded microphone. He took my arm and pulled me to his side.

'*Bon soir*! Good evening! Ladies and gentlemen, now that I have your attention, allow me to introduce you to ze very young, the very 'andsome and as you can see –' he gesticulated towards my photographs that were still projecting themselves along the walls '– ze very talented, Monsieur Awstin Jacobs!'

A loud applause erupted from the crowd gathered below. Their attention and applause was overwhelming and surprisingly enjoyable. This was a validation of my talent like I had never dreamed of. I had never experienced anything like this; I felt like a goddamn rock star. I was being recognised and applauded for my work by people that could actually make or break my career.

The applause came to a natural end and the music began to play again. The bass still thudded and the volume was still as potent, but the style and pace of the music had taken a dramatic and sudden change of direction.

The dancefloor below us had emptied and everyone was gathered around it.

Mia and Louise suddenly appeared. They began to dance seductively towards each other. Their dance was so captivatingly graceful and alluring, even though I wanted to look away, my eyes wouldn't let me.

They glided across the floor, their bodies spinning and entwining their way around each other as they finally made physical contact. This was just like the image I'd seen earlier tonight in the restaurant. I had seen their bodies swoon and dip in rhythmical harmony like this before. Along with the rest of the room, I was mesmerized by their fluid and seamless sensual dance.

'Good, aren't they?'

Monsieur Medone was still standing firmly by my side.

'Yes,' I replied. 'They look like professionals.'

'They are sisters. They learned to tango before they even learned to walk,' he explained.

I turned back to look at them and they were looking up at me and beckoning me towards them. The crowd was cheering and Monsieur Medone grabbed my arm.

'Go, Awstin, everyone wants to see you dance with them ... go and give them what they want, and have some fun!'

To say that I was feeling under pressure would have been a gross understatement. It seems I had no choice I had to go and join them.

I made my way down the stairs and towards the dancefloor.

They were both standing firm, thrusting their hips sideways in perfect time with the music, waiting for me to arrive. I moved towards them; my head was spinning but still I kept walking. Mia took my hand and pulled herself towards me. She was stronger than she looked. Louise took my other hand and wrapped herself around my back. I was sandwiched in between the two of them. They pulled away from me in turns as they began an intricate, perfectly-timed seductive dance, spinning, moving and twisting their bodies. With my head still spinning, I closed my eyes. I could feel them moving seductively around me.

***

It was 7am, and I'd just woken up. My eyes were still shut, but my consciousness had begun to stir and awaken. I opened my eyes with trepidation.

Thank goodness, I was in my Marie Antoinette bed in the Imperial Suite at the Ritz, exactly where I should be.

As I slowly awoke I began to formulate more lucid thoughts and I quickly realised that the last thing I could remember was dancing with Mia and Louise in the club with Monsieur Medone. I sat upright in bed and began digging deep into my memories for some kind of recollection of the events after that.

My head was pounding and no matter how many times I went over it, after my dance with Mia and Louise I couldn't recall a damn thing. My struggle to remember continued, and then a sudden gut-wrenching thought entered my mind.

Rachel! I hadn't rung her last night.

I knew that she would be frantic by now. I reached for the phone; it was already 12pm — it would be 11am in London. I called her number.

As soon as she answered I began apologising profusely.

'Rachel, hi it's me, Austin. I'm so, so, so sorry that I didn't ring you last night. I had to attend an end of campaign party with Monsieur Medone, I just couldn't get out of it. It was too late to ring by the time I got back to the suite. I can't wait to get back to London to see you. I'm missing you like crazy. Are you okay?'

Her voice swept sweetly down the phone and I was relieved by her response.

'Yes, I'm fine now that you've rung. I was worried when I didn't hear from you last night.'

'I'm so sorry, Rachel, but I really couldn't get out of going to the party. There were important people there that Monsieur Medone wanted to introduce me to, but I'd much rather have been in my bed and on the phone to you.'

I didn't tell her about Mia and Louise, or that I couldn't remember a thing after my dance with them. I ended the call by telling her that I couldn't wait to see her and that I'd ring her from the airport as soon as we landed in Gatwick.

As I put down the phone I felt a mixture of relief and guilt wash over me.

I got up and went to check on Dad. He was nowhere to be seen, but there was another one of his notes on the table.

He had gone to the last destination on his list: the Eiffel Tower. He had left it until last because of its outstanding symbolism. It was the most renowned and famous landmark in Paris: its signature piece. Just as I finished reading the note the phone rang. Its sudden shrillness made me jump.

It was Monsieur Medone.

'Awstin! How are you feeling today?'

'Monsieur Medone, hello. I'm fine thank you, and thanks for last night and for hiring me for your campaign. It's been such a pleasure working for you.'

'Awstin, the pleasure is all mine. You are worth every penny, your photographs and last night's party were a hooge success.'

I desperately wanted to ask him about last night. Find out what had happened, and how I'd got back to the hotel. I didn't ... I couldn't. How could I let him know that I had no earthly idea, no recollection whatsoever of what had happened after the dance with the girls? This would have been really unprofessional, so I let the matter slide and pretended everything was fine.

'Thank you, monsieur, you are very kind.'

'Nonsense it is what you deserve. *Au revoir*, Awstin, we will speak soon.'

'*Au revoir*, Monsieur Medone.'

Silence filled the room once more and my head was still laced with confusion as to what had happened last night. I paced around the suite, slowly packing my belongings. Within a few hours Dad and I would be making our way to the airport, and we'd soon be back in London.

The afternoon passed slowly as I continued to agonise over my lost memories. No matter how hard I tried to remember I couldn't recall a single thing. I was sipping a steaming hot, freshly-brewed cup of coffee when the door to the suite opened: it was Dad.

'Hello, Son. Good to see you up and about. You were sound asleep when I checked on you earlier. You must have come back very late last night, I didn't even hear you coming in.'

Okay, decision time. Should I tell Dad that not only did I have no idea what time it was when I came back, but that I didn't even know how I got there, or should I just lie? I chose the latter option.

'Yes, Dad, it was quite a party. It went on much longer than I expected.'

Dad sat down and let out a loud sigh. 'Well as long as you enjoyed yourself, Son. I guess I'd better start packing my stuff, we'll have to leave soon. Any chance of a coffee before I make a start?' He looked at me and smiled.

'Yes, Dad, of course. I'll get one for you now.'

We sat for a while discussing the Eiffel Tower and the events at the party that I could remember. Our conversation continued as Dad packed his suitcase, and before long we were ready to leave the hotel.

The journey to the airport went quickly, and when we arrived Philippe insisted on carrying our cases into the departure lounge.

By the time we boarded the plane and took our seats in the first class compartment, I was beginning to feel tired, so I lay back and waited for takeoff.

As soon as my eyes closed a spike of adrenalin suddenly coursed through me, and a disturbing image flashed through my mind. It was of me, Mia and Louise together. We were all lying on the Marie Antoinette bed in the Imperial Suite. My heart began to race nervously as more images swiftly followed. What I saw was so intimate that it made me feel sick.

I opened my eyes and breathed deeply from the confusion that now engulfed me. Perplexed by the origin and authenticity of these crazy images, I couldn't work out if what I was seeing was just my imagination, or if they were actual memories from the night before: I honestly had no idea.

CHAPTER SEVENTEEN
RACHEL COAST

Austin had been in Paris for three long weeks and the day of his return had finally arrived. It was almost 9.30pm and his flight from Paris would soon be arriving at Gatwick airport.

I had hardly slept a wink the night before, staying up waiting for a phone call from him that never came. He had rung me every day, and so I was quite distraught by the time I eventually heard from him at around 11am this morning. His call was fuelled with apologies and explanations. The fact that he said he'd gone to a party and got home too late to call me was, I have to admit, a little concerning, but I refused to allow myself to get worked up about it. Instead, I focused on the fact that he was on his way back to London.

The compulsion I felt to jump in my car and drive to the airport to meet him was overwhelming. I kept imagining myself running across the runway and flying into his arms. Unable to concentrate on anything else, I paced around my room, looking at my watch obsessively.

The clock hit 9.45pm and my phone rang. It was Austin – my heart leapt out of my mouth.

'Rachel, hi ... it's me.'

'Hi, Austin, are you back?'

'Yes we are, we're on our way home now.'

'How was your flight?'

'It was fine ... Rachel, I know it's late and I know you're coming over to us in the morning to sort out the next report ... but I can't wait until then. I really need to see you tonight, is that okay?'

'Yes, of course it's okay. I can't wait to see you either.'

'Great. I'll be there as soon as I can.'

I put down the phone and caught a glimpse of myself in the mirror. *Crap*! I looked like a bag lady. He'd just spent three weeks photographing some of the most beautiful women in the world; I couldn't let him see me like this.

Then I looked around my bedsit. Even though I could afford something better, I just hadn't got around to flat hunting. There was so much going on in my head, moving on from this claustrophobic living space was the last thing on my mind

Austin had never seen my extremely humble home, and he had just spent three weeks in the luxury of the Ritz in the Imperial Suite of all places! Both I and my bedsit had some tidying up to do, so I set to it straight away.

I span around my room like a tornado and I managed to shower, dress and put my makeup on in record time. The adrenalin that was coursing through me was both assisting and delaying me in my lighting quick actions. Then my phone rang again.

'Hi, I'm outside fancy letting me in?'

'Y-yes,' I stuttered, 'I'll be down in a minute.'

Austin had arrived a little sooner than I'd expected. I quickly glanced around the room, it didn't look great, but it would have to do. Then I stopped in front of the mirror and checked myself for the last time. With no more time to preen myself, I would have to do too!

Heading down the stairs, I took an extra deep breath before opening the door. A huge bouquet of flowers greeted me. It was so big that it almost hid Austin's face.

'Austin?' I shrieked – I couldn't stop my excitement from spilling out of me.

He lowered the bouquet and revealed his glorious, enthusiastic smile. Paris had agreed with him. He looked even more handsome. I could feel my legs starting to wobble and my heart grinding to a halt.

'Rachel, these are for you.'

'Austin, they're beautiful! Thank you, come in.'

As I walked up the stairs to the first floor I felt so conscious of him walking up behind me. I hadn't looked at myself from behind – I hoped I looked okay.

We reached the door to my bedsit and before we walked in I turned to him and apologised. 'Please excuse the mess. Oh, and I have to warn you ... it's really, really small.'

It really was a small room with almost everything in it. My three-quarter bed was positioned in the middle of the back wall. One corner was sectioned off and housed a kitchenette whist the other housed a very small shower. One wall consisted of wardrobes and a space for my TV. My small two-seater sofa lived by the bay window, and that was it.

'Rachel,' he said, 'I've come to see you, not your bedsit.'

We walked into the room, and without even taking a glimpse at the surroundings, he span me around, took the flowers out of my hands, and threw them on to the bed. Then he held my hands and pulled me close to him.

'Rachel, you have no idea how good it is to see you. I'm so sorry that I haven't been here for you over the last couple of months. Since the first time I got ill I really haven't felt myself. I care about you so much, Rachel, and I beg you, please don't hold my terrible behaviour against me.'

I broke my silence. 'Austin,' I whispered, 'I don't hold anything against you.'

This moment was so perfect I didn't want to explain to him that his behaviour had actually been driving me mad, and filling me with consuming and veracious doubts about his true feelings for me. In that moment I just wanted him here with me, holding me close. The last two months of madness had been so hard. I had spent most of it wondering if his lack of contact with me was his way of letting me down gently.

I'd hoped in my heart that this wasn't the case.

In this perfect moment I had the confirmation that it was not. My feet wanted to dance, and my voice wanted to sing. Austin was here with me at last, thwarting my doubts and filling my heart with confidence.

We stood clutching each other, neither one of us wanting to break away. Eventually, we parted slowly and reconnected once more with a long, lingering, gentle kiss.

My temperature soared. His kiss was so soft so tender and so full of temperance.

Then he pulled himself away from me, quickly and

abruptly. 'Rachel, I have to go.'

What? So soon? I didn't understand. 'But Austin, you've only just got here.'

'I know and I'm really sorry, it's just a fleeting visit tonight, I really can't stay any longer but I had to see you.'

Just as he was about to walk out of the door, he reached into his jacket pocket and pulled out a small box. 'Before I leave, I want you to have this. I hope you like it. Oh, and there's a card with the flowers too.'

He kissed me quickly on the lips and fled out of the door.

Alone again, I sat on the edge of my bed staring at the flowers and the small box in my hands. I reached for the flowers and looked for the card. It was hidden neatly between a rose stem and some gypsophila. It was a tiny card in a tiny envelope, the type that typically accompanied flowers. It made me wonder if florists thought a verbose amount of words were not necessary when you had just said it all with flowers.

I opened the envelope and read the words on the card inside it.

I see forever when I look into your eyes.
All my love, Austin
xxxx

My heart swelled as my emotions cracked with relief; I burst into tears.

Forever was the exact amount of time that I had in mind to spend with Austin. His beautiful words staring at me made me feel ten feet tall. I felt like I could jump out of my window and fly around this wonderful, crazy world, whooping and cheering on my way.

I was so carried away with these affirming words that I had almost forgotten about the small box.

With the words from the card still swimming around my head and filling my heart to the brim I picked it up and took off the wrapping. Beneath it was a black and gold leather case; it looked really expensive. A small gold button protruded from the front of it. I pressed the button and the box opened... I gasped.

A small raindrop-shaped crystal glistened against the red

velvet interior. It was attached to a beautifully delicate silver necklace.

A raindrop, a crystal raindrop … I was completely dumbfounded. I'd never told him about the raindrop that had landed on my cheek and how it had affected me. This must be serendipity at work. It was by far the most appropriate and beautiful gift I had ever received.

I took it out of the box and made my way to the mirror. Pulling my hair to one side, I clasped the necklace firmly into place. The crystal raindrop seemed to draw every light in the room towards it.

I lay back on my bed, watching the reflections bounce and dance around the walls. Then I closed my eyes and wrapped my arms around myself.

Yes, I was alone again, Austin had left very suddenly, but his visit tonight had thwarted my doubts. For the first time in a long time I felt content, warm, loved and wanted.

Chapter Eighteen
Austin Jacobs

I left Rachel in such a hurry. As much as I wanted to stay with her I couldn't. As we clutched each other tightly in her bedsit, a gut-wrenching guilt began to slowly wash over me. The images of me, Mia and Louise began to fill my mind again. I tried to push them away but they were relentless and they kept bombarding me with their veracity. I had to leave before I did or said something stupid that I'd regret. I made my heartfelt apologies, hoping that my sudden departure hadn't upset her.

What had happened to me on my last night in Paris? Had I really spent it with Mia and Louise in my Marie Antoinette bed as the images suggested? I had planned on spending much more time with Rachel this evening but these damn images kept getting in the way.

On my way home the images began to fade and subside, and by the time I got to my bed they had finally stopped haunting me. I pulled my quilt around me and buried my head in my pillow.

CHAPTER NINETEEN
RACHEL COAST

7.30am. My daily alarm buzzed loudly, dutifully fulfilling its purpose for the day. I reached out and hit the cancel button. I was up, and I was awake.

I'd fallen asleep fully-clothed on top of the bed again. Over the last couple of months this had become a bit of a habit.

I undressed, took a quick shower and readied myself for work.

The November sun was shining brightly, and the world seemed like quite a wondrous and extraordinary place. The drive to the office was slow and traffic-bound as usual, yet today the miserable faces in the office that greeted me had no effect on my effervescent mood.

I busied myself with paperwork for an hour or so, and then the clock struck 10.30am, this was my cue to leave. I grabbed my briefcase and hurried out of the office. I was scheduled to be at Jacobs' by 11.30am to finalise this month's report and take the photograph.

Ding-dong ding ... how I loved that bell on Jacobs' Photographic shop door. It had without a doubt become one of my favourite sounds in the whole world, and my heart soared as its chimes filled my ears. Mr Jacobs was overjoyed to see me.

'Rachel, how the devil are you?'

He looked about ten years younger than the last time I'd seen him. His ravaged features were somehow smoother and his face looked more relaxed than before.

'Mr Jacobs!'

He came over and hugged me.

'You know, Rachel, it's about time you called me Ted — this Mr Jacobs won't do anymore, it's Ted from now on.'

'Ok, Mr Jacobs ... I mean, Ted,' I said warily, not yet comfortable with this change of address towards him. 'Did you enjoy Paris, Mr Jacobs?'

He tipped his head and glared at me as if to berate me for addressing him like this.

'Sorry, Mr Jacobs — I mean, Ted.'

His face now widened, his avuncular smile beaming at me once more. 'Yes, Rachel, I had a wonderful time.'

'You look really well Mr ... sorry — Ted.'

'Why thank you, Rachel! I feel pretty good too! But enough about me, I'm sure you're eager to see Austin. He's in the studio working again ... he worked so much in Paris, Rachel, he had no time to enjoy the sights. He didn't even get to enjoy the incredible French cuisine — well not until the last night anyway. Go on, I'll see you later.'

I bounced towards the door at the back of the shop and into the studio.

Austin was mid-shoot. He didn't notice me walking in so I stood there, silently watching him work for a few moments. It was only when he stopped to change the film in the camera that he spotted me standing there.

As soon as he saw me that enthusiastic smile beamed its way towards me and bowled me over. He ran towards me and wrapped his arms around me hugging me tightly. 'Rachel!' he said. 'I've been longing for you to get here.' He looked at me and saw that I was wearing the necklace. 'You liked your present then?'

'I *love* my present,' I responded.

The models began coughing in the background, making it quite obvious that they were trying to draw Austin's attention.

'Rachel, give me five minutes and I'll be with you,' he said. 'I've just got to finish this shoot, I'm almost there.'

'No problem,' I replied.

This would be the third report I had compiled for Conik Penster Dewe and the third picture I would have taken. It was all a bit mad really.

I understood that Conik Penster Dewe needed a written report. He had taken a financial interest in Austin. Of course he would need a report, this made perfect sense, but I couldn't for the life of me work out why he needed a photograph. I couldn't really understand how this would benefit his knowledge of the business. But hey, who was I to question it? Any excuse to see Austin was warmly welcomed.

He finished the shoot, and I had his full attention as we quickly ran over some of the figures in the report. Then it was time to take the photograph. He pulled a typical male model type expression and flicked his hair back before placing one of his hands on his hips. He looked so funny it made me laugh, and I paused to compose myself before taking the photograph. He held his pose and I pointed the camera at him.

Click.

Austin's arms dropped to his side and he shook his head. Then he doubled over and rested his hands on his knees.

I moved towards him. Something was wrong. Before I reached him, he was standing upright again.

'Austin! Are you all right?'

'Yes, I'm fine, I just felt a bit dizzy for a second. I'm okay now.'

He didn't look fine, the colour had drained from his face, but he insisted that he was okay. Then he shooed me out of the studio, kissing my hand as I left.

'We've both got work to do, Rachel. I need to prepare for this afternoon's shoot, and you need to get back to the office with the report.' He kissed my hand again and looked up into my eyes. 'I'm fine! Stop worrying! I'll pick you up later and we'll go out somewhere nice,' he added.

I left him to his work somewhat reluctantly, and returned to the office with the finished report.

***

All afternoon I kept running over the course of events in the studio. My mind was totally distracted from my work. All I could think about was seeing Austin later.

He was supposed to pick me up at 7.30pm, but he rang me at 6.30pm and cancelled our plans. He was feeling really ill again. This was crazy; I couldn't understand how he could feel fine one minute and then feel so ill the next?

Of course I was absolutely devastated that I wouldn't be seeing him tonight, but I was more concerned about his state of health. He sounded terrible on the phone; he could hardly speak to me.

I called Mr Jacobs.

'Hi Mr – sorry, hi Ted.' It still felt really awkward addressing him like this.

'Hi is that you, Rachel?' he whispered.

'Yes it is.' I don't know why, but I whispered my response. 'Is Austin okay?'

'I'm really worried about him, Rachel. He's in bed, he's not feeling well again ... this is not normal.' Ted sounded really concerned.

'Oh Ted, I'm really worried about him too! Do you think he should see a doctor?'

'I'm one step ahead, Rachel. The doctor is on his way now.'

I was so relieved to hear him say this.

'Ted, please let me know what he says.'

'Will do. I'll ring you as soon as he's left.'

'Bye, Ted ... thank you.' I put the phone down, and not knowing quite what to do with myself I began pacing around in ever decreasing circles, wide-eyed, worried and waiting for Ted's call. I would usually have rung my parents for a quick chat around this time of day, but I didn't want to miss Ted's call, so I delayed calling them.

An hour dragged by but still nothing. I turned on the television and flicked mindlessly through the channels. Two hours later my phone finally rang.

'Rachel, it's me, it's Ted.'

'Hi! I've been so anxious. Is Austin okay, what did the doctor say?'

'Well, Rachel, he's examined him and it seems that he's in good health. The doctor isn't sure why he's feeling ill. All of his vitals are in tip-top condition, but just as a matter of course and to be on the safe side, he's arranged an appointment for him at the hospital this week. Then they can carry out some tests and check a few things.'

A sense of relieved confusion swept over me. On the one hand I was relieved that the doctor had said he was in good health, but on the other hand my concern had deepened. If everything was okay, why did he keep getting these bouts of illness?

'Thank you so much for getting back to me, Ted. I've been sitting here worried to death about him.'

'Don't fret, my dear, he's okay. Now you take care of yourself and stop worrying. I'll see you soon.'

'You too, Ted ... goodnight.'

'Goodnight sweetheart ... sleep tight.'

Chapter Twenty
Conik Penster Dewe

Conik Penster Dewe stood straight and tall with his head held high. He tilted his head back and shot off the ground. His flight upwards appeared effortless as he hurtled his way along the face of the vast metal wall. He came to a stop hundreds of feet above the ground and the metal door just in front of him slowly creaked open; he glided gently forwards into the vault that had just opened itself to him.

After landing quietly inside, he stood poised and prepared as he readied himself to offer the third photograph of Austin Jacobs to the Cantartis.

The words 'Cantartis awaken!' bellowed from the depth of his stomach.

The Cantartis reacted immediately to his command and began to rock slowly from side to side before spinning wildly and leaving its plinth. As it became airborne, it lost its solid shape, and transformed into a glowing, gaseous mass that circled and swooped in the air above him.

It descended slowly, twisting and spiraling until it finally swooped down and hovered above the photograph. Its delicate tendrils reached out tentatively before pouncing and enveloping it completely. The photograph safely inside its smokey bosom, it shot into the air, dancing and skipping as it made its way back to the crystal plinth. It reverted back to its solid state and the light inside it glowed even brighter than before.

Conik Penster Dewe folded his arms with delight and squinted as its luminosity refracted around the room, lighting up his cold, dark violet eyes. A sinister grin began to sprawl slowly across his face. He held his macabre expression perfectly as he admired his handiwork. The light that shone so steadily and brightly in the Cantartis suddenly flickered for a moment, and a troubled expression began to mask his delight as a crease in his brow gave his concern away. His smile was not quite as sinisterly enthusiastic as it had been, and a more troubled look occupied his eyes. He stared quizzically at the incandescent light, watching and wanting it to stop and be still again.

His troubled wait was over. The light finally stilled itself. He watched carefully for a while to make sure that its glow was stable, still and steady.

The flickering he had just observed in the shining light before him meant one thing only: Austin was resisting the extraction.

He drummed his chin slowly with his index finger before turning promptly. He cricked his neck to the side and in a lightning flash movement, he projected himself like a bullet away from the Cantartis and out of the vault. He shot downwards at some speed until he suddenly stopped twenty-five feet off the ground. His arms stretched outwards and his coattails billowed around him as he hovered in midair before slowly floating downwards.

He was now sitting comfortably in the leather armchair that stood alone in this vast, never-ending room, save for a raggedy old standard lamp that stood loyally by its side. Its loneliness welcomed him and he seized its leather arms, gripping them tightly as he closed his eyes. His hands gripped tighter as he dug his nails into the old worn-out leather before pulling himself forwards and opening his eyes.

'Release your locks!' he screeched.

The hinges began to creak as the thousands of metal doors flew open in one collective movement.

Each light ripped its way around the room as if they were trying to blind his soulless eyes. The light in the middle of the wall that had once looked so small was now much bigger than before. It was not quite as large as the others, but the darkness that had initially surrounded it was slowly disappearing.

He sat silently in his leather-clad chair, his eyes straining to widen under the brightness of their glory. He began to move his head and tap his feet. His fingers were drumming his chin as if he were listening to a symphony that only he could hear. He struggled to widen his eyes and as he did, their violet colour intensified.

Unable to bear their brightness any longer, his eyes closed, and he dropped his head towards the floor. His raven-black hair fell loosely around his face, and he held his pose for a few seconds before gripping the arms of the chair tightly once more. His head flew back with a jolt as the lights continued to bombard their way around the room.

A babble of unintelligible words streamed from his mouth and what started as a whisper ended up as a thunderous roar. 'Enough! *Velieris vestri lux lucis.*'

The metal doors reacted immediately to his command. In one seamless movement, they slammed shut, throwing the room into darkness. He remained seated, apparently soothed by the sudden visual silence, and his voice groaned deeply like a man who had just had his every desire satisfied.

He rose out of the chair and flew towards the lift, stepped inside it and muttered the words, '*Reverto mihi iam.*'

The lift shook violently as it made its return journey upwards. It stopped, opened its doors, and before him stood the two hooded guards and the long corridor. Three of the seven candles were now lit and they burned brightly as he made his way along the corridor to the elevator at its end.

Underling was poised and ready to open the birdcage doors on the floor above, and when Conik Penster Dewe arrived, Underling yanked them back. Conik Penster Dewe flew out of the elevator and whizzed past him towards the large oak doors of his office. The doors flew open and the fire roared its greeting on his arrival like a loyal pet acknowledging his masters return.

'Underling!' he bellowed in a loud, piercing voice.

Underling jumped and was there in a matter of seconds 'Yes, sire?'

'We are now almost half way through the process, yet Austin Jacobs is *still* resisting the extraction ritual. His resistance is being influenced by his feelings for this damn girl.'

Underling looked nervous. 'Yes, sire.'

'We must destroy the love he holds for her, Underling! And it has to be *his* decision to let her go!'

'Yes, sire.'

'The Lamborghini, the imperial suite at the Ritz Paris, and Mia and Louise were not enough to lure him away from her.'

'Yes, sire, they were effective. He was taken in and seduced by the car and the opulence of the suite at the hotel Ritz exactly as you planned it, sire. Though, for some reason, he has no recollection of the events with Mia and Louise ... it seems he has some sort of mental block shielding his actions from him. I believe it is because of the situation with the girl.'

'Enough!!! The girl has to go, we must put more distance between them.'

'Yes, sire'

'After the next extraction, his resolve should not be quite as robust as it is now. In the meantime, I want him kept busy and far away from that girl. I want you to surround him with further distractions and temptations and I want you to organise a fashion campaign with Francois. Fly him and his father to Milan in a private jet, I want no expense spared; give him an open-ended expense account and make sure he spends some time at Lake Como.'

'Yes, sire. I will arrange everything immediately.'

CHAPTER TWENTY-ONE
AUSTIN JACOBS

The thumping headache and the churning stomach pains I had been experiencing throughout the night seemed to have disappeared. That awful sense that my lifeblood was being siphoned from me was finally gone, and the chink of light that always seemed to creep its way through a small opening between the shut curtains cast its morning beam across my bed.

I opened my eyes and stared again at the dust particles trapped in the sunbeam. My eyes became lost in their trance as I watched them bounce and spin, basking in its warmth. My alarm startled me out of my stupor as it buzzed loudly.

My head felt as clear as a bell and as I stretched my arms towards the headboard and tensed my legs, my limbs felt strong and agile. Leaping out of bed, I looked in the mirror and – even though I say so myself – I looked really good. Dad was in the kitchen and he looked surprised to see me bouncing through the door with such energy.

'Austin! I was just about to bring you a cup of tea, I didn't expect to see you up. How are you feeling?'

'I feel fantastic, Dad, as good as new. Sit down and don't worry about making tea. I'll make us breakfast.'

I whisked some eggs and added some milk and flour before firing up the gas and getting the frying pan out. Before long, we were sitting opposite each other eating hot pancakes and fresh blueberries.

He gulped it down and sipped at his tea. As his cup chinked back down on the saucer he looked up at me and gave me that half-worried, half-loving furrowed brow smile that I knew so well.

'You know how much I love you son, and I know you think

you can take on the world, but I've got to tell you ... I'm really worried about you.'

I pushed the sugar bowl towards him and smiled. I wasn't faking it; I really did feel great.

'Dad, I feel great, I swear — and anyway, I'm sure I heard the doctor say I was fine.'

Dad squinted at me as if he were examining me and trying to determine if I was telling the truth or just fobbing him off.

'You do look pretty good, son, I have to say. And yes, the doctor did say that you seemed to be in good health, but he also said that he wants you to have some tests in the hospital just to make sure.'

'Yes I know, Dad. I heard him.'

'Good. Well in that case, I want you to promise me that you'll go this week no matter how good you feel now.'

I reached across the table and took Dad's hand in mine. 'Dad, I promise I'll go to the hospital for the tests.'

He placed his other hand on top of mine and nodded. We then chatted about Paris as we cleared up the breakfast dishes, and when we'd finished we made our way downstairs to open the shop.

We'd only just unlocked the door when Mr Underling walked in. He hadn't rung to say he would be coming and I wasn't expecting him — my initial thoughts were panicked ones. Was everything all right? Had I done something wrong? Was I in trouble? Was it anything to do with my last night in Paris?

'Austin, Mr Jacobs, good morning.'

'Good morning, Mr Underling,' Dad and I replied in unison.

Mr Underling tipped his head towards us as if he had every intention of bowing. He would do this quite often throughout conversations. It was such an unusually subservient mannerism for a man in his position.

'I trust you both enjoyed Paris?' he enquired.

'Oh yes, beautiful place,' Dad replied. I agreed with his reply and repeated his sentiment.

'Yes, it is a beautiful place, Mr Underling. We had a wonderful time.'

Mr Underling's presence always made me feel a little

nervous and anxious. He was my lifeline, my one and only agent, my link to the amazing clients I'd been working for, and ultimately the key to my success. He had the power to make or break me, and I was acutely aware of this.

'You impressed a lot of people in Paris Austin ... well done,' he said in a very matter of fact manner.

Relief swept over me. 'Thank you, Mr Underling.'

He nodded. 'As a direct result of this success, you have been booked to cover another fashion campaign. It will be another three week schedule and you'll be based in Milan for most of the time.'

My mind began to race as his words began to hit me. Milan – this was unbelievable, I was being sent to another fashion capitol! I really was becoming an international fashion photographer: Paris and now Milan.

'When do we leave?' I blurted out excitedly.

'Tomorrow evening,' he replied. 'A car will pick you up at six o'clock and drive you to Heathrow airport. A private jet has been chartered for your flight. You will fly from Heathrow to Linate airport in Milan.'

My father and I looked at each other in disbelief. Mr Underling went on to explain that we would be staying in the Presidential Suite in the Principe Di Savoia Hotel. He handed us a copy of the itinerary and added that I would be working for a client called Francois Frettere. I would be taken to meet with him and he would brief me on the detailed schedules of the shoots over the three-week period.

He tipped his head forward.

'Good day, gentleman.'

The doorbell rang out as he closed the door behind him, and my father and I stood silently, listening to its chimes. Just before it stopped ringing I leapt off the ground and punched the air with excitement. This was unbelievable. *In only three short months, my dreams of becoming an international fashion photographer were coming true.*

Dad turned to me with a worried look on his face.

'Austin,' he said, 'are you feeling up to this? I know you're feeling okay today, but last night you were in a really bad way, and Dr. Albright has booked you in for those tests.'

'Dad, Dad, don't worry! I feel great, I'll see if I can arrange to go to the hospital first thing tomorrow morning to get the tests done before we leave. Will that make you happier?'

'I'm sorry, it's just that I worry about you son, I can't help myself. The last couple of months have been a bit of a whirlwind for you. Maybe too much of a whirlwind? You haven't had a second to stop and catch your breath.'

I jumped up and down on the spot and ran up and down the shop.

'Dad, look at me – I'm fine, I'm young, I can take this. Look at our life now compared to what it was. Our debts have been paid; we've got no more money worries. Opening up the studio and working for Mr Underling has been the answer to our troubles.'

Dad nodded and his face broke in to a weak smile. Then his expression changed and a more serious look followed.

'Austin, we haven't really talked about your mother since all this madness began, I know your time is completely taken up, but I don't want us to forget about her. I know she's still out there somewhere and we need to find her.'

He was right; I had avoided the subject of my mother completely. I didn't have time to go and look for her. The truth was that recently, I had begun to wonder how realistic it was that my mother was still 'out there', as he put it. It had been almost twenty-two years since she'd disappeared. I had begun to wonder if my father was just hanging on to this quest so that he could hang on to her memory. His love for her knew no bounds and I understood this, but it was different for me. I was young, I had my own life to live, my own dreams to follow. After the events of the last couple of months, even though my health and my relationship with Rachel were suffering, I was still enthralled with the reality of achieving my dreams and making enough money to make Dad's life less stressful. I knew that he needed some sort of positive response from me so I placated him.

'As soon as we get back, Dad, I'll find time to look for her. I promise.'

His face finally broke into a genuine smile. 'Okay, son, you go to the hospital tomorrow morning and as soon as we get back from Milan you'll start looking for your mother again ... yes.'

'Yes, Dad!'

With my father now happy again I relaxed for a moment ... then my thoughts swiftly turned to Rachel. All of the plans I had in mind to make things up to her would have to be put on hold.

This was not what I wanted – I wanted to spend time with her, and I knew that I needed to, but this was my career. I was finally achieving my most distant dreams; dreams that I had pretty much given up on, dreams that I thought were virtually lost to me.

I couldn't give up on them now, I just couldn't. I had to go to Milan. I needed to establish and concrete my career before being able to call the shots and work when I wanted to. If I was ever going to become a man that had the character and the means to be the rock that Rachel and Dad needed, then this was the time to make myself that man; these were still early days and I had to establish myself. There would be sacrifices made by all, but the long-term goal would be worth it.

With my decisions justified, and just one night left in London before leaving for Milan, I knew that I would be spending every hour of it with Rachel. I picked up the phone and rang her.

'Morning, Rachel.'

'Austin! Hi how are you feeling? Are you all right?'

Her voice sounded concerned and anxious. I quickly reassured her.

'Yes, Rachel, I'm fine. I feel great, I'm so sorry again about last night, Dad told me that you'd rung to see how I was. Thank you.'

'I was worried about you, Austin, I'm so glad he called the doctor. He told me that you were okay but that the doctor wanted you to go for some tests,' she said, an air of concern in her voice.

'Yes he's booked me into the hospital – just as a routine. To be honest, Rachel, I feel amazing today. On top of the world ... honestly, I'm much better and I'd really like to take you out tonight. Can I come over and pick you up at about seven?'

Her voice sounded brighter and less strained when she replied. 'Yes, of course, Austin.' Then it changed back again. 'But only if you're feeling up to it.'

'Wild horses couldn't keep me away from you, Rachel,' I replied reassuringly. 'I'll be there by seven. See you later.'

***

My Lamborghini Diablo was such a dream to drive. It certainly caught the attention of every man, child and beast that it passed. I made it to Rachel's just as the clock hit seven, and she ran out to meet me as I pulled up outside.

Her auburn hair shone like a glorious sunset, and fell down around her face as she moved towards the car. She looked so happy as she flashed her beautiful smile at me. My stomach flipped with anxiety as she got closer. I wanted tonight to be perfect, exciting and wonderful, but my stomach churned with dread from the thought of telling her that I would be leaving for Milan the next day.

It had taken some doing, but I had managed to book a whole restaurant just for us. It was a small Italian bistro near Leicester Square and it had a reputation for offering the finest pasta dishes in the whole of the London.

We pulled up outside and the valet took my keys.

The staff stood to attention when we walked in. The sound of acoustic guitars, and sweet violins spun through the air embracing our ears. Dimly lit lamps with soft amber lights were dotted around the room. Candles graced every table and flickered to the music. The atmosphere was perfect. Rachel looked suitably impressed with my efforts; when I explained that I'd booked the whole restaurant just for us, she looked satisfyingly stunned.

It wasn't just the romantic connotations of my gesture that had made me think of doing this; it was also because I didn't want to run the risk of bumping into any females that may distract my attentions from her. For the first time in a long time, everything had gone as planned: the evening was just perfect.

It was almost time to take her home, and I still hadn't told her about my impending trip to Milan. During dinner she had tried suggesting things that we could do over the next couple of weeks. It had got harder as the night progressed, but I managed to brush her suggestions aside by continuously changing the subject.

We walked outside hand in hand and stood under a streetlight as we waited for the valet to bring us the car. Its warm glow shone down on us, and Rachel looked breathtaking; her pale auburn hair shone like pure sunlight under its beams and her eyes sparkled like innocent jewels. How I wished I had my camera on me. If I could have captured the image of her glowing so beautifully under that streetlamp it would have been the ultimate photograph of pure unadulterated beauty. Rachel was it — she was beautiful inside and out. Her eyes shone with honesty, and as I stared at her I knew that I could never even contemplate the thought of ever loving anyone else. The feelings I held for her were imprinted on every atom inside me. She was it, the whole package. I knew there and then that no matter what: she was the one.

She laughed and teased me as we waited for the valet to bring the car to us and it felt like old times. Like things used to be. I hoped that this was a sign that things were getting back on track. Perhaps all of the madness of the last couple of months was finally behind me.

About halfway along the journey to her bedsit she asked if I wanted to meet up tomorrow night. I couldn't delay telling her about Milan any longer. As we drove along, I began to explain.

'Rachel, I'd love to, there's nothing I would like more, and I need you to know this when I say that I'm really sorry, but I won't be able to.'

Her beautiful, happy, glowing face dropped and a sad, hurt look took its place. 'Oh okay, guess you're busy. I'm sure you have lots to do, that's okay,' she said, faking a smile.

I pulled the car over, took off my seat belt and turned to look at her. She was silent and staring straight ahead.

I lifted up my hand to touch her cheek and I turned her face towards me. 'There's nothing I'd like more than to see you tomorrow night. I'm sorry, I know I should have told you earlier but I didn't want to spoil our evening. Mr Underling has booked me on another three-week shoot. It's in Milan and I leave tomorrow evening at six o'clock.'

She looked stunned at first, then she quickly smiled. 'Austin, that's wonderful news, it really is — you'll be working in another fashion capitol.'

Her mouth was smiling but her eyes were full of sorrow. I reached over and wrapped my arms around her.

'I'm going to miss you, Rachel. I know going to Milan is great for my career, and thank you for being so supportive, but I'm really going to miss you.'

She hugged me tightly and whispered, 'I'm going to miss you too.' She pulled back from me a little and then gently punched my arm. 'I want you to go and knock them dead, hotshot international fashion photographer. You go and slay them.' Then her arm dropped on to her lap and her head bowed, and in a quiet voice she whispered, 'But I'm still going to miss you.'

It had to be said that Rachel Elizabeth Coast, the girl I loved, was seriously amazing. I looked at her in awe as I pulled her close to me. She pressed against me and I could feel her heart beating loudly in her chest. I lifted her chin up and pressed my lips against hers. They were so soft, warm and inviting. I pressed my lips harder against them and our kiss deepened. My head began to spin and my legs began to feel hot and prickly. Soon, I was oblivious to my surroundings and lost in the passion of the moment.

Then – *bam!* Images of Mia and Louise began to sear through my mind. I quickly pulled away from Rachel and pulled my seat belt around me.

'Well, Miss Coast, we can't stay parked up here forever. We'd better make a move and get you home.'

The journey back to her bedsit was, for the most part, silent. We held hands all the way, only releasing our grip when I needed to change gear. The images of Mia and Louise were plaguing me constantly and when we finally got there, I brought the night to a sudden end. The last thing I wanted to do was upset Rachel in any way but I didn't know what else to do. I had to get away. It wasn't over: the images were still taunting me.

***

The next day was frantic; I had so much to do before leaving for

Milan. Besides packing for a three-week trip, Dad had insisted that I go to the hospital for the tests before leaving.

Dr Albright had been very accommodating and he had managed to fit me in for an eleven o'clock appointment at the hospital. By three o'clock I had been prodded and poked for four hours, and by four o'clock I was home, packed and ready to leave.

Dad had decided to research the hotel we were staying in on account of the fact that I was up to my neck, and had no spare time to do it.

He had discovered to his delight that our suite had its own private spa and swimming pool. When he relayed these details to me I was sure that he must have got them wrong, but I didn't bother to question him about them, not when he had such a huge smile on his face.

He was like an excited child, speedily spewing out facts about Milan and the Presidential suite we would be staying in. He was particularly delighted about the fact that Frank Sinatra had stayed in the very same suite on countless occasions. It was apparently the suite most favoured by royalty and the rich and famous. It had been this way since the hotel first opened in 1927.

The chauffeur-driven limousine arrived promptly at ten past four to take us to Heathrow airport, and by five thirty we were boarding a private jet.

The stewardesses that greeted us looked more like catwalk models than aviation employees. The captain welcomed us on to the plane and held a brief conversation with us about the weather before we settled in our seats. The luxurious interior was incredible, like something out of a glamorous film. We had flown first class to Paris and had been amazed, but this private jet was something else.

The white leather chairs, huge white leather sofa, and fifty-four inch TV were all ours to enjoy; a whole plane occupied by only the cabin crew and us. Glamorously gilded and absolutely heavenly, this travelling space was more like a plush apartment than a means of transport.

This life that my father and I had recently embarked on was the complete polar opposite compared to the life we had led before; it really was another world.

The luxury that surrounded us was faultless. It was beyond comprehension or dispute and it inspired surreal feelings of awe as the senior stewardess gave us the grand tour.

We took our seats and prepared for takeoff. I listened to the engines as they began to fire. The plane began to move and we were soon speeding down the runway. Faster and faster, it accelerated until we felt that gentle push backwards. We were off the ground and on our way.

In a few short hours we would be in Milan.

Dad and I had only just begun to relax and really enjoy the facilities on board, when the captain announced that we would we be landing in twenty minutes. After a very smooth landing, we were soon making our way speedily through customs. A chauffeur called Mario was waiting for us and we followed him to a limousine parked up outside.

When we arrived at the Principe De Sovoia we made our way to a private lift that led directly to our suite. Mario pressed the button for the tenth floor.

When the elevator doors opened we gasped at the suite that lay beyond them; the sight that greeted us was nothing short of breathtaking.

Dad was absolutely right – I couldn't quite believe it. The suite actually did have its own pool and spa, and its setting was incredible. As we explored room after room, I couldn't stop wishing that I was sharing all of this opulence with Rachel.

It had been such a long day and even though I was fuelled with excitement, I was starting to feel a little tired. I checked my watch; it was getting late and I had to be up early for a breakfast meeting with Francois Frettere at seven o'clock the next morning. I needed to get some sleep and I needed to ring Rachel.

'Rachel, hi it's me it's Austin, can you hear me ok?

'Yes,' she replied. 'It's a really good line.'

'We've arrived safely and we're in our suite, it's amazing! I wish you were here with me.'

'I wish I was there with you too.'

Even though my eyes were nearly closing, we chatted for nearly an hour. I told her all about the private jet and the layout of the suite, describing all of its grand features in detail until my fatigue finally got the better of me.

'I'm sorry, Rachel, I don't really want to put the phone down but I'm going to have to go. It's been a long day and if I stay on the line any longer I'm going to fall asleep on you. I've got a breakfast meeting at seven in the morning. I miss you so much, I'll ring you tomorrow.'

My eyes closed the moment I put down the phone and I fell into a deep sleep.

CHAPTER TWENTY-TWO
AUSTIN JACOBS

My alarm shrilled loudly through the early morning Italian air. Mario, our designated chauffeur, was due to pick me up at quarter past six and I had less than an hour to wake up and get ready for my breakfast meeting with Francois Frettere.

Mario was exceptionally prompt and arrived exactly on time. He was an older man, possibly in his early fifties; his stature was short and squat and he was bridled with a very large midriff. When he opened the limo door, I noticed that he wasn't wearing a wedding ring. I wondered if his roundness was a credit to his mother's home cooking, and imagined him sitting at an old wooden kitchen table with a huge bowl of pasta and meatballs lovingly laid out in front of him, his spoon and fork shoveling the delicious dish into his eternally starving stomach.

I was still in the process of waking up properly as we drove along. Unfortunately, I first saw the modern and ancient architecture that graced the Milan skyline through slightly bleary eyes; I wasn't awake enough to be able to appreciate it at all.

We suddenly entered a long tunnel. It was much like the tunnel Philippe had driven me through in Paris when I went to meet Monsieur Medone. Just as we left the tunnel, I saw a building ahead of us that looked familiar. As we drew closer I was amazed to see that it was pretty much the exact same design as the building in Paris. Mario pulled up right outside and got out before opening my door and tipping his head towards me. My eyes drifted upwards, scanning the glass structure, and as we walked up the steps Mario pushed the glass entrance doors open.

As we entered the foyer I noticed that the layout was exactly the same as the building in Paris. Mario directed me to the elevator and told me that Signore Frettere's office was on the fourth floor. If my memory served me correctly I was sure Monsieur Medone's office was on the fourth floor too.

As I made my way upwards I wondered if Monsieur Medone and Signore Frettere worked for the same company. Branding was everything in the fashion world – perhaps this extended to their office buildings too, perhaps they all had to be exactly the same. After all, the business they were in depended entirely on image and projecting an immaculate perception.

I arrived on the fourth floor where a very attractive woman in a sharp black suit greeted me. She led me down a corridor and stopped in front of a large oak door. She knocked twice before opening it. The smell of freshly-brewed ground coffee wafted through the air and hit the back of my throat. It smelt delicious.

I stood still in the doorway for a moment. The interior decor of the office was very similar to Monsieur Medone's office in Paris; dark wooden panels clad the walls, and the atmosphere felt distinctly familiar.

Signore Frettere was sitting in a large leather chair behind a grand old desk. He smiled broadly as I walked into the room.

He was quite a striking looking man, graced with classic tall, dark and handsome looks. He must have about thirty or so and his whole persona screamed wealth, power and confidence. His white shirt hung loosely from an obviously athletic physique; although casual, it was definitely designer and very expensive. His trousers were casual chinos but I knew without a doubt that they were made from the finest cashmere. This was a man in control of everything, and his grand smile broadened as I walked in.

'*Buon giorno*, Signore Jacobs, welcome to Milan.' He stood up and made his way towards me. He placed his hands on my shoulders and kissed me squarely on both cheeks.

'*Buon giorno*, Signore Frettere,' I replied, a little shocked from his gregarious greeting.

He stood back from me and gestured towards the chair in

front of the desk.

'Please take a seat, Signore Jacobs. Would you like a coffee?'

I moved towards the small leather chair opposite his large antique desk and sat down.

'Yes please, Signore Frettere, a coffee would be lovely. It smells delicious.'

'Now there is a word that I haven't heard for a while. "Lovely" really is one of the quaintest British words ever. Don't you think, Signore Jacobs?' He went on without giving me a chance to respond. 'How do you take your coffee?'

'Black with one sugar, please.'

He nodded towards the very attractive woman in the sharp suit. She nodded back. Then he began to exchange pleasantries with me about my journey, the suite at the Principe Di Savoia Hotel and various other superficial topics until the attractive woman had finished pouring my coffee and placed it on the desk in front of me.

After I'd taken a couple of sips, Signore Frettere got down to business and began running through the schedule for the next three weeks in painstaking detail. His energy was exhausting, and his attention to detail was simply obsessive.

My schedule, it seemed, was jam-packed, but thankfully not quite as hectic as Paris. Dad would be delighted; we could finally spend some time together.

After three long hours the meeting was over. I was exhausted, but at least I had been briefed fully and I had my itinerary.

Mario drove me back to the hotel. The traffic was gridlocked and it was almost lunchtime by the time we arrived.

As I walked out of the private elevator and into the Imperial Suite, its unbelievable grandeur hit me again. Five hundred square meters of absolute luxury and overt opulence. I called out to Dad as soon as I arrived back. I heard a faint voice calling back to me.

'I'm in here, Austin.'

I called out again. 'Dad, I'm back. Where are you?'

'I'm in here, in the pool.'

Dad was floating peacefully in our private pool whilst Frank Sinatra's voice sang quietly in the background. The room itself was amazing. It was like walking into another time in history.

'Wow this place is amazing, Dad!'

He gently opened his eyes and stood upright in the water.

'Yes, it certainly is,' he said. 'How was your meeting? I hope they're not going to run you ragged like they did in Paris.' His relaxed expression turned to one of concern.

'No, Dad.' I looked at him and smiled. He looked so content standing there in the water. I knelt down close to the water's edge and looked at him. 'Dad, I won't lie to you, the schedule is a bit hectic. My first shoot is at a villa on Lake Como. I have to be ready to leave by 4pm, but it's not as mad as Paris.'

He looked at me with concern still etched across his face. It only lightened when I repeated and promised again and again that it was not as busy as Paris and that I'd be having dinner with him tomorrow night.

He finally lay back in the water and closed his eyes.

'Good ... that's good,' he said, as he bobbed along, humming quietly to the dulcet tones of Frank Sinatra.

'I'll leave you to it, Dad. See you later.'

He raised his hand out of the water and waved to me.

I made my way to the master bedroom. The softness of its velvet-studded walls surrounded me as I lay there on my bed. Even though I only meant to close my eyes for a second I ended up drifting off into a deep sleep.

It was the phone ringing loudly in my ear that woke me up.

'Signore Jacobs, we have to leave ... we have to leave now. Where are you? I was expecting you ten minutes ago.'

It was Mario, the chauffeur. I'd slept all afternoon; it was ten past four – he was waiting for me and I wasn't ready! This was not good. I leapt out of bed and grabbed my jacket. I didn't even have time to say goodbye to Dad – I just ran out of the door.

It was a good hour's drive to Lake Como from Milan. This was both a good and bad thing. It was good that I had time to wake up and collect my thoughts, but bad that we may arrive late because of my tardiness.

This was so unprofessional and it bothered me. I tried to excuse it by convincing myself that I must have needed the sleep. That's what Rachel's dad would have said. As this thought flew through my mind, the memory of Rachel and me falling asleep on the packaging in the studio raced through my mind. A feeling of contentment and warmth ran through me.

Mario's voice interrupted my thoughts.

'We are almost there, Signore Jacobs, do not worry, we will arrive on time'

He was right; within the next few minutes we had pulled up outside a twelve-foot-high wrought iron gate.

Mario pressed the intercom and announced our arrival. The gates opened slowly and we drove through them. A long driveway lay ahead of us, with trees full of pink and white blossom lining the way. A large white villa with a red terracotta roof was just visible in the distance. As we drove towards it, music began to filter quietly through the air. The closer we got, the louder the music became, and by the time we reached it the bass was thumping underneath us.

There were models and people everywhere. The atmosphere was more like a party than a photographic shoot. We walked in through the front doors and Signore Frettere appeared at the top of the sweeping marble staircase, a model draped on either arm.

He looked down at me and shouted very loudly over the music. 'Austin, you've arrived!'

He descended the stairs and glided over to greet me. He placed his hands on both of my shoulders and gave me a kiss on each cheek.

'Follow me Austin, let me show you around. I have some strong ideas as to where I'd like some of the shots to be taken, but I want you to have a look for yourself! See what you think!'

The villa was huge and absolutely magnificent. It had an outdoor pool that was adorned with marble statues on each corner and a formal, well-manicured parterre dominated the grounds. Signore Frettere showed me around, pointing out suitable backdrops that he had chosen. I suggested a few variations. Some he warmed to, others he kindly dismissed.

It was decided the first shoot would be outside, the scenery was breathtaking. The lake was like a millpond and shimmered gloriously for miles into the distance. The snowcapped mountains rising above it were mirrored perfectly in its reflective surface. Lake Como was truly some of nature's finest work, and a place that should be seen by everyone. I stood drinking in the view for a few moments; I wished that Rachel were here with me, she would be as mesmerised as I was.

Being presented with this beautiful setting was going to make it hard to remember that the model was the subject, and the location the backdrop. Outside, shoots were a lot more challenging than studio or inside shoots because the light was constantly changing. Luckily, I always carried a compass – especially for cloudy days. Trying to establish which direction the sun was shining in was impossible with heavy clouds above, but it was vital to know where the light was coming from and the human eye alone could not evaluate this. My compass would help me locate the sunlight today.

A team of technicians rushed around setting up tripods, flags and umbrellas, and I instructed them as to where I needed everything to be placed. I checked the light, adjusted a couple of the reflectors and the shoot began.

The models were open to all my directions and I was getting some really interesting shots. I had been quite taken aback and a little apprehensive when I first arrived to what seemed to be a swinging party but, despite my initial impressions, the models were incredibly professional. We wrapped it up after about two hours and everyone took a break for refreshments before moving onto the next setting. Signore Frettere had selected four other backdrops around the villa and it took us a further six hours to eventually arrive at the last setting of the day. It was getting late and I was starting to feel tired. I wanted to finish this last shoot and get back to the hotel so that I could ring Rachel and get some sleep.

We made our way up the sweeping staircase to the first floor of the villa. Just down the hallway to the left was the bedroom that Signore Frettere had chosen for the last shoot of the day. This was the lingerie part of the collection. I suggested that perhaps it was a bit clichéd and obvious to photograph them in a bedroom setting and offered him alternative ideas, but he was firm in his choice and would not be swayed.

The bedroom looked like an eighteenth century boudoir. Deep red velvet drapes splattered with gold inlay dominated the room and adorned the four-poster bed. An intricately carved wooden walnut dressing table stood out from the wall. Its mirror was edged with gold guilt and golden cherubs clung to each side of its base. It was a fascinating and regal period piece. This was an extremely grand looking room, and I began to warm to the idea of this as the setting. The technicians were there, everything was set up, and we were ready to start.

The models were fantastic and they were making my job really easy. As we were nearing the end of the shoot, the two models that had previously been draped on Signore Frettere's arms walked in. The lingerie they wore was by far the most seductive of the whole range: long, golden toned legs adorned with black sheer stockings and French knickers that revealed more than was required when certain poses were offered to me. Something suddenly stirred in me and as I began to photograph them, I began to imagine them wandering around my bedroom in the Presidential suite. I could see myself sitting in the Jacuzzi, sipping champagne whilst watching them gracefully remove one garment after another as they paraded provocatively in front of me. I heard the whispering voice again, encouraging me to look at them in a way I shouldn't.

I struggled to focus on getting the final shots of the lingerie shoot in the can. It was finally over. The relief I felt was incredible but the energy it had taken to ignore the images and the whispers had left me feeling exhausted. The last half hour had drained every last drop out of me.

Signore Frettere thanked me for my work as he walked me to the front door.

'I won't keep you any longer, Austin, we have an early start tomorrow.' He smiled as he bid me goodbye.

Mario made it back to the hotel in good time, and by the time I arrived in the Presidential Suite I was ready for bed. Dad was still up and he was floating in the pool again. I don't think he'd changed out of his swimming trunks since we'd arrived here.

We had a quick chat and I wished him goodnight. I lay back on my bed, closed my eyes for a second, and when I opened them again it was 4am. I sat up. My brief second had turned into hours and I hadn't got around to ringing Rachel. It was too late to ring her now. I crawled back into bed and pulled the expensive sheets tightly over me. I needed more sleep. I had to be up and ready to leave by 7.30am.

I awoke feeling quite refreshed and the day passed quickly and effortlessly; by 5pm I had finished the shoot and I was back at the hotel. Dad was in the pool again and I wondered if he was ever going to get dressed. I was sure that if he carried on like this, by the end of the three weeks he would have grown gills or webbed feet at the very least.

'Dad, hi, I'm back, I thought I'd find you here.'

'How was your day, Son?'

'It was good, Dad, it went really well. How's your day been?'

'Fabulous, I've always dreamed of being able to take a swim in my very own pool every day, and you know what, it's even better than I imagined.'

'I had noticed, Dad ... I don't think I've seen you out of your trunks since we got here. Have you been out at all today?'

'No, not yet. I thought I'd wait for you to come back'

'Well, I'm here now, so how do you fancy getting dressed? We could pop out for a stroll and find somewhere to have dinner on the way.'

'Oh yes! I'd like that, we could catch up on the last couple of days. Give me an hour and I'll be ready'

Before I did anything else there was one thing I had to do. I made my way to my bedroom and lay back on the bed as I dialled Rachel's number.

'Rachel, hi, it's me.'

'Oh, Austin, hi! Are you ok? Is your father ok?' Her voice was flat and almost sarcastic.

'Yes, Rachel, we're both fine. I'm sorry, please don't be angry because I didn't ring you last night, I didn't finish the shoot until late. When I got back to the hotel I lay down, closed my eyes for a second and the next thing I knew it was four o'clock in the morning. It was too late to ring, and I've been on a location shoot since the crack of dawn. I miss you so much Rachel. I wish you were here with me.'

Her voice softened. 'Sorry, Austin. I'm not angry, I was worried, that's all.'

The last couple of months had been so hard for the both of

us. Spending so much time apart from each other wasn't easy. Before my career took off I had time to think about her all day long. Time to take her out and lavish her with my attentions. Since my studio and my career had been catapulted into overdrive I'd hardly seen her.

As if this wasn't enough, the bouts of illness I'd suffered and the images and conflict I was dealing with had contributed greatly to making the situation between us even more difficult.

She gracefully accepted my apology and while I waited for Dad to get ready I stayed on the phone to her. I'd just finished telling her about the shoot at Lake Como and the very handsome Signore Frettere when I heard Dad shouting out.

'Austin, I'm ready.'

'Rachel, can you hold on a second?' I turned my head and shouted towards the door. 'I'll be there in a minute, Dad! Rachel, I'm sorry, I have to go. I'm taking Dad out for dinner. I'll ring you tomorrow.'

We said our tender goodbyes, and Dad and I left the hotel to explore the sights of Milan. We found a quaint, friendly restaurant on the corner of a narrow street and spent the evening eating fabulous food and catching up.

I filled him in on all of the events of the last couple of days, omitting the details about the crazy imagery of the models that had filled my mind and distracted me. This was definitely not something that I felt comfortable talking to my father about. In fact, this was something that I couldn't talk to anyone about. I had to keep this madness to myself.

When we got back to the hotel I wasn't quite ready for the silence and tranquility of the suite.

'How do you fancy a night cap, Dad?'

Dad's eyes were sparkling and he looked enthused. 'Yes Austin I think I would like that very much.'

We made our way to the bar and ordered two double brandies. I had never really been bothered either way about alcohol. I could take it or leave it, but tonight I had a burning desire for a smooth warm intoxicating glass of cognac.

I swirled it around in my glass and breathed in its aroma before taking a sip. It was as satisfying as I had imagined it would be.

Then a familiar voice called out my name. It was Signore Frettere with the two models that had sparked off the images on the shoot at Lake Como.

I put my hand up politely and waved as they walked over to us.

'Signore Jacobs, good evening.'

'Hello, Signore Frettere, how nice to see you.'

'And you too, Austin. We were hoping you'd arrive back at the hotel soon. Lucia, Marietta and I made a special trip over here to see you. This must be your father!'

He stepped forward and kissed my father on both cheeks. Dad looked a little taken back but smiled graciously as Signore Frettere stood back.

'I'm very pleased to meet you, Signore Jacobs.'

'Pleased to meet you too! Shall we take a seat?' Signore Frettere gesticulated us towards a quiet corner in the bar.

We followed him and we all sat down. Signore Frettere raised his hand suddenly. 'How rude of me!' He looked firstly at me. 'Austin,' he said, 'you remember the girls from Lake Como?'

'Yes,' I replied, and nodded politely at the both of them.

Then he looked at my father. 'Mr Jacobs, this is Lucia and this is Marietta, my favourite models.'

The girls both smiled as he complimented them.

'So, Austin,' he continued, 'the shoot doesn't start until 10pm tomorrow night, what do you say we take the girls out on the town and get to know each other a little better? I like your work and I'd like to discuss the possibility of booking you again. You have a real skill and an incredible eye for a composition. If your last two days work is anything to go by, I won't be able to afford you soon.' He was now complimenting and flattering me and I liked it. 'So what do you say Austin?'

My father looked at me, nodded and smiled. 'Go on, Son, have a good night out. Goodness knows you deserve it.'

I glanced over at the girls. They were both wearing incredibly tight little black dresses that left very little to the imagination. These were the girls that had sparked off the images, and the last thing I wanted was to spend any time with them. This was like Paris all over again. My plans of having a quiet night with Dad were flying out of the window.

Signore Frettere was an important client. He wanted to discuss future bookings with me. Everything considered, I felt that I really had no choice but to accept his invitation.

Dad successfully wriggled his way out of coming with us and bid us goodnight. I knew that he was having withdrawal symptoms. He was desperate to get back into his trunks and assume the position of a fish once more.

A limo pulled up outside the hotel and within twenty minutes we were in a very upmarket and incredibly modern bar. We had drinks in our hands and beautiful people all around us. I knew that I needed to keep my wits about me so I opted for a soft drink — especially after what had happened in Paris. No way was I going to go down that road again.

Signore Frettere led me to a VIP lounge where we sat alone and discussed the numerous events he had coming up, and how he would like to book me as the main photographer to cover them all.

My head was swimming with excitement and it was a relief to be away from Lucia and Marietta. I really didn't want to party, I was here to ensure that my career would continue on the upward trajectory it was on, and if this was the way I had to do it, then I had to play the game and go with the flow.

I managed to get through the rest of this hedonistic party sober and blissfully free of any unwanted images. Finally, Signore Frettere called an end to the evening and led us all out of the bar.

The limo was waiting outside and Mario drove us back to the hotel.

As he pulled into the private entrance I prepared myself to say goodnight and get out of the limousine. Just as I was about to step out of it Signore Frettere asked if Lucia and Marietta could come up briefly to look at the suite. It had a worldwide reputation for its luxury and the girls were intrigued to see it. Signore Frettere had apparently frequented it on many occasions and was all too familiar with the luxury it offered.

I didn't want the girls anywhere near me, but my brain wouldn't work fast enough to come up with a feasible and plausible excuse to say no.

Lucia, Marietta and I entered the private elevator together

and they giggled annoyingly all the way to the tenth floor. When the elevator doors opened I turned to them both and said quite curtly, 'Would you mind waiting here a moment please.'

This was unbearable; I just wanted them to go. I needed to check where dad was, and what state he was in before giving them the grand tour. He'd be so embarrassed if they saw him in his trunks.

I made my way to the pool, but dad was tucked up in bed, snoring loudly. Relieved that I'd avoided any embarrassment for him, I went back for the girls but they had disappeared.

Then I heard faint bouts of laughter and water splashing loudly.

Lucia and Marietta were bouncing around in the pool, stripped to their underwear and playing like children.

I stood at the water's edge and called to them in a loud whisper.

'Lucia, Marietta ... please, I need you to get out and get dressed.'

They looked at each other and pulled sarcastically sad faces at me as if they were mocking my request.

Then they both giggled loudly before swimming towards me. I was still leaning over the water's edge when Marietta flew up out of the water and grabbed my shirt. I lost my balance and she pulled me head first into the pool.

It was all happening so quickly. One moment I was standing on the edge of the pool, the next I was completely submerged in the warm turbulent water.

My legs kicked and my arms instinctively reached up to break the surface and gasp for air. I wasn't getting anywhere — I was still under. I stretched my arms upwards and pulled hard against the water in front of me. Again and again, I desperately tried to propel myself upwards. I needed air. I needed to breath, but I just couldn't reach the surface. No matter how hard I tried, I remained submerged. Panic started to set in; I began to flap and flay franticly, grabbing at the water above me. I was sure that I was going to drown. I had to reach the surface. I needed to breathe.

Suddenly, my lungs took a sharp intake of air — but I was no longer in the pool.

I was lying down.

My eyes were closed.

I was warm and dry.

Where was I? What the hell had happened?

Relief and concern swept over me when I opened my eyes and saw the green velvet walls of the Imperial Suite.

I was lying in my bed, very naked, and very confused!

I sat up and looked around me. The room looked like it had been ransacked. Pillows were strewn all over the floor; sheets and towels lay scattered amongst empty bottles of champagne.

'What the —?' I whispered under my breath.

I jumped out of bed and threw on some jogging bottoms.

Dad was nowhere to be seen. He had actually resisted the temptation of the pool for once and gone sightseeing. I wondered if he had any idea of what had happened last night. Had he heard or seen anything? Could he shed some light on the dark nothingness that was my memory? I retraced my steps from the night before as I made my way to the pool. It was so quiet and the water was clear and warm. I knelt down to touch its surface. As my fingertips skimmed along it, a flashing image of Lucia and Marietta coursed through my mind.

I could see them clearly. They were strutting around the edge of the pool, displaying their signature catwalk moves and teasing me with their provocative displays. The images progressed into more intimate visions of the three of us together. These detailed images made my stomach churn with guilt. I pulled my hand quickly out of the water and returned to my bedroom.

My head was spinning. Was the image I had just seen an awful memory resurfacing, or a figment of my imagination? Was this related to the bouts of illness I'd experienced?

I poured myself a cup of coffee and drank it in a state of turbulence.

I quickly concluded that I could ponder over this forever and I began to think a little more analytically as I appraised the situation.

Fact: something was wrong with me, and by the time I'd finished my second cup of coffee and third bagel I had decided to ring Dr Albright in London to see if the results of my tests were back.

The receptionist answered and put me through to him.

'Hello, Austin, how's Milan?'

'Its great thank you, Dr Albright. I wondered if the results from my tests were back?'

'Yes, they are, and I'm happy to say that everything is absolutely normal. You're in great shape, Austin, there's nothing wrong with you at all.'

'Thank you, Dr Albright, that's wonderful news. Dad will be thrilled.'

'Pleasure, Austin. Send my regards to your father and enjoy Milan.'

It felt like a huge weight had just been lifted off one shoulder and deposited firmly on the other. This was great news in one way. Physically I was fine, there was nothing wrong with me, but I knew deep inside of me that something wasn't right.

Frustrated and shaken, I paced around my bedroom, picking up wet towels and clearing away the champagne bottles. These weren't figments of my imagination – that was for sure. As I paced around, a chilling thought ran through me. If there was nothing wrong with me physically then maybe I had a psychological problem? The incident last night with Lucia and Marietta had definitely left me shaken; I couldn't remember a thing and it was driving me mad. All I could remember was that one minute I was drowning and the next I was waking up in bed, gasping for air. I'd obviously suffered another blackout ... but why?

Trying to pull myself together, I focused my thoughts on Rachel and my reasons for being here, and I decided that no matter what was wrong with me or how it affected me, one way or another I was going to battle on and get through the next two and a half weeks.

The rest of my stay travelled at a seriously giddy pace. Signore Frettere kept inviting me to all sorts of parties and various events. My work itinerary might have been less hectic than Paris but the demands I was expected to meet socially were far more taxing.

During my three-week stay, I suffered four episodes of memory loss in total. These blackouts and memory loss had become more frequent. All of them occurred whilst I was in the company of Lucia and Marietta.

By the time dad and I boarded the private jet to fly home, my head was in a mess. Was I losing my grip on reality as well as my sanity?

I sat back on the leather chair and strapped myself in ready for takeoff. At last we were leaving Milan – I was desperate to leave this madness behind me and even more desperate to get back to London ... to get back to Rachel.

CHAPTER TWENTY-THREE
RACHEL COAST

Austin was about to arrive back from Milan.

As I sat waiting for him to pick me up, I thought about how unfortunate and typical it was of me to have fallen in love with a guy whose career was taking him away from me for weeks on end. I was lost and lonely without him.

Countless long nights spent alone in my tiny little bedsit with nothing but my own thoughts to converse with had reinforced the fact that I was so in love with Austin, I would have put up with all sorts of atrocities just to be with him.

Since graduating, I had received a few phone messages from my university friend, Julie, asking me to meet her for a drink, but we kept missing each other's calls. Every time I'd phone her back the call would go straight to answer machine, which was a real shame as I could have really done with her company on many an occasion over the last couple of months. The last time we'd actually spoken to each other was just after I ended my relationship with Julian.

Whilst a part of me was urging Austin on to achieve his ambitions and realise his dreams, another part of me was chronically concerned that the success he was enjoying was creating a growing distance between us. I worried that it would ultimately lead to the end of our relationship.

To rationalise and control my concerns, I kept telling myself that when you truly love someone, you're happy for them to have space to grow and explore their ambitions, even if it does take them thousands of miles away from you for long periods of time.

I had watched my mum and dad try to cope with a similar situation. Dad had a great job that he really enjoyed, working for a global computing company. He tried to explain to me on many occasions what exactly it was he did, but no matter how many times or in how many different ways he put it, it was obvious that his skills were quite specialised and that you needed to be a rocket scientist to know exactly what he was talking about.

As a result of his sought-after skills, he spent a lot of time working for large international companies away from home. It was really tough on my mother not seeing him for weeks on end. She told me that she coped with my father's long absences from home because she had the security of marriage and the commitment from my father to rely on. This gave her fortitude and strength, and an unquestionable belief in their relationship and his love for her.

I, however, didn't have that kind of security to hold on to. Austin and I had only just begun our relationship and, though he had expressed strong feelings for me, I was still unsure of their longevity. I fretted over our future together. I knew without question that Austin was the only one for me; I knew with every atom in me that I would never want anyone else.

This left me wide open and vulnerable, and I was petrified of losing him to his success and his new life. We'd only seen each a few times in the last three months and I worried constantly that this long distance love affair was the beginning of the end. That someday he'd meet some stunning model, fall in love, and that would be it.

Watching the clock in my now familiarly obsessive way, I paced around my bedsit as I waited for his call. His plane would be landing soon and he'd be calling me to let me know what time he'd be getting here.

I kept fiddling with my hair and re-applying my lipstick over and over again.

I was on edge and about to explode with excited anticipation when the phone finally rang – it was Austin!

He said that he was about to leave the airport to come and pick me up. That he'd be with me in about forty minutes.

I'd spent three whole hours plucking and preening and making sure that everything was perfect, that I was perfect, or as perfect as I could be. I was no supermodel, that was for sure, and I couldn't even begin to compete with the stunning models he photographed ... I just wasn't born that way.

Before meeting Austin I had never worried so much about my appearance, but since his career had taken off and he was faced with impeccable beauty every day I was more conscious of my flaws than ever. I wanted to be perfect for him. I wanted him to look at me in a way that he would never look at anyone else, as if I was the only girl in the world.

Dressed in my new black dress that had taken me two weeks to find, I was as ready as I was ever going to be.

Ten minutes passed and my phone rang again; it was Austin.

'Rachel, hi, it's me.'

'Hi! Are you nearly here?' I asked.

'No I'm bloody not.' He sounded flustered and angry. 'I'm sorry, Rachel, something's come up. Mr Underling has just rung me and insisted that I meet with him tonight to discuss how things went in Milan. Why it couldn't wait until tomorrow I don't know. I'm so sorry, Rachel.'

I was silent. It seemed that his apology was sincere — his frustration was obvious.

'I've got to go, Rachel, the traffic's really bad ... I can't wait to see you tomorrow.'

As I put the phone down a sick growing knot began to fill my stomach. It grew, rising slowly until it sat uncomfortably in my throat. It felt like I had been gutted. Three long weeks waiting for this night to arrive and at the last minute my reunion with Austin had been brutally snatched away from me.

I understood that Austin couldn't say no to Mr Underling's request to see him. He was his agent and he was responsible for Austin's success. He had more than spring-boarded his career ... it was more like a NASA rocket launch. Even though I understood this, it didn't make me feel any better about being let down, so I skulked around my tiny bedsit.

As the hours passed and the walls closed in on me, the intensity of my disappointment began to slowly subside. It wasn't his fault, and besides, within a matter of hours I'd be with him. The next report was due, and I was due to call into Jacobs' Photographic at about 1pm the next day.

***

That sweet, sweet bell caressed my ears. Its sound was so familiar and so comforting it reminded me of how things used to be before Austin's stellar career began.

The memories of our long painting sessions and drinks at the pub began to flood my senses. Back then all of our ambitions were just wonderful small talk and hopeful dreams. How things had changed ... well, for Austin at least. He was really living his dreams and it had all happened so quickly for him. My dreams, on the other hand, had faded in to obscurity and I had no one to blame except for myself. I had allowed my thoughts and energies to be consumed with Austin, and I was finding it hard to focus on anything else.

There standing in his usual spot was Mr Jacobs. He was a sight for sore eyes. I'd never seen him looking better; these trips with Austin were certainly doing him the world of good.

'Ted, you look wonderful! How was Milan?' I said, unable to hide my joy at seeing his familiar face.

He greeted me with his usual smile; open, broad and sincere. Enthusiastic tales of the Presidential Suite and the marvelous sights ensued. He was so excited to impart the details of his trip I didn't want to stop him, but I was eager to see Austin.

I tried not to show it but he seemed to notice my anxiousness. It wasn't that I wasn't interested in his tales of Milan; I had all the time in the world for Ted.

Ted suddenly, thankfully, cut his monologue short, saying, 'Rachel, I'm sorry, I could go on about Milan for hours, but I'm sure you must be anxious to see Austin. Go on through, he's in the studio waiting for you.'

My heart was already in overdrive and my stomach was churning. Not seeing Austin for so long had broken any familiarity that had grown between us and I could feel my nerves tingling out of control as I walked towards the door. It was slightly open, so with my heart pounding, I peeked through.

He was bent over the light box studying negatives. I stood

there in the doorway for a few moments, peeping through at him. I didn't want him to see me ... not yet. He looked much more handsome than the last time I'd seen him. I wasn't sure if it was because it had been so long since I'd set eyes on him, or if it was because he really was hotter than I had remembered. Either way, he looked glorious standing there with his black shirt hanging loosely off his shoulders. His dark, wavy hair was just touching its collar and it flicked up slightly at the nape of his neck. He stood up straight and began walking towards the door.

I opened it quickly and walked in. As soon as he saw me, that large enthusiastic smile beamed its way across to me.

'Rachel!'

He ran forwards picked me up and spun me around, kissing me as we twirled around the floor.

Heavenly-fuelled feelings washed over me as he held me tightly, yet gently. My heart began beating faster and faster as we span around. As he kissed me, all of my doubts began to dissipate. A peaceful veil cast itself over me. I didn't want this moment to end.

He kept spinning me around until we eventually slowed to a natural stop. Pulling away from me gently, he held me at arm's length.

'Rachel, let me look at you.'

He smiled as he stared into my eyes. He pulled me close once more and hugged me tightly. As he did, we heard the shop bell ring and the sound of laughter and chatter filled the air. We both turned and looked towards the studio door. Five models walked in, complete with their entourage of dressers and makeup artists. They were laughing and chatting amongst themselves. Austin broke our embrace.

'Sorry, Rachel, looks like my afternoon shoot is about to start. I'll just get the details you need for the report.'

He handed me some paperwork and proceeded to greet the party that had just walked in.

I hung around until the shoot began before getting the camera out to take the photograph. I didn't want to leave, not yet — I'd only just got there.

I watched him for ages through the lens of the camera. I could have stayed in this spot all afternoon but time was getting on; I had another appointment to get to. I'd dragged my time here out for as long as I could.

He turned to me and smiled, I had to take the photograph now. His image filled my lens – that was it – *click!* I had it.

Just as I got the shot, Austin put down his camera and rubbed his forehead, looking faint. He told the girls to take a minute. I called to him but he didn't respond. I began making my way towards him but before I got to him, he stood tall and turned to face me.

'Don't panic, Rachel, I'm fine. I only stopped for a second to change the film, that's all.'

He could see I looked concerned and I knew that he was lying. This was the fourth time I'd seen him react like this. It suddenly dawned on me that he seemed to react badly every time I took the photograph for the report. This made no sense at all! Taking his photograph couldn't possibly have anything to do with his reaction.

He smiled at me.

'Don't worry, Rachel. I'm fine. I'll see you later ... pick you up at 7pm.'

'Okay ... are you sure you're alright?'

'Yes, I'm fine, honestly. See you later.' He winked at me, then turned around and continued working.

Perhaps I was wrong; perhaps he had stopped to change the film.

After a quick chat with Ted, I left the studio and fought my way through the traffic back to the office. After a few phone calls it was time to make my way home and get ready to see Austin.

My excited and elated state proved to be short lived. Unbelievably, he rang to cancel our date; he was apparently feeling ill again. Here I was on my own, confused, worried and absolutely devastated.

The doctor couldn't find anything wrong with him. He'd had the results from the hospital tests whilst he was in Milan and he was given the all clear. What the hell was going on with him?

I rang Ted.

'Ted, it's me. It's Rachel'

'Oh, Rachel, my dear, hello! Are you all right?'

'I'm fine, Ted, thank you, but I'm worried to death about Austin. Is he okay?'

'Honestly Rachel, I don't know. I'm beside myself, I don't know what to do!' He sounded really worried. 'He's in bed, just like before ... I'm going to get a second opinion, something is wrong and it needs to be put right. He shouldn't be getting ill like this. Rachel, I'll ring you back later. I'm going to ring another doctor now.'

'Oh! Good, Ted, that's a relief, please let me know what he says.'

'I'll ring you as soon as he's seen him.'

'Thank you, Ted. Thank you!'

Something was definitely wrong with Austin ... but what? And why couldn't the doctors find anything? He was in great shape physically – the tests had confirmed this.

Sitting on the edge of my bed, I thought back to the very first time he had fallen ill. I began checking my diary and analysing the time line of events over the last few months. My conclusions confirmed that his bouts of illness happened every time I'd taken the photograph and finalised the report for Conik Penster Dewe.

Then it hit me as clear as day and I berated myself for not seeing it before. His illness coincided with Conik Penster Dewe taking an interest in his career, and wanting these damn reports. The pressure of having one of the most successful business magnets in the world watching your every move would be incredibly stressful for anyone to cope with.

If there was nothing wrong with him physically, then perhaps it was stress related. I'd read that stress could do strange things to you. Affect your health in all sorts of ways. Surely this could be a feasible prognosis.

I paced and deliberated for nearly two hours, mulling over my theory, then Ted rang back. The second doctor had said exactly the same as the first – he couldn't find anything obviously wrong with him. He had, however, booked Austin in for more hospital tests.

Somewhat relieved by Ted's phone call, but still a little distressed by the whole thing, I found it hard to get to sleep.

My mind kept mulling over the last few months and the more I thought about it, the more I was convinced that his bouts of illness were because of the pressure he was under.

He'd taken a massive leap in his career and that came at a price. It wasn't all fun and games. He had to deliver the goods and keep doing it. I wanted to talk to Ted about it, see what he thought, but not over the phone. I'd talk to him in person.

***

The dawn light burst through my window. It was 6.30am. As I opened my eyes my first thought of the day, as always, was Austin.

It was too early to ring him so I waited until 8.30am. This was a far more reasonable and civilised hour.

Ted answered the phone. He was surprised that Austin hadn't rung me already. Apparently he had got up really early, about 6.00am. Ted said that he looked great and apparently Austin had said he felt great too. Ted went on to say that he had made several phone calls, got dressed and left for a location shoot at about 7.30am.

I put the phone down and stared blankly into space. Austin would have known that I'd be anxious about how he was feeling. Why hadn't he called me?

The day progressed, and one meeting ran into another with little distinction between them, but still no word from Austin.

I tried ringing him several times but his phone kept switching to answer machine.

It was getting harder to keep my spirits up. I had expected to hear from him by now. It was almost time to pack up and go home; the day was almost over and my mood was at an all-time low. I kept looking at my phone willing him to ring it.

As I drove home to my empty bedsit my heart sank even further at the prospect of another lonely night ahead of me. Hurt and angry tears began to fill my eyes. How could Austin be so bloody thoughtless and inconsiderate? One little phone call to tell me he was okay, that's all I wanted. Was that too much to ask? Obviously it was and it was really getting me down.

I'd just arrived home and flopped on to my bed when my

phone finally rang.

'Rachel, hi it's me. I'm sorry I haven't rung before, I've been rushed off my feet and I haven't had a chance to contact you.'

At last: the call I had been waiting for, accompanied by a heartfelt apology and, as always, a perfectly plausible excuse.

'I just spoke to Dad, he said you rang this morning'

'Yes I did, I was worried about you, I was checking to see if you were okay after last night.'

'Yes, I'm fine, Rachel, it's so weird. I felt awful last night then this morning when I woke up I felt as right as rain, fighting fit and full of life, I feel great.'

'Good, I'm so relieved.' I hesitated for a second. 'Austin ... your father said that the doctor wanted you to go for more tests at the hospital. I know you're feeling better but you are still going to go and get checked out, aren't you?'

'Yes, Rachel. I've promised Dad that I will and now I will promise you. I'm still going to go for the tests.'

I sighed with relief. 'Good, that's good.'

'Rachel, I am really sorry about letting you down. Will you please allow me to pick you up at seven and take you to dinner? Please say yes. I'm officially desperate to see you.'

My mood lifted immediately. 'Yes of course, yes.'

I hurried into the shower, preened and plucked as quickly as I could. For the third night in a row, I pulled out my new black dress.

A car horn beeped outside. I looked out of the window – it was Austin! The car horn beeped again. I grabbed my bag and ran downstairs. I stopped dead in my tracks when I saw him ... he was wearing a black tailored dinner suit. The top two buttons of his crisp white shirt were open and a bow tie hung loosely around his neck. He looked like a film star! He was standing there holding the passenger door open for me, and as I reached him he took my hand and kissed it.

'*Enchanté, mademoiselle.*'

I blushed as he helped me into the car and as I lowered myself into the seat he bent down towards me.

'Rachel,' he whispered. I looked up at him.

He kissed me on my lips and his hand brushed my cheek gently. I felt a sudden bolt of energy run through me, and my stomach flipped. He pulled slowly away and our lips parted.

'You wouldn't believe how good it is to see you, Rachel. You look beautiful.'

My heart skipped several beats and my whole body tingled from my head to my toes. Nothing had got in the way tonight. He was here, I was in his car with him. We were finally together again.

Seeing him dressed so immaculately intrigued me as to where he was taking me. Despite my persistent questions throughout our journey. He had kept on saying that it was a surprise, and that I'd find out soon enough.

We started heading west out of London and as soon as we got on to the M4 my curiosity was uncontainable.

As we neared the Heathrow airport turn off he started indicating.

'Please,' I begged, 'tell me where we're going.'

We were off the motorway and heading into the airport.

'Rachel, I wasn't really on a shoot today. The truth is I've been running around trying to get your passport.'

He paused while I stared at him, uncomprehending.

'Your mum and dad are lovely people, Rachel. And they were really helpful.'

What the hell was he talking about? I was perplexed and intrigued and excited all at the same time.

'Sorry, Austin, I'm completely lost.'

We had arrived on a runway next to a small private plane. He turned to look at me and held my face in his hands.

'Rachel, I wanted to do something really special. I've booked dinner in Paris. I needed your passport to take you there, so I rang your mum and dad and asked for their help. Your mother said you kept your passport at home with them for safekeeping. I drove to Wales and back today and picked it up.' He paused and looked at me with a concerned look on his face. 'Please don't be annoyed with me. I know I took a liberty contacting your mum and dad, but I figured that I was going to meet them one day anyway, and I really wanted to take you to Paris.'

I had no time to respond or think, I was on cloud nine hundred and ninety-nine. This was the stuff that my wildest dreams were made of. Not because I was going to Paris, but because of the incredible grandness of the gesture and the sheer effort involved in organising it — just for me.

We walked towards the private jet, and as we approached it two air stewardesses that looked like they'd come straight off the cover of a magazine greeted us. This was like being in a fantasy.

The contrast of this night compared to my usual nights alone with my TV dinners was startling. I'd spent weeks cooped up in my bedsit, rattling around it on my own. Tonight, here I was with Austin, flying to Paris for dinner ... in a private jet.

Truthfully I couldn't have cared if he'd walked me to the local fish and chip shop on the High Street; I just wanted to see him and spend time with him. Though saying that, I have to admit that the potency of the surroundings began to yield its power over me. This was incredible and I couldn't quite believe it. In no time at all we had taxied the runway and we were in the air and on our way to Paris.

It seemed like we were only in the air for five minutes when the captain announced that we would be making our descent and arriving at Charles De Gaulle airport.

A chauffeur driven limousine was waiting for us on our arrival. And within the hour we were seated in the dining room at the beautiful Hotel Meurice. It was right in the heart of the city and its mosaic floors, crystal chandeliers and heavy damask curtains surrounded us with their splendour.

The view from the windows was breathtaking and overlooked gardens across the street. Austin informed me that they were called the Tuileries Gardens. Apparently they were created by Catherine de Medics in 1564 and eventually opened to the public in 1667. In the nineteenth century it was the place where Parisians celebrated, met and relaxed. His knowledge was as impressive as the restaurant. It truly was quite a magnificent place and the service was impeccable, and as precise as a minuet.

This was the kind of place where being overdressed for the occasion was an impossibility. Though it was truly amazing to be here in this grandeur, I had to admit that it was completely overwhelming and I was most definitely out of my comfort zone. Austin, on the other hand, appeared to be in his element;

he looked very relaxed and quite at home.

'Did you come here with your father whilst you were working here?' I asked.

'No, I didn't get the chance to. I worked and slept most of the time, but Dad managed to get here. It was on his list of places to see and places to eat – he loved it, said the food was amazing.'

The menu was in French and I studied it for ages looking for anything that looked familiar. I understood a couple of words like *pommes frite* and *boeuf* but that was about it.

Austin sat back and peeped at me over his menu. I couldn't see his mouth but I could see by his eyes that he was smiling at me. He was obviously amused by the fact that I had no idea what any of the dishes were. He dropped his menu and beamed at me with that broad enthusiastic smile.

'Would you like me to go through the menu with you, Rachel?' he asked confidently.

Tonight I could see quite clearly that the last three months had changed him significantly. The confident and totally in control man that now sat opposite me, was a far cry from the Austin that came bursting in through Jacobs' Photographic shop door on the first day I ever saw him.

Even though his newly found self-confidence made me feel safe and secure in these grossly unfamiliar surroundings, this new and unfamiliar air of self-assurance also troubled my fragile insecurities.

As they began to surface I reminded myself that it was me that he had brought to Paris, not one of the supermodels he had photographed, and the real clincher, the one fact that really kicked my concerns into the sidelines, was the incredible lengths he had gone to just to get me here. Driving to Wales and back was a hell of a journey. Repeating these facts like a mantra helped to beat these troubled thoughts into submission.

I was back on track and Austin helped me choose a dish from the menu. After he finished ordering he took my hand gently and placed it in his.

'Rachel,' he said softly, 'tonight is the first time in weeks that I am exactly where I want to be ...'

'Yes, Paris is quite something,' I said, 'and this restaurant is amazing.'

He smiled to himself as he tipped his head downwards. 'Rachel ... I don't mean here, in this restaurant, or here in Paris. It's because I'm with you.'

I opened my mouth to respond but he stopped me.

'Rachel, a lot has happened over the last couple of months. I've accomplished and achieved so many of my dreams and ambitions. Things that I thought may never come true.'

He paused, then pulled me close and whispered in my ear so nobody else could hear.

'As wonderful as this seems, none of it compares to being here with you tonight. I've missed you so much.'

His words were perfect. In a few beautiful sentences he had quashed my concerns and made me feel more desired and wanted than ever.

My whole body felt warm and complete. My mind was calm and still. It felt as though I was frozen in time. Lost in that perfect moment where the past is forgotten and the future not thought about. I knew there and then that I would treasure and remember this moment and this feeling forever.

He looked so happy and relaxed. It made me question my thoughts about the possibility that stress was the cause of his mysterious bouts of illness.

Just as we were about to eat two very French, female voices broke our concentration.

'*Bon soir*, Awstin'

Two creatures that looked too perfect to be real were walking towards us. They must have been six feet tall with legs that went on forever. One was a glorious brunette the other a very sexy blonde.

'Awstin, you look so handsome tonight, how good it is to see you.'

Austin looked up, and as his eyes met theirs an uncomfortable look swept across his face. He quickly composed himself, but his initial reaction had not gone unnoticed, certainly not by me.

He stood up and introduced me. 'Rachel this is Mia and this is Louise.'

I stood up and looked up at them. They towered in their

glory above me; they were so tall and elegant. They made me feel like a dumpy umpa lumpa.

'Hello, pleased to meet you,' I mumbled feebly, and sat back down very quickly.

Before my mind could process any thoughts about who exactly these two women were, Austin explained that they were two of the models that he'd photographed in Paris. That they were also very dear and close friends of Monsieur Medone, the client he had worked for in Paris.

They said their goodbyes and glided away like swans, gracefully navigating their way through a lake of tables and people.

He hadn't mentioned Mia and Louise when he had relayed his tales of Paris to me. The green-eyed, insecure monster that slept quietly in the pit of my stomach had been stirred. Throughout dinner I couldn't stop myself from watching him; I kept checking to see if he was looking in their direction.

It was just as our desserts arrived that Austin announced he needed the restroom. His timing was terrible. The waiter had just placed the most glorious looking crème brûlée right in front of me.

This was one of my favourite desserts and I was delighted that it was on the menu. The vanilla essence in this small pot of heaven was irresistible. I tried to do the right thing and politely wait for him to come back before starting to eat, but it was just too good. I couldn't resist. I began by just taking small little tip of the spoon bite sizes. Before I knew it, I'd eaten it all and Austin still hadn't returned.

I sat patiently, for what must have been at least another ten minutes, occasionally scanning the room whilst trying to avoid eye contact with anyone. This was crazy. Where was Austin?

A waiter approached our table. I blurted out that my boyfriend had left for the restroom at least half an hour ago and that he hadn't returned. I asked him if he could show me where it was. He was very calm and he reassured me that everything would be fine as he led me to the bathroom.

'I will go in and see if he is there, *Mademoiselle*. What is his name?'

'Austin Jacobs ... his name's Austin Jacobs.'

He nodded and I thanked him.

'Thank you ... merci.'

He walked in through the heavy wooden door, and I waited anxiously outside. After a few minutes he reappeared. The restroom was empty. Austin wasn't in there.

Where the hell had he gone?

Okay I thought, think logically: maybe our paths have crossed? Perhaps he's already back at the table.

I thanked the waiter for his help and explained that I was going to check the restaurant again.

I walked in and looked over to our table. It was empty – he wasn't there.

Without wasting a second, I looked carefully and purposefully at every table and every diner. Mia and Louise's table was empty and Austin was nowhere to be seen. Where was that waiter? I needed his help.

I found myself walking towards the rather grand foyer.

Up until now I had been quite calm, all things considered, but as I stepped into the foyer the realities of my predicament began to sink in.

I had no clue as to where Austin was, and even less of a clue as to how or where to find him, or even where to begin looking for him? Then I had the awful thought to deal with, the one I didn't want to have to consider: what if I couldn't find him?

Under a sudden attack of sheer determination I began describing him to all of the staff as well as the guests. I asked everyone who'd give me the time if they'd seen my handsome boyfriend.

This was tough going as most of the people I spoke to only spoke French and my persistent enquiries were met with one confused look after another. I wasn't getting anywhere. Austin was missing. Should I inform the French police? Should I ring Ted?

After walking up and down the street just outside the hotel for the umpteenth time, I made my way back into the foyer.

To both my relief and horror, I found Austin.

Chapter Twenty-four
Rachel Coast

He was standing right at the top of the sweeping staircase with Mia on one arm and Louise on the other. They were taking it in turns to kiss him on the cheek and stroke his chest as they made their way down the flight of stairs.

The three of them were totally unaware that I was standing in the foyer watching them. My heart sank and hit my stomach with such force that I nearly fell over with the sickening feeling this sight induced.

This vision of Austin with these two girls on each arm filled me with dread, fear and anger. These three gloriously attractive people walking down this ornately stunning staircase was a strikingly beautiful sight ... but to me it was the ugliest thing I had ever seen.

Where the hell had they all been? What the hell had they been doing? I had to stop the searing thoughts tearing through me. It didn't bear thinking about.

Rooted to the spot, I silently watched their every move as the confusion hurt and anger began to well and grow inside me.

As they reached the bottom step, Austin fell to the floor in a sudden and dramatic movement.

Still rooted to the spot, unable to move a muscle, I watched the scene in front of me unfold. Every member of staff along with several customers began flocking around him with concern. A healthy crowd had completely surrounded him and I couldn't see what was going on.

It was at this point that I finally managed to animate myself. I ran towards him, fighting my way through them. One of the staff was kneeling next to him. He was checking his pulse and feeling his forehead. I knelt next to him.

'Is he okay?' I asked.

'He has passed out,' he replied.

I knelt down and grabbed Austin's hand. It was limp and lifeless. I held it tightly.

'Austin, wake up. Wake up.'

I lay my head on his chest and I could just about hear his heart beating.

One of the receptionists came running over to us with a small bottle clutched in her hand. She knelt down and waved the bottle under Austin's nose. She looked at me and, in a strong French accent, said reassuringly, 'Smelling salts.'

Austin began to cough violently and his hand reached up towards his mouth to cover it. He was conscious again.

'Austin. Are you all right?'

He squinted his eyes open and looked up at me and smiled. Then he looked at all of the people surrounding him. His smile disappeared and now a puzzled and confused look occupied his face. He pulled me gently towards him. 'Rachel, what's going on?'

I suddenly remembered that ugly vision of Mia and Louise walking down the stairs with him. I looked up before answering him, searching for them in the crowd.

'You've been missing for two hours Austin. I've been frantic. I couldn't find you anywhere. I was just about to ring your father and inform the police, but then I saw you walking down the stairs with Mia and Louise, the two women you introduced me to at dinner. When you got to the bottom of the stairs, you collapsed.'

He listened to me intently as I explained what had happened. He looked fraught and more worried than I'd ever seen. He didn't say a word as he picked himself up from the floor, refusing to accept help or assistance from anyone. He turned to me and held my hand tightly. His head hung low and his eyes stared at the floor.

'Rachel, we need to talk.'

He looked up and searched the room. Still holding my hand tightly, he guided me towards a quiet seating area in the lounge. The vision of him with Louise and Mia kept flooding my mind and I wanted to pull my hand away: I didn't want him to touch me.

What explanation could he possibly have for disappearing for two whole hours with the two leggy models? Anger began to rise in me. I didn't like the answers my imagination was conjuring up.

Then a sickening thought crossed my mind. Was this it? Was he about to tell me that he didn't want to be with me anymore? Was this what he needed to talk to me about? No! This couldn't be it. Why bring me to Paris to end our relationship in this cruel and callous way? This evening had been full of mixed messages and nothing made sense anymore.

'Rachel,' he said. 'I really didn't want to have to tell anyone about what's been happening to me over the last few months. I was hoping and praying that they would just stop and go away.'

What was he talking about? Hoping what would go away?

'Rachel, I really didn't want to worry you or dad, I've been trying to deal with this on my own.'

Deal with what? My mind was racing and I wished he'd just get to the point.

'Rachel, I'm so sorry that you've just spent the last two hours looking for me and worrying. I wanted this evening to be perfect. I'm so, so sorry.'

He did sound genuinely sincere, he always did, but he still hadn't explained himself. I stayed silent, feelings of impatience mingled with curiosity growing inside of me.

'Rachel, the honest truth is that I don't know what happened. I have no earthly idea of where I've been for the last two hours.'

I looked at him incredulously; I didn't understand what he was trying to say. How could he not know where he'd been? How could he say that he knew nothing when I'd clearly seen him walking down the stairs with Mia and Louise?

He carried on. 'Please, Rachel ... please promise me that you won't tell my father what I'm about to tell you.'

Exasperated by his drawn out explanation, I assured him that it would go no further.

'Rachel, over the last few months I've been experiencing blackouts... total memory losses,' he said. 'It's happened a few times. I black out and hours pass by. When I wake up I have no recollection of what's happened to me, or where I've been. Tonight I had another one; I remember our desserts arriving, I remember leaving the table to go to the restroom, I recall opening the restroom door ... and that's it. The next thing I remember is waking up on the lobby floor and looking up at you.'

'And Mia and Louise?' I questioned him. 'Do you remember walking down the stairs with them?'

'No,' he said, 'I don't. I just can't remember a thing.'

A worried look rushed across his face and mine.

My preoccupied thoughts of what exactly had gone on with Mia and Louise had temporarily left my mind and now I was seriously concerned.

'Austin this is serious ... I respect the fact that you don't want to tell anyone, but I really don't think it's sensible to keep this to yourself. You really need to see a doctor and soon.'

He looked so anxious and his grip on my hand tightened.

'I know you're right, Rachel ... but I can't tell dad, he'll only worry about me ... I *will* talk to the doctor about it when I go for more tests this week I promise. I'm so sorry, Rachel, this evening has been a disaster and it's my fault. Please forgive me for putting you through this.'

This evening in Paris had indeed been a disaster and all I wanted to do was go home. We returned to the airport and boarded the private plane. Oblivious to its captivating luxury, my mind twisted and puzzled throughout our flight. This disturbing information about Austin's blackouts was all I could think about.

In between my thoughts of concern I kept seeing Austin standing at the top of the stairs in the hotel with Mia and Louise hanging off his arms, kissing him. It made no sense. How could he not remember this? How could he be alert and conscious and yet not remember a thing? A cynical paranoid streak in me wondered if this was just a cunning and perfect excuse to not have to explain his two-hour absence. The two hours that I was sure he had spent with them.

As we neared Heathrow my head began to hurt – I couldn't think anymore. Tonight had been a crazy mix of elation, deflation, anger and concern. I didn't know whether I was coming or going. Austin was as quiet as a mouse all the way home, a perplexed look across his face. We left the plane and got back into the Lamborghini. He started the engine and we were soon on our way into London. We had been silent for some time; I kept turning to look at him and saw that his brow was furrowed and his eyes were fixed on the road. His mouth was tight and strained.

'Penny for them?' I broke the silence.

It was as if he didn't hear me. I spoke again.

'Austin! Are you ok?'

'I'm sorry, Rachel, what did you say?'

'I asked if you were okay … and I said, a penny for them?'

'Rachel, I'm sorry, I'm so angry with myself I just can't explain it.'

His voice was loud and berating. It startled me.

I responded quietly and gently. 'Angry? Why?'

'This wasn't the evening that I had planned for us, Rachel, and it's made me feel so damn mad, it's just that I wanted tonight to be special and perfect … Look what I put you through. I'm a damn liability.'

We pulled up outside my bedsit. I turned to look at him. He was staring straight ahead and his hands were still gripping the steering wheel tightly. I reached out and placed my hand gently on top of his.

'Austin, please don't be angry. I'm actually relieved that this happened tonight.'

He looked at me with sad, puzzled eyes.

'If it hadn't, I still wouldn't know about the blackouts you've been experiencing.' In a teasing tone, I went on to say, 'And I wouldn't be able to nag you to death, as I will be doing, to tell the doctor about them.'

A hint of his enthusiastic smiled flashed across his face for a second. I hadn't seen a glimmer of it since he'd left for the restroom in the restaurant this evening. He reached into his inside pocket and pulled out a box.

'I had planned on giving you this after dinner.'

I looked at the small box as he placed it on my lap.

'Please open it.'

I scooped the box up from my lap and gently opened the lid. Inside it was a small pair of heart-shaped earrings. I gasped when I saw that the heart shape was formed by two sparkling crystal raindrops entwined together.

'I hope you like them ... I thought they'd match the necklace.'

The evening may have not been perfect but this present certainly was. I stared at them for a moment.

'I love them, thank you!' I said, as I fought back my tears.

He hugged me tightly and kissed me gently on my forehead. 'I'm so, so sorry about tonight, Rachel. I hope you can forgive me.'

I squeezed him tightly. 'Austin, it's okay, as I said, I'm glad it happened.'

'I don't deserve you, Rachel, I'm an ass,' he said, taking my hand and kissing it gently. He got out of the car and walked me to my front door. 'I'll ring you tomorrow.'

After one more hug and several more apologies, he was gone.

CHAPTER TWENTY-FIVE
EARLIER THAT AFTERNOON IN CONIK PENSTER DEWE'S OFFICE

This would be the fourth time that Conik Penster Dewe had visited the cavernous vault room in so many months.

His arrogance went before him as he paced confidently down the hallway of torches towards the two hooded figures that guarded the golden lift doors.

He had the fourth photograph of Austin nestled safely inside his long black coat.

The two hooded figures stepped aside and the golden ornate doors opened.

The words '*Camera Cellar*' spewed effortlessly out of Conik Penster Dewe's miserly mouth. The lift responded and began to shake violently.

The vibrations rattled every bolt, nut and hinge that held it together. Conik Penster Dewe held out his arms and steadied himself on either side of the lift walls as it made its descent from the hall of torches to the cavernous vault room; finally and frantically, it oscillated its way to a sudden standstill.

The doors flew open. Conik Penster Dewe stood straight and upright with his feet tightly fixed together. He reached upwards and spread his fingers widely before running them through his thick, black, wavy hair and brushing himself down.

Composed and preened, he glided out of the elevator. With an assured arrogance he flew gracefully towards the never-ending metal wall of doors in front of him.

He stopped abruptly two feet in front of the wall just as he had done before. He looked forward, closed his eyes, and uttered the words '*denique unus.*'

He left the ground in a sudden bolt of movement and shot up vertically with incredible speed. After hovering momentarily, he whispered a series of sounds and the vault door swung open.

Once inside, he reached into his pocket and once again he held up the photograph of Austin and bellowed the words, 'Cantartis, awaken.'

The solid glass box reacted immediately, and it was soon rocking on its plinth and spiralling into the air. Within moments it had travelled across the room and engulfed the photograph of Austin.

With anticipated victory, Conik Penster Dewe rose off the ground and licked his lips. His face began to contort with excitement as he watched the box return to its solid state. His arrogance was fuelled by the knowledge that this offering was the hinge pin. This meant that he was beyond the halfway mark in the extraction process. Austin should now be more susceptible and more controllable.

The light inside the Cantartis was visibly brighter and its glow was both glorious and constant.

Conik Penster Dewe stilled himself and looked at it intently.

Then he let out a deep, chilling scream. The light in the Cantartis had begun to flicker frantically. His face contorted as he watched it slow from its frantic pace to a periodic pulse until it eventually stopped.

'STILL HE RESISTS!' he yelled, his voice like thunder.

He clenched both hands and twisted them, skillfully punching the air above him before flying out of the vault room and bolting towards the lift doors that would take him back to the hallway of torches. He had no time to sit and admire his celestial collection today, no time to slumber in his leather armchair bathing in their glorious light.

He hurried his way down the hallway of torches. There were now four flames lighting his way and they glowed silently as he flew past them towards the next elevator.

Underling was waiting to open the birdcage doors on his master's arrival. The moment the lift arrived Underling pulled back the doors on cue. Conik Penster Dewe bolted out of them and flew down the hallway to his office with a furious energy.

'We have work to do. My office in exactly ten minutes!' he bellowed to Underling, after screeching to a smoke-billowing halt.

Underling nodded.

Conik Penster Dewe took a seat in his large armchair and stared into the flames. He looked up at the large picture of the woman on the wall and waved his hand in front of it. The red velvet curtains unhooked themselves and the woman was soon hidden from view. He stared into the flames in front of him. His fingers were busily beating against his chin and the odd whisper occasionally leaked from the narrowed corners of his mouth.

He was quite obviously in the middle of intense deliberation, weighing up the predicament that lay before him.

Somehow he had to find a way to destroy Austin's love for Rachel. His efforts so far had not been effective. Only three more photographs to procure and the extraction process would be complete. The protection that Austin and Rachel's love was affording Austin had to be destroyed. It was clouding matters and causing him concern. By the time the fifth and sixth installment was secured, he needed Austin to be ready to hand the seventh piece over of his own free will. He knew that he would have to manipulate the situation even further if he were to complete the extraction process.

The door knocked. Conik Penster Dewe's voice snaked its way around the room. 'Enter.'

Underling entered.

Conik Penster Dewe sat perfectly still and continued to stare into the flames that lapped and cackled in his grand fireplace.

He bolted forward and turned to look at Underling. 'It seems, Underling, that our efforts are not working so well.'

'No, sire.' Underling hung his head low.

'You stopped him from seeing Rachel when he returned from Milan, Underling?'

'Yes, sire. I did as you asked. As soon as he arrived back I rang him and insisted that he attended a meeting with me immediately.' Underling looked very agitated and he hesitated before speaking again. 'Sire, I was waiting on your return to update you on Austin's most recent activities.'

Conick Penster Dewe sat forward in the chair. His eyes narrowed in his stoney face and a look of frustrated anticipation swept across him. 'And? Spit it out, Underling.'

Underling bowed his head towards the floor. 'Yes, sire, despite our attempts to keep him and Rachel apart he has gone to great lengths and great expense to take her to Paris tonight ... for a romantic dinner, sire.'

Underling bowed deeply, shaking as he waited for his master's response.

Conik Penster Dewe gripped the arms of his chair tightly. 'What lengths? What expense?'

'He has hired a private plane to take them to Paris, and he has driven all day just to get Rachel's passport from her parents' home in Wales.'

Conik Penster Dewe shot out of his seat. His violet eyes darted violently around the room, and his voice sounded enraged and sinister when he next spoke.

'Where are they having dinner, Underling?'

'The Hotel Meurice, sire.'

'Really!' Conik Dewe's face twisted with glee. 'Perhaps things are not as bad as they seem Underling. Young Austin is obviously succumbing to the extravagance of the life that I have laid before him.'

He drummed his chin slowly. His violet eyes darting around the room.

'Call Mia and Louise! I need them to work their magic tonight. Book them in to the best suite at Hotel Meurice. Arrange for them to be in the restaurant at the same time as Austin and Rachel.' Conik Penster Dewe smiled to himself. 'Tomorrow morning, ask Celia to pay him a visit. I want her to inform him that he and his father will be moving into the Mayfair Town House with immediate effect.'

Conik Penster Dewe began to pace backwards and forwards in front of the large black glass windows.

'Grace and Albert must be told of their arrival and informed that, as from tomorrow, they will be attending to their daily needs. Arrange for a team of Gustlings to pack and move their belongings. I want them settled in Mayfair by the end of tomorrow, and I want him and his father on a private plane to New York by 6pm the following day. Book him on another international fashion shoot. They will stay in the New York Plaza. I want him kept in New York for the next two months.'

Underling nodded. 'Yes, sire, straight away. But what about the reports, the photographs, who will –?'

'I really couldn't care who writes the report. You will arrange for a suitable low-ranking employee in New York to take the photograph. I want to put as much distance between Austin and Rachel as possible.'

'Yes, sire.'

Conik Penster Dewe rubbed his hands together as he paced back and forth. Underling stood silently, his head bowed, waiting patiently for his dismissal. Conik Penster Dewe began to rap his finger against his chin once more, a pensive look etched across his face.

'Underling, one more thing: you and I will also be visiting New York. The time is drawing closer. I want to keep a very close eye on Austin and I will take drastic measures if necessary to break this love he holds for Rachel.'

Conik Penster Dewe sat back once more in his leather armchair. His facial muscles eased for a second, and a look that almost resembled satisfaction flashed across his face. It was short lived, arriving and departing in a second as his brow quickly furrowed. His hand flicked in front of the painting and the drapes pulled back again, revealing the painting of the woman.

With his fingers drumming his chin, he spoke. 'I think you will like it in New York, Catriona.' The woman in the painting remained still as always. He spoke to her again as if he were having a two-way conversation. 'Don't look so surprised, my dear. You know what draws near. Did you really think that I would leave you here all alone at this crucial time?' The woman in the painting stood still, unmoved by Conik Penster Dewe's words of address. 'We are so close, my dear! So close to the end!'

Conik Penster Dewe stared into the flames and continued drumming his chin with his fingertips. Then he flicked his hand again and in one graceful movement, the large red velvet curtains that hung above the painting swished shut again.

Amused by his imaginary conversation with the woman in

the painting, he laughed loudly as he threw himself back into his large leather armchair.

'Goodnight, Catriona.'

His eyes closed and his thoughts turned once more to the troublesome relationship that had developed between Austin and Rachel.

His plan had not accounted for Austin falling in love and it was becoming increasingly obvious that its power was having a remedial effect on the whole extraction process.

If distance and a variety of temptations didn't cure the problem, he knew that he would have to take more drastic actions.

Austin was the last of the Crystal Bloodline. He alone was its last stand. The fight for its survival was inherently and unconsciously battling inside him. He was also in love with Rachel, and her with him. This love was strengthening and protecting him.

Conik Penster Dewe had thrown riches and beauty, lust and greed in front of Austin, but the power of the Crystal Bloodline, coupled with the love he held for Rachel, had almost made him immune to all of it.

He would not make the mistake of underestimating this power or its capabilities.

Chapter Twenty-six
Austin Jacobs

Dinner in Paris with Rachel was supposed to be a new start, but all of my careful planning, trying to make sure it was a perfect evening, had gone to hell in a basket.

As I drove away from her, anger began to well up inside me and my foot pressed hard on the accelerator.

Planning this evening had been like a military exercise that started very early this morning with a phone call to Rachel's parents. The drive to Wales to get her passport was a much-preferred option to breaking into her bedsit and ransacking her home, no matter how honourable or romantic my intentions. Rachel's parents had been overwhelmingly welcoming and absolutely wonderful. Rachel had apparently told them all about me, and they knew that we had been dating for a while. They both seemed genuinely pleased to meet me, and I hoped that they could see how serious I was about their daughter. They certainly seemed impressed with my plans to surprise Rachel and take her for dinner in Paris.

Yes! I had pulled the whole thing off perfectly. Everything had gone completely to plan, right up until dessert in the restaurant. Why did Mia and Louise have to be there? Why did I have to have one of my blackouts? Why did it all have to go so horribly wrong?

As I drove home I became more distraught with every passing yard.

Tonight had given me my first real insight into what was really happening to me during these blackouts, and I was beginning to believe that my worst fears could be true. I had been so desperate to believe the images I was seeing were just figments of my imagination. Now it seems I had to consider the real possibility that this was not the case at all.

Rachel was the only person who had seen me when I was right in the middle of one. She had said, quite categorically, that I was fully aware and in control of myself as I walked down the stairs with Mia and Louise apparently draped all over me.

Where had I been with them? More importantly, *what* had I been doing with them?

The memories of the girls tangoing in Paris began to flash through my mind. Then vague blurry images of the Imperial Suite in The Ritz blazed into my conscious. Disturbing images of me and the girls cavorting on my Marie Antoinette bed bombarded me. The guilt I felt was growing, and I feared now more than ever that these images were very real memories.

After Rachel's insight tonight, there was one thing I was sure of: somehow or other, I was fully functional during these blackouts. By the time I arrived home it was hard to accept that, even if I didn't have any memories of the things that had happened, I still felt accountable.

My stomach knotted. Rachel did not deserve to be with someone like me; this wasn't fair on her. Broken, devastated and guilt-ridden by tonight's revelations, I took to my bed.

Dad was already fast asleep when I arrived home and I could hear him snoring loudly as I lay tossing and turning under the strain of my guilt.

New images began to flash through my mind. Mia, Louise and I were sprawled across a huge, luxurious bed. Mia was lying across my legs and Louise was delicately unbuttoning my shirt with her perfectly manicured fingers.

Why could I only remember small flashes? Why couldn't I remember everything? I had never wanted to be in Rachel's arms so much.

It turned out to be a long night and I was relieved to see the morning arrive. Lying fully clothed and sprawled across my bed as the sunlight chinked its way through my curtains I smelt the unmistakable aroma of bacon cooking. I could hear dad whistling happily to himself in the kitchen.

I was about to launch myself out of my bed when my phone rang.

The woman's voice on the other end of the line was unfamiliar and it had a gravelly texture, as if it had been soaked in vodka.

She said her name was Celia Compton and she asked if I could please make my way to the front door of the shop to let her in. She was here on behalf of Conik Penster Dewe and wanted to see me straight away.

Puzzled by her unexpected arrival, I replied, 'Yes Miss Compton I'll be there in a moment.'

I quickly tidied my hair and straightened my shirt, then ran into the kitchen.

'Dad!'

He turned to look at me. 'Morning, Austin. Bacon sandwich?'

'Dad! I just had a phone call from a woman. She's waiting outside the shop door. She works for Conik Penster Dewe and wants to see me right away, I have no idea what she wants ... I've got to go!'

A woman in her late twenties, standing six feet tall, stood by the front door. This must be Celia Compton. She looked extremely sophisticated and absolutely flawless in her black, tailored business suit. I hastily opened the door to let her in and she strutted across the threshold.

'Austin Jacobs, I presume?'

Her voice was curt and businesslike ... I didn't like the feel of this and I wondered what was coming next.

'Yes, I'm Austin.'

She looked me up and down with a look of distain. 'Conik Penster Dewe is very pleased with you.'

I let out a small, inaudible sigh.

She glanced around the shop, her nose pointed upwards. 'He has decided to give you a Mayfair Town House to live in. It comes complete with a state-of-the-art photographic studio and an indoor swimming pool. I am to take you and your father to see your new home immediately ... I'll be in the car waiting.'

WHAT! A new home with an indoor pool and a studio? My head was awash with questions and wonder. I bolted back upstairs, taking them two steps at a time.

'Dad!' I shouted.

He was still in the kitchen, eating a bacon sandwich.

'Dad, you need to get dressed straight away.'

'Let me finish my sandwich and I will.'

'There's no time, Dad! Get dressed now!'

Dad looked concerned. 'Why? What is it, what's wrong?'

'Nothing's wrong, Dad — in fact, quite the opposite. Conik Penster Dewe has given us a house in Mayfair. It's got a photographic studio and an indoor swimming pool. This woman, Celia Compton, is going to take us there to see it. She's waiting for us now.'

Dad nearly choked on his sandwich as he bolted out of his chair. 'I'll be dressed in no time, just give me a minute.'

Dad and I had lived in two-bedroom flats for as long as I could remember. They were usually situated right above whatever business we were running at the time. Living in a house in Mayfair with a state-of-the-art studio and a pool was unimaginable, unbelievable!

Then I thought about our shop and the practicality of keeping it open. In reality the shop had been losing money for a long time, which was the reason for setting up the studio.

My career was soaring and so was my bank balance, I was making so much money we didn't need the shop anymore. Dad didn't need to work anymore. Moving to this house in Mayfair was perfect; we could let the shop go and dad could finally retire.

Dad was dressed and ready in record time and he had a definite spring in his step as we bounded towards the limousine parked right outside the shop.

The chauffeur stood on command with the door open. Dad and I stepped backwards, looking at the shop front for a moment. It was almost as if we both knew that we would soon be saying goodbye to Jacobs' Photographic.

We entered the chauffeur-driven limousine. Celia sat upright and businesslike in the back. 'Good morning, gentlemen.'

'Good morning,' we replied simultaneously.

'Gentleman, we will shortly arrive at your new home, Copper Beech Hall. Conik Penster Dewe has gifted it to you,

Austin. It is an eight-bedroomed property situated in the heart of Mayfair, and is a traditional and luxurious residence.'

She never relaxed from her bolt-upright position as we travelled along, and continued to brief us on our new home in her old, professional manner.

'It has been modified over time and has staff quarters, which are occupied by Alfred and Grace, your butler and housekeeper. They will attend to your everyday needs.'

Dad and I stared incredulously at each other. This really was another world. A large, wrought iron gate opened up in front of us. Copper Beech trees lined the drive as we drove slowly towards what looked like a stately manor. It was three floors high, and architecturally stunning. Huge pillars stood like centurions guarding the front door. As the limousine glided to a smooth stop, two figures appeared in the doorway.

The chauffeur opened the door and Celia stepped out, we followed her lead and walked towards the twelve-foot high mahogany doors.

'Grace! Alfred! How good it is to see you again.'

'Good morning, Miss. Compton, and you.'

'Please allow me to introduce you to the new occupants of Copper Beech Hall. Grace, Alfred, meet Mr Austin Jacobs and his father Mr Edward Jacobs.'

Both Grace and Alfred nodded their heads and replied in unison. 'Pleased to meet you both.'

'We are looking forward to serving you,' Alfred added. Grace nodded her head in agreement.

My father coughed and cleared his throat. 'Yes we're very pleased to meet you, too.'

'Yes,' I said. 'Very pleased to meet you.'

My father and I were so bowled over by the events of the morning. Neither of us could quite comprehend what was happening; it was too incredible to be true.

Alfred pushed the large mahogany front doors open and we walked into a huge, marbled hallway. A wide sweeping staircase dominated the centre of it.

'Austin, Mr Jacobs ... to the right of the stairs is the East Wing and to the left the West,' said Celia Compton, her eyes firmly fixed on the top of the stairs.

Several doors led off the hallway and she proceeded to take us on a grand tour.

The rooms were all lavished with expensive velvets and original oil paintings. Huge chandeliers and decorative lamps illuminated each one.

We finally arrived at my state-of-the-art studio. It was incredible and four times the size of my studio at the shop.

Celia Compton then led us down a small flight of stairs that led to a huge games room. A clear glass wall ran down the side of it. Beyond the glass wall was a fifty-foot long swimming pool.

I thought Dad was going to have a cardiac arrest there and then when he saw the pool. He gripped my arm tightly with excitement as we walked through the glass doors to take a closer look at it.

'Now that you know where everything is, Grace and Alfred will assist you with whatever you need.'

Celia Compton's voice had an officious tone that simply commanded attention.

'Conik Penster Dewe has arranged a team to help you move your belongings. They will arrive at the shop by 12pm today to assist you in any way they can. Grace will prepare an evening meal for you.'

Dad and I walked swiftly behind Celia Compton as she led the way back to the grand hallway.

Alfred was standing straight and tall in front of the Mahogany front doors. He was a very distinguished-looking elderly man, dressed in black pinstriped trousers, a crisp white shirt, and a pinstriped waistcoat. A gold pocket watch peeked out of the top of his waistcoat pocket.

'Alfred! Mr Jacobs senior and Mr Jacobs junior will be leaving soon to collect their belongings. They will return in a few hours.'

'Yes Miss. Compton ... Mr Jacobs ... Mr Jacobs.'

We arrived back at the shop to find two removal lorries parked up outside.

In a matter of hours, our daily lives had changed beyond recognition. This realisation was up close and personal, and mixed with conflicting emotions. I had spent so many happy times here with dad, just the two of us in our flat above the shop. I had met Rachel here *and* built the studio with her here.

Rachel! I hadn't thought to ring her. I'd been so carried away with Celia Compton's visit and the house in Mayfair. The events of this morning had served as a distraction from my worries and concerns. To be honest it felt good to forget about them, if only for a little while. The excitement that this morning had brought began to subside rapidly as I recalled how awful our dinner in Paris had been last night. The blackouts, the girls ... putting my beautiful Rachel through all of that.

Just as I was about to ring her, Mr Underling arrived at the shop.

'Ah! Austin, good afternoon.'

He looked around at all the people carrying our belongings out of the shop and taking them to the removal vans outside. Before he could say another word I began explaining the morning's events and the outrageous generosity of Conik Penster Dewe's gift.

He smiled at my obvious enthusiasm and excitement.

'Well, Austin, Conik Penster Dewe will be even more delighted when he hears that you've been booked for the next two months by a prestigious client in New York! You and your father will leave tomorrow at six o'clock in the evening. Just make sure you're packed and ready to leave by four.'

Mr Underling left and I turned to look at Dad.

'New York, Dad, we're going to New York! Can you believe it? I'll have done it. I'll have worked in all of the fashion capitols of the world!'

Dad looked quite happy about the news at first, then a concerned look flashed across his face. 'Two months, Austin ... That's a long time.'

He was right, two months was a long time.

'I know, Dad.'

'We seem to have forgotten about your mother again, Austin, we haven't looked for her at all. It's not anyone's fault, I know this. We've been away so much we haven't had the time and now we're going to be away for another two months.'

'I know Dad, I've had no time to spend with Rachel either.'

Dad stood silently for a moment. I knew that look in his eyes too well. He was busy evaluating the situation. He smiled and took my hand.

'Look, Austin, another two months won't hurt, let's just go to New York. You will, as you say, have photographed in the four great fashion capitols of the world. That was your dream — you can't stop when you're almost there. We've coped so far, two more months won't hurt, and I'm sure Rachel will understand.'

He was right ... I had to go to New York, but right now I had to ring Rachel. I only had one night in London and I'd be gone again.

'Rachel, it's me, Austin.'

'Hi, Austin.'

'Rachel, I'm sorry about last night.'

'Austin, you don't have to apologise, it's fine. Have you been to the hospital today?'

In all of the madness I'd completely forgot that I'd promised her I'd go.

'No ... Rachel I haven't had time to get there yet, but I will, I promise. I need to see you tonight — I have so much to tell you.'

I hadn't planned to tell her about the house over the phone but I couldn't stop myself and I blurted it out.

'Conik Penster Dewe has given me and dad a house in Mayfair to live in. Well, I say house — it's an eight-bedroomed mansion and it's amazing. I'll pick you up at 8.30pm and tell you all about it if that's okay with you.'

Rachel's voice sounded stunned.

'Yes 8.30pm is fine. Austin, what do you mean he's given you a house, I don't understand?'

'I'll explain later — I have to go, we're in the middle of packing everything up. See you later.'

Within hours we were in our new home, Copper Beech Hall. Our belongings were being carried through the mahogany front door by the team of people that had helped us pack and move.

In and out of the front doors came box after box. We were amazed at how much stuff we'd accumulated since living in London. We hadn't had time to sift through everything properly so there was a lot of junk that we didn't need, mixed in with our sacred sentimental belongings. A stranger wouldn't be able to tell them apart. Items that hold sentimental value are, by nature, only identifiable and of value to the one with the sentiment.

We directed the team with the boxes to the various rooms. Some were for upstairs, others for down. Eventually all our belongings had arrived safely.

When all of the helpers had left I ran up the huge flight of stairs and took a right turn. There were four bedrooms in the right wing. I ran down the corridor and headed to the left wing where I found another four bedrooms. A spiral staircase stood at the end of the corridor. I spun up it and there in front of me was one huge suite covering the whole of the top floor. An enormous bed — bigger than I'd ever seen — stood in the centre of the room. There was a small, beautifully decorated living area and when I opened up the double doors on the back wall I found the bathroom, fully equipped with a Jacuzzi and a wet room. Tiny lights were dotted all over the ceiling and cream marble and travertine tiles lined the walls and floor.

This was where I decided to stake my claim. Dad could have the rest of the house in its entirety, apart from the studio of course, but this top-floor suite was definitely going to be mine — even though it would be two long months before I could really enjoy it.

The time had run away with itself, and I needed to get washed and changed. Dinner would be ready soon and Rachel would be waiting for me to pick her up. I didn't really want to stay here for dinner, but I was trying to keep everyone happy.

Grace welcomed us into the dining room. She wore a long black dress that didn't quite reach her ankles, and flat, sensible shoes clung sturdily to her feet. Her white apron strings were wrapped around her middle and tied in the front. She was a stout, portly, friendly-looking woman who must have been in her mid-fifties, and after an hour of sitting at the table I can say without a doubt that her cooking skills were of an international chef's standard. Dad and I were going to have to watch our waistlines.

Dad looked so relaxed, the lines on his face had mellowed into nothingness. All of the stress I used to see erased. He smiled at me and winked. 'Shouldn't you be off soon?'

He knew I'd arranged to see Rachel tonight and he knew

that I was anxious about telling her that I'd be away for so long.

'Go on,' he added. 'Off you go, give my love to Rachel ... and don't worry, two months will fly by. She'll probably be a bit upset when you tell her that you'll be away for so long, but I've seen the way she looks at you. She'll be waiting here for you when you come back. I know she will.'

'Thanks, Dad, see you later.'

Alfred opened the door for me as I ran out of Copper Beech Hall. The Lamborghini was parked right outside.

Alfred's voice followed me down the steps as I made my way to my car.

'I took the liberty, sir. She's ready to go.'

Having your own butler was amazing. I felt like a superhero, an A-list celebrity, a royal prince of the realm.

My foot hit the accelerator and the engine roared. The back wheels began to spin as I gently pulled my foot off the clutch and headed down the driveway.

***

The traffic was hindering my progress tonight, and even though the official rush hour was over, bumper to bumper queues heralded their way from one road to another. Somehow despite the delays, I managed to get to Rachel's on time.

Just as I was about to ring the doorbell she opened the front door.

She looked so beautiful. She was wearing a fitted black lace dress that clung beautifully to her figure. The crystal necklace lay delicately against the black lace at the top of her dress.

'Rachel, you look amazing.'

She flicked her loose auburn hair over her shoulder. The streetlight caught the crystal earrings. They glimmered and sparkled perfectly as they nestled her lobes. My hand reached out and I gently brushed one of the exposed earrings with my thumb. Her skin was so soft.

Pulling her close I began hugging her desperately.

'Rachel, I hate being away from you.'

Her arms tightened around my waist. She hugged me closer and whispered in my ear, 'Me too.'

The warmth and security of holding her tightly in my arms both engulfed and baptised me. We held each other silently, our bodies fixed together. Safe in her arms, I closed my eyes. My heart and soul were present and accounted for, and exactly where they wanted to be.

Then my phone rang. I ignored it. Then it rang again and again. I pulled away from her reluctantly; it was Mr Underling. This was a call I couldn't ignore.

'I'm sorry, Rachel. I have to take this.' I pressed accept. 'Hello, Mr Underling.'

'Austin, I need you to come over to my office before eleven tonight. Charlie, my chauffeur, will pick you up at ten thirty. The client in New York, Len Ganfeall, wants a video conference call with you. He wants to discuss your itinerary in New York.'

This couldn't be happening, not at this time of night. I did a quick calculation and worked out that it was only 5pm in New York. I quickly resided myself to thought that these untimely interruptions during my free time were another part of the price I had to pay for my success.

'How long do you think the call will take, Mr Underling?'

'I would imagine that it would take about an hour or two.'

'Okay, Mr Underling, thank you I'll see you later.'

The call ended and I looked longingly at Rachel. My time with her tonight had just been snatched away from me. My heart sank, and began free falling into a deflated and dense descent.

Longing for this call to have never happened, I looked up at her. She could see by the disheartened look on my face that I had nothing but bad news.

'Austin ... it's okay. I couldn't help but hear the conversation.'

'I'm so sorry, Rachel, I'm going to have to cut our night short to get to this meeting.'

She tried to look pleased for me.

'New York, wow! Sounds amazing! When do you leave?' Her voice was cheerful but she looked like a broken doll, her eyes haunted with sadness and her mouth desperately trying to smile.

'Tomorrow ... I leave tomorrow. Rachel, you don't have to

pretend that you're all right with this, because I'm not all right with it either.'

She sat there silently. I needed to let her know how I felt; she needed to know that my love for her was absolute.

'Rachel, I need you to know how much I want to be with you. The last few months have been crazy, and even though it's been wonderful achieving my goals and dreams, being away from you so much is really starting to get me down. I didn't realise that my success would take me away from you so much.'

She took my hand, and cupped it in hers; her touch was so soft and gentle. 'Austin ... as much as it hurts me when you're away, I wouldn't have it any other way. I want you to realise all of your dreams, and be everything that you can be. I do miss you like crazy when you're not around, it's true, and not seeing you for weeks isn't easy I won't lie, but I know that these opportunities don't come around every day. You have to follow your dream. I'm not going anywhere ... I'll be waiting right here for you when you come back, but you really need to see a doctor. I'm worried about you ... please promise me you'll go and see someone in New York.'

Her sentiment was completely genuine and sincere but she couldn't hide the sad, broken look in her eyes.

'I promise I'll go and see a doctor. Rachel, it's been so hard being away from you. I need you to know this. I don't want you to think that it's easy for me, or that it doesn't bother me.'

She smiled and her hand reached up to my face. She gently held my chin and turned my face towards hers.

'Just make sure that you come back to me ... because if you don't, I *will* come and find you!'

Her teasing tone lightened and relaxed the moment, and the words that I had meant to say to her on so many occasions came flying naturally out of my mouth.

'I love you, Rachel.'

Her beautiful blue eyes widened and welled. She wrapped her arms around my waist and whispered, 'I love you, too.'

We held each other tightly unable to let go. This was a special moment and one that I wanted to hold on to for as long as possible.

We stayed like this, clutched silently to each other, for so long that we had to hurry to the restaurant and hurry through our courses. We only had two hours together before I had to leave for the meeting with Mr Underling.

With so little time I hadn't got round to telling her that I'd be away for two months. I didn't want to tell her, not yet.

Savouring every moment of the drive back to her bedsit I avoided breaching the subject all the way. It would be a long time before we would be together again and I wanted what little time we had together to be perfect. I was acutely aware of the fact that very soon I would have to return to the house in Mayfair to meet Mr Underling's chauffeur. My original intentions were to take Rachel there after dinner, but this it seems was not to be.

We only had time for a very quick goodbye. Walking her to her front door, knowing that it would be two long months before I'd see her again, was tearing me apart.

I looked into her beautiful, kind face before kissing her. Her pale blue eyes looked at me with such love and compassion, that I couldn't survive their penetrating beauty; I closed my eyes, pulled her close and pressed my lips down hard on hers.

In my wisdom, I had decided not to tell her about the length of this trip to New York. I would, of course, have to tell her at some point, but tonight was not the right time. We'd had such a glorious evening, as short-lived as it was ... it was perfect. No distractions, no crazy images haunting me. I was filled with nothing but pure, unadulterated feelings of adoration and devotion for Rachel.

Chapter Twenty-seven
Austin Jacobs

I'd pushed my punctuality to the limit tonight and I arrived at Copper Beach Hall with about two seconds to spare. Alfred was standing at the top of the steps, waiting to greet me when I arrived.

'Good evening, Mr Jacobs.'

'Good evening, Alfred.'

'I'll park the car in the garage for you, sir.'

He took the keys off me and took the Lamborghini to its heated garage. Dad and I had never really had a reliable heating system in any of the places we'd lived, yet now Dad and I lived in a house where even the garage had a state-of-the-art heating system that was as accurate and reliable as a Swiss watch.

I stared at my reflection in the huge, gold-framed mirror hanging on the wall. As I began straightening my tie it suddenly struck me: this big – no, this *enormous* – building was my home. My circumstances had changed dramatically and in such a short space of time. In that one defining moment the enormity of this staggering change really hit me. The front door opened and I turned to look. Alfred had returned. As he came through the door I could see a black limousine crawling slowly up the driveway.

The chauffeur, a thin, gawky-looking chap, got out of the car and opened the back door to let me in. 'Good evening, Mr Jacobs. I'm Charlie,' he said in a broad cockney accent.

'Good evening, Charlie, pleased to meet you.'

He opened the door for me and we were soon on our way.

The drive was smooth and peaceful and I didn't take any notice of where exactly Charlie was taking me. I was too lost in my concerns about leaving Rachel without telling her that

I would be away for so long. By the time we arrived at the mouth of a long, thin tunnel I didn't have a clue where we were. Charlie announced that we would soon be at Mr Underling's office. I had never visited him at his actual office before, he'd only ever met me at the shop.

We exited the tunnel and a building suddenly appeared straight ahead of us. It looked exactly the same as the office blocks I had visited in Paris and Milan, and the tunnel we had just driven through looked just as familiar.

'Where are we, Charlie?'

'Why, we are at Mr Underling's office, sir.' He stopped the car and opened the door to let me out. 'If sir would like to follow me.'

'Yes of course, but what I meant was, where in London is this?'

He hurried up the steps and through the door. He ignored my question as if he hadn't heard me posing it, and directed me towards the lift.

'His office is on the fourth floor, sir.'

With no more time to pursue or think about the exact location of our whereabouts, I made my way into the lift and up to the fourth floor.

The lift opened and a long hallway spanned in front of me. Mr Underling suddenly appeared.

'Austin, you've arrived, come in.'

He led me into a large boardroom; I could hear a lot of chatter and laughter. The large screen on the wall was filled with four strange faces talking amongst themselves. They stopped and looked at us when we entered the room. The older gentleman in the tailor made suit spoke first in a broad New York accent.

'Austin Jacobs, Len Ganfeall. It's good to meet you.'

He was incredibly loud and the enthusiasm of his greeting was quite overwhelming.

'Mr Ganfeall, pleased to meet you too.'

His broad New York accent bellowed out of the screen again as he said, 'Let me introduce you to my team Austin.'

He introduced me to the other strange faces on the screen and in no time at all, the meeting had commenced. There was a lot to take in. Mr Ganfeall was so full of energy and ideas. He was already the loudest and demanding client I had come across.

It was almost half past one by the time we concluded the call, and I was more than ready to go home and crawl into my bed. My mind momentarily imagined my old bed in our flat then it dawned on me: Mayfair was now my home. The enormous bed at the top of the house would be where I would sleep tonight.

***

By 6pm the following day both dad and I were seated on a private jet and on our way to JFK airport. We were both so exhausted from our jam-packed day of preparations for the trip that we slept most of the way.

When we arrived at JFK we were greeted by our chauffeur, who informed us that his name was Larry and that he would be at our service throughout the duration of our stay in New York. He drove us to the Hotel Plaza which, he informed us, was one of the best hotels that New York had to offer.

When we arrived we were shown to the Royal Terrace suite. This beautiful suite bathed in natural sunlight would be home for the next two months. It offered a terrace to sit on with a spectacular view of the city. Dad was delighted that the hotel had a pool – though this time it was not a private one. He would have to wait until we got back to London to enjoy that luxury again. Our Mayfair manor house was quite something and we were both looking forward to being able to really spend some time there and sample more of Grace's cooking.

New York was new territory for me and though I'd seen its sights in films, being here was something else. I marvelled at the hundreds of people purposefully rushing along the cities busy streets. Each and every one of them looked like they had somewhere important to be, or someone important to meet.

Observing their urgency brought new meaning to the term a New York minute. My work schedule was in New York minute time too, and before I knew it, three intense weeks had passed. Three weeks of no free time at all. Eat, sleep and work were the best three words to describe my time there. Dad, on the other hand, was having a ball; he was steadily making his way around the tourist spots of New York City.

Liberty Island, Times Square, the Meatpacking District and The Museum of Modern Art were just a few of the places on his list.

Rachel had spent the last three weeks under the impression that I would soon be home. I had delayed telling her every time she mentioned my return during our daily calls. It was cowardly of me, I know, but I just hated hearing that sad tone in her voice and I just wanted to delay her disappointment for as long as possible.

At the beginning of my fourth week I knew my time had run out: I had to tell her. I blurted it out and followed it up with a barrage of apologies and excuses for not telling her sooner. She tried to sound fine about it but I could tell that she wasn't. I wasn't fine about it either. The thought of not seeing her for another four weeks was becoming harder to cope with.

This constant distance between us was getting me down. I was finding being apart from her just as difficult as she was finding being apart from me. Her concern for my health was obvious in our daily conversations, and she kept badgering me to go and see a doctor here in New York. She also asked on a daily basis if I'd had any more blackouts. Not wanting to worry her, I lied and said no.

The truth was that I had blacked out several times. The last one was two days ago. I was working on an afternoon shoot in an exclusive nightclub. The VIP area of the club was quite something; it was adorned with red and purple velvet sofas and soft furnishings, and violet lights sparkled along the walls.

Two models, Blayze and Caden, lay on the velvet sofas in designer evening gowns. Blayze had an ethereal, dangerous look to her. She was modelling a black satin gown that had been perfectly designed to make her look like a fierce goddess. A long, silk, loosely-draped train fell seductively around her bare ankles, and her perfectly pedicured toes peaked delicately out of diamond clustered peep-toe stilettos. Caden wore a red, figure-hugging gown. A split that ended just above her knee revealed her beautifully shaped legs. Her long, red, flowing hair and ruby-red lips created a startling colour clash that worked perfectly with Blayze's ice-white hair, ruby lips and black gown. The effect was strong and inspiring.

Dry ice had been brought in to add some mystery to the composition and the smoke began to lick around their ankles before rising slowly upwards from the floor. Blaze stood up and walked through the smoke towards the camera. She lifted her hand up and held it, her palm facing upwards, just under her chin as she puckered her mouth and blew a cloud of it towards me. The smoke's transparency disappeared as it thickened to an opaque density. I lost sight of the composition in front of me as it swirled itself around me. The next thing I remembered was waking up on my bed in the Royal Terrace Suite.

These blackouts were not going away and even though I knew I should have gone to see a doctor weeks ago, I hadn't.

It wasn't that I was putting it off; I genuinely hadn't had the time. Dad was still clueless about them and thought I was okay, but the longer I was away from Rachel, and the more blackouts I experienced, the more I questioned my whole situation.

Yes, my career was soaring and dad and I were out of debt, which was wonderful. It had to be said that dad looked really well too! The pressure was off him completely, and it showed.

On the other hand, my health was still suffering. Something was wrong with me, this I knew. The blackouts I kept experiencing and the visions I kept seeing made me feel sick with shame and disgustingly disloyal to Rachel. My relationship with her was suffering from more than just the distance between us and it was becoming unbearable.

Every night, when my head hit my pillow, I found myself deep in deliberation about what I should do.

Should I throw the towel in — give all of this up? There was so much to consider. Conik Penster Dewe for a start. I was committed to him big time for his investment in me. Besides the initial set up costs, he had been incredibly generous. Mr Underling ... I owed him so much, too, for believing in me. He was an amazing agent and I pretty much owed my success to him. He had taken a chance on me and had catapulted my career into the stratosphere.

There was also Dad to consider ... he was getting older. If I turned my back on all of this what would the outcome be?

I'd probably have to give the Lamborghini back. The house in Mayfair would no longer be ours to live in. We'd be back in the shop in no time, lumbered with even more debt than before.

***

It was a couple of days before the report was due, and I'd just arrived back from a long day. Hungry and exhausted, I made my way through the lobby of the Hotel Plaza, and towards the lift. Just as I was about to press the button someone called me.

'Austin.'

I turned to see who it was. I was shocked to see Mr Underling standing there

'Mr Underling, hello! I didn't know you were here, in New York.'

'I arrived a couple of days ago. I have some business I need to attend to. How are you finding New York, Austin?'

'Very good, Mr Underling. Very demanding but everything seems to be going really well.'

'Good, glad to hear it. Come, sit with me and have a drink.'

We made our way into the Oak Room and found a free table in a quiet corner. Walls adorned with detailed wood panels surrounded us, a barrel-vaulted ceiling hovered above us, and murals of German feudal castles filled the arches in three carved niches.

My lack of interest in what Mr Underling had to say must have been apparent. He stopped mid-sentence and asked me if I was all right. I was so tired that my mind kept wandering. All I'd thought about all day was being back in London with Rachel.

Before I had time to censor what I was about to say, the words rushed out. 'Mr Underling, I don't know if I can do this anymore.'

'What do you mean, Austin? Do what?'

'Travel all the time, Mr Underling. Being away from London, from Rachel ... I'm finding it really difficult. I'm tired and confused and I don't know if this is the life I want ... constantly on the move and living out of a suitcase.'

Mr Underling looked troubled and concerned by my

outburst. I suddenly realised the implications of what I'd said.

'Mr Underling, I'm sorry. I don't want to let you down, I won't let you down and I don't want to sound ungrateful in any way. In fact I can't thank you enough for everything you've done for me ... it's just that ... at the moment I feel that I am letting down one of the most important people in my life: Rachel.'

Mr Underling looked worried. A look of incertitude that I hadn't seen before flashed across his turbulent face. 'I see. Perhaps we have been working you a little too hard, Austin.' He looked at his watch. 'I'm sorry, I must go. I have an appointment to get to. I'll speak with you about this tomorrow.'

Too tired to even think about what had just happened, dazed and exhausted I made my way to the luxury of the Royal Terrace Suite.

Dad was out. He'd left one of his little notes for me.

Hi Son,
Gone to see El Cid (the statue by that woman sculptor Anna Hyatt Huntington. Not the old Hollywood film!)
See you later,
Dad
X

Our suite came complete with butler service; a very traditional, nice British man called Brian was our designated butler. Dad reckoned he overhead the staff referring to him as 'Blighty Brian'. This I could believe: he really was your stereotypical quintessential British butler. He was very polite and ever so professional; he never expanded on any question you asked him. A polite but simple 'yes sir' or 'no sir' was his standard answer to every question.

Blighty Brian was preparing some food for me whilst I took a desperately needed bath.

As I was drying myself the phone rang. I answered.

'Austin, it's Mr Underling ...'

I spluttered my response. 'M-Mr Underling, hello.'

I hadn't expected to hear from him again until tomorrow, and wondered why he was calling me.

'Austin, in view of our conversation this evening I've arranged for you to have some time off with immediate effect. I think that a little rest will do you the world of good.'

This was not what I had expected him to say.

'But there's a shoot booked for tomorrow, Mr Underling.'

'Don't worry, Austin. I've rearranged it with Mr Ganfeall for the day after and you don't have to be there until ten o'clock in the evening; they've decided to change it to a night shoot.'

'I don't know what to say, Mr Underling — thank you!'

'Pleasure, Austin. You have a well-deserved rest, I'll see you at the next shoot.'

CHAPTER TWENTY-EIGHT
RACHEL COAST

Almost a week had gone by since Austin had divulged the devastating news that he would be staying in New York for another four weeks. Up until this unforgivably late disclosure, I had been living under the assumption that he would be away for just a few weeks. He hadn't actually told me that he would be away for this long, but his other trips had lasted this length of time; I'd had no reason to think that this one would be any different.

On this basis, I had prepared myself for the exact amount of alone time I was about to endure.

Not wishing to do anything else with my abundance of free time, I sat night after night, alone in my bedsit, waiting for Austin's daily call.

Tonight wasn't any different: just before his call I had been lying down, reliving our last night together whilst staring blankly at the lightshade above me.

Under normal circumstances it would be around now that I would be visiting Austin to finalise the monthly report. The thought of some stranger in New York doing this really bothered me. I didn't like it one bit.

I had just about come to terms with the fact that I would have to wait a little longer before seeing him again when the phone rang.

It was Austin.

'Hi.' His voice sounded rushed and excited.

The line kept cutting out, so I had to struggle to hear what he was saying.

'Rachel I'm on my way back to London. I'm ... we're leaving JFK at ... forty-five. So I'll be at Heathrow by ... thirty ... can't wait to see you.'

The line died. I tried ringing him back but to no avail. The line was so bad all I'd managed to hear was that he was on the something forty-five flight from JFK, and that he would be landing in Heathrow at something thirty. After several failed attempts at calling him back, I launched myself off the bed and leapt to my feet.

The realisation that he was coming back to London hit me and my heart began to pound with thunderous percussion. Agitated and excited, I tried to think logically. I had such limited information – I hoped he'd ring again. If he didn't, I'd just go to Heathrow airport in a few hours and find out what flights were leaving JFK at something forty-five and arriving at something thirty. It was ridiculous really, but it was all I had to go on.

I rushed around, trying to gather my thoughts as well as my bag and keys.. His last words, 'Meet me at Heathrow', resounded in my head as I rushed excitedly around. Showered, changed and ready, I drove to the airport.

***

After several visits to several different information booths I discovered that there were two flights that matched the limited information I had. They were arriving from JFK within an hour of each other. He had to be on one of them. If he wasn't on the first arrival he would definitely be on the next and I had time to get from one to the other.

With time on my hands I settled myself in the arrival lounge. Hours filled with nothing but clock watching and reading magazines passed by as I waited for the first plane's arrival.

At long last the screens changed; the plane had landed.

On tiptoes, and with my neck craned, I searched the crowd that soon came flooding through.

Frantically scanning the room for him I watched intently as the last few stragglers filtered into the lounge area, until finally the door behind them closed. All of the passengers had disembarked and there was no sign of Austin.

It was time to speed my way to the next terminal for the second planes' arrival.

Crowds of people slowed my way as I politely tried to skim past them. After a couple of wrong turns, and several near collisions with both people and a few stationary objects, I eventually arrived at the second plane's arrival lounge.

My nerves tightened, the plane had landed and the passengers were just about to start filtering through.

This was it ... Austin would be here any minute.

Passenger after passenger arrived.

Where was Austin?

One unrecognisable face after another flooded through but still there was no sign of him.

I was just about to start questioning myself. The phone call had been so brief and garbled. Had I got the times wrong? Had I got it all wrong? Was he coming back to London at all?

The blur of faces suddenly cleared and my concerns disappeared with them.

There he was beaming his wide, enthusiastic smile towards me.

As soon as I saw him; the full-blown reality of the effect he had on me began to manifest itself. My hands began to tremble and my knees began to feel like they were about to cave in on me.

'Rachel! You're here!'

His voice was on top of me; he was standing right in front of me.

He picked me up and kissed me. His lips were warm, his touch soft and gentle. I'd missed him so much. A million tiny explosions burst through every atom in me and I could feel my body crumbling into an ecstatic blur.

Our lips slowly parted and he brushed his head against my cheek.

My back arched with excitement as his warm breath whispered its way into my ears.

'I've missed you so much, Rachel ... so, so much.'

My knees gave way again. I was limp, caught in his trance. My heart was full, my soul was complete!

If ever a girl wanted confirmation that a guy really loved her ... really cared and missed her, and would do anything just to be with her. This was it! All the confirmation I needed.

He took my hand and I followed him unquestioningly as he led me through the airport.

We were just about to enter a tunnel when he turned to me.

'I hope you don't mind but I didn't want to waste this time I have with you, I've booked dinner here at one of the airport hotels – it's just down here. The Imperial Suite is ours for the night. It'll be just you and me.'

Did I mind? Of course I didn't mind, I didn't care where we were going or what we were going to do.

Before we entered the suite through the large door in front of us, he stopped quite suddenly and turned to me.

'Rachel before we go in, I'd like you to close your eyes.'

His tone was excited and imploring. I responded without thinking.

'Okay! Done, my eyes are closed.'

Completely intrigued and spellbound, I scrunched up my eyes as tightly as I could. He was suddenly standing behind me. His breath was the only part of him touching me. It was warm and temperate and as it hit the back of my neck my shoulders began to rise involuntarily. My back arched from the base of my spine upwards. He didn't even have to touch me; his breath alone inspired intense feelings in me. Then I felt him pressing against me, nudging me playfully forwards. His arm stretched around me and his body jolted slightly as he pushed the door open, then he guided me a little further forward.

'You can open them now.'

I opened my eyes slowly, one at a time.

Austin was standing two feet in front of me holding a long, satin, blood-red gown. The carpet was scattered with red petals leading the way into the suite. Ruby-red candles glowed from every corner, perfectly complementing the deep red velvet drapes adorning the walls. Large sofas sprawled comfortably in front of the open fireplace. There were trees in ornate pots in every corner, filling the room with their life and vibrancy; tiny lights twinkled playfully around their branches.

My eyes were wide open and I was immediately intoxicated with the magic of the scene in front of me.

'Rachel, I bought this dress for you. I hope you like it? I thought you may like to wear it for dinner this evening.' Austin handed me the dress and pointed me in the direction of a door to the left. 'That's the bedroom, you can put it on in there.'

I kissed him and rushed towards the door.

The bedroom that lay beyond it was spectacular. A huge four-poster bed stood in front of me; two small boxes lay on it with 'open me' written on them. Inside one of the boxes were shoes that matched the dress perfectly, and in the other beautiful lingerie. I ripped off my jeans and sweater, replaced my best – but not so great in comparison – underwear with the lingerie in the box.

I stepped into the gown and sat on the bed to put on the shoes. I stood up and looked at myself in the mirror. Wow! I had never imagined that I would ever wear a gown like this. I stared at my reflection and hoped beyond hope that I looked just as he'd imagined I would.

As I walked back into the suite, Austin took an audible gasp. 'Rachel, you look like a goddess.'

I blushed at his reaction – my cheeks were surely as crimson as my dress. His eyes burned into me as he looked me up and down with an unusually assured look.

'Rachel, you look absolutely breathtaking. I have to say it again. You look like a goddess ... like a goddess!'

A sudden knock on the suite door interrupted us.

A suited gentleman entered the room. 'Mr Jacobs, I'm Mr Forbes. I'll be looking after you during your stay. We were wondering if you were ready to begin dinner, sir?'

Austin looked at me. 'Rachel, are you ready to eat?'

I didn't know if I wanted to eat or not but I responded with a yes anyway.

He turned to the suited man. 'Yes, Mr Forbes, we're ready.'

Mr Forbes nodded in acknowledgement.

Austin took my hand and led me through the double doors to the right. A grand dining room lay beyond - beautiful delicate china and carved silver cutlery lay upon the table.

Austin pulled my chair out as I sat down. After taking his seat he leant over the table and poured me a glass of wine. The suited man, Mr Forbes, returned with several staff, all carrying a variety of silver dishes billowing steam from their edges as they floated past us.

Austin turned to Mr Forbes. 'Thank you, Mr Forbes, that will be all for now. I think we can take things from here.'

Mr Forbes nodded. In no time, he and his staff had left the room.

It had been so long since we had been alone together, I couldn't stop myself from feeling incredibly nervous. My hands were perspiring and it was hard to steady them.

Austin got up and sat next to me. 'Rachel, I don't have much time here ... in a few hours I'll have to leave to catch my flight back.'

He leant over and kissed me confidently and passionately. The intimacy I felt just kissing him like this was debilitating.

Before I knew what was happening, I was being carried out of the dining room and into the bedroom. My arms wrapped around his neck as I gazed into his glorious face. He placed me gently onto the huge four-poster bed.

My head began to swim and my eyes lost focus as a blurred vision of Austin stained my senses. I felt his knees either side of my legs and his hands leaning on the bed either side of my shoulders. Then the room began to spin and my head began to roar, and then nothing.

***

The next thing I remembered was being lost in that waking moment, that fraction of a second when you suddenly awake and become aware of the world once more. Your eyes are still closed tightly but your consciousness has stirred from its slumber.

In lightening quick flashes my brain began to function.

Austin! I was with Austin in the hotel suite. My eyes opened. In one swift move I sat up and looked around me.

I was still dressed in my beautiful red gown, lying on top of the glorious four-poster bed. Austin had laid me down on this bed. What happened after that? And where was Austin?

Chapter Twenty-nine
Rachel Coast

By now I was on my feet and pacing around the bedroom trying to piece my memories together. I got as far as remembering Austin leaning over me after laying me down on the bed. After that I couldn't remember a thing. Where was he?

'Austin?' I called out.

Nothing but silence responded.

Then I heard a knock on the bedroom door. The voice of the suited gentleman Mr Forbes filtered through it.

'Good morning, Miss Coast. I'm afraid Mr Jacobs is not here. He extends his apologies. He had to leave to catch his flight back to New York. He said he would ring you when he has arrived there. Would you like me to serve you breakfast now or later?'

What? Austin had left without saying goodbye? Caught up in my confused thoughts, I unintentionally ignored Mr Forbes question about breakfast.

'Miss Coast, would you like breakfast now or later?'

His second prompt triggered a response from me. 'Could I just have a coffee for now please?'

'Certainly, Miss Coast. I'll have it waiting for you.'

My head was spinning as I headed for the bathroom. I picked up my jeans and my sweater on the way. As I stood there, splashing water on my face, questions and concerns ripped through my mind.

What *had* happened last night? *Why* couldn't I remember? *Why* had Austin left without saying goodbye?

Then the smell of freshly brewed coffee hit me. The effect it had on me was surprisingly calming and warming. I walked through the bedroom doors into the living room but as I sat sipping my coffee, a feeling of devastation and confusion began to engulf me.

Last night had passed so quickly, and I couldn't even remember all of it. *Why* had I passed out? And *why* hadn't Austin woke me up to say goodbye?

By the time I left the hotel and returned to the car park my head was in a total mess and I had no idea where my car was.

I reassured myself that, under the circumstances, it was a bit too much to expect me to remember exactly where I'd parked it. Rushing to get here, I'd taken no notice at all of where I'd left it. Two and half hours of head scratching, cursing and pacing from one car park to another ensued before I eventually found it.

My bedsit, my little space, was now the only place I wanted to be. I wanted to bury my head deep in my pillow and wrap my quilt around me and wait for Austin to call. I was desperate to speak to him, desperate for answers.

The last twelve hours had been crazy.

Austin had travelled all the way from New York to see me; this was the thought I held on to.

As I drove home, I tried really hard not to think about the fact that he was now thousands of miles away from me, or the fact that it would be at least another month before I would see him again.

Lunchtime came and went, and by mid-afternoon I had fallen asleep. It was early evening by the time I awoke again. My stomach rumbled loudly as I stirred from my sleep and the first thing I did was check my phone for any missed calls. Mum and Dad had rung twice but there was nothing from Austin. Hungry and drowsy I made my way to my kitchen. Living alone had never really inspired me to cook, and the limited kitchen appliances that occupied my kitchen did nothing to enthuse me. A few pieces of dry bread and some chocolate spread were the only things edible in my cupboard.

Sitting on the edge of my bed, a steaming hot cup of tea in one hand and my chocolate-coated toast in the other, I stared at my phone, wishing and willing it to ring. The minutes and hours ticked by. Nothing but silence filled the room. Surely I should have heard from Austin by now, he must have arrived back. Not able to wait any longer I picked up my phone and dialled his number.

His voice and a flurry of excuses as to why he hadn't rung me yet was what I was hoping to hear. Unfortunately, nothing but disappointment met me at the end of the phone line in the form of his answer phone. I hesitated before leaving a short message.

'Hi, Austin, it's Rachel. Hope you're okay, I don't know what happened last night but you left without saying goodbye. Hope everything is okay ... speak to you soon ... love you.'

Looking around my pokey little room I recalled last night's events once more, from his grand entrance in the arrival lounge at the airport, to our time together in the hotel. The beautiful gown, the rose petals on the floor, the lights that twinkled on the trees ... then finally waking up to an empty hotel room. The memory of him leaning over me whilst I lay on the bed just before I passed out kept flashing through my mind.

Rattling around my bedsit for the next few hours was mentally tortuous. I just needed him to ring me, tell me everything was ok, that we were ok; explain to me what exactly had happened. I was prepared for plodding through another few lonely weeks until he came back to me, but right now, I desperately needed his reassuring call.

Two hours, three hours, four more hours went by. Nothing but silence ensued. I tried ringing him several times. His answer machine greeted me on every occasion. It was getting late and I had to get some sleep. I had work the next day.

I'd had one false alarm throughout the evening where my heart momentarily soared, but it wasn't him, it was my mum and dad calling again. Tonight my conversation with them had been especially brief. Though I loved them dearly, attempting to discuss superficial weather and gardening details with them was more than my patience could tolerate. Frustrated and anxious, I made my excuses and ended the call as quickly as I could. Hanging on to my dwindling hope of hearing from Austin I lay back on my bed before drifting off to sleep.

***

Monday morning arrived and I had slept through my alarm. I only had ten minutes to get ready before I had to leave for the office. I checked my phone. There were no missed calls. Why hadn't Austin rung me? What was going on? Was he ok? Had something happened to him?

These were the thoughts that occupied my mind as I drove to work. The traffic was an absolute nightmare and my lack of concentration on what I was doing caused me to almost run into the back of several cars.

When I arrived at the office I was still totally distracted. Lost in my confusion, I didn't hear Mr Turnbull calling me.

His loud monotone voice finally caught my attention and made me jump out of my stupor.

'Miss Coast! Would you *please* come into my office?'

I put down the paperwork I had been pretending to study and hastily made my way to meet him.

'Rachel, please take a seat.'

He stood bolt upright behind his desk with his hands clasped behind his back. His face was stern and serious.

'Rachel, I'm afraid to say that we have received an official complaint about you.'

My attention to the job was now fully restored by the shock of what Mr Turnbull had just said.

'I'm sorry, Mr Turnbull?'

I knew that my mind hadn't been fully on the job, but I was certain that I was on top of everything. I couldn't imagine any of my clients making a complaint about me.

The next sentence that left his mouth made my stomach churn and my head explode. I couldn't believe what I was hearing.

'The complaint has come from Mr Austin Jacobs, Rachel. He has asked that you no longer handle his account. He insists that you have acted in a very unprofessional manner, and no longer wants you to deal with his affairs. In view of this, I need you to gather all of the paperwork relating to the Jacobs' Photographic account and bring it to me as soon as possible.'

Shell-shocked, numb and dumbstruck I sat open mouthed staring at him.

'Could you get it for me now please, Rachel?'

I just about managed to respond to his second request for the paperwork.

'Yes, Mr Turnbull, it's in my desk ... but ...'

He cut me short. '*Now* please, Rachel.'

'Yes, of course.'

I returned with the paperwork and handed it to him.

'This complaint will be documented on your employment record and we will be keeping a close eye on you from now on. We do not take kindly to complaints of any kind.'

Still trying to comprehend what exactly was happening and no longer able to contain myself, I blurted out, 'This can't be right, Mr Turnbull, you must have misunderstood him – you must have got it wrong.'

He stared at me with a frown that indicated I was to ask no more questions, and my self-defence was not required or welcomed.

'I can assure you, Rachel, there has been no mistake regarding this matter. That will be all, if you could get back to work please. Oh just one more thing, I'd like you to spend today on the phone canvassing for some new accounts. As you no longer have the Jacobs account to look after, you will need to find a new one to replace it.'

I was too devastated and confused to utter one more word, so I left his office and took my seat at my desk.

Fighting back the tears I wondered what on earth was going on. Was this really it? Was this the horrible moment I had feared would come? Surely not, it couldn't be.

This couldn't be Austin's way of dumping me? No! This was not the answer. Something was terribly wrong – why had he bothered to come all the way from New York to see me if he had intended to dump me in such a cruel, cowardly and callous way?

All I knew at this point was that one thing was certain: I desperately needed to speak to him, I couldn't wait a moment longer. I had to find out what was going on.

Picking up my phone, I called his number.

The line was completely dead.

I tried calling him again and again, but every time I tried there was nothing but that awful, dead, droning tone.

Mr Turnbull was watching me like a hawk, and even

though I was close to bursting into tears and running out of the office, somehow I managed to hold it together.

In between canvassing calls and touting for new business I kept ringing Austin's number, hoping that it would ring again and that I'd get through to him and clear up this madness. Then it dawned on me — the hotel! Of course, I could ring the hotel he was staying in! I already had the number logged into my phone.

A very polite receptionist answered my call and informed me that Austin and his father had checked out of the hotel that morning.

What was going on? The situation just seemed to be going from bad to worse. His phone was dead. He had checked out of his hotel, and on top of that I didn't even know where he lived anymore, not since his swift move to the new house in Mayfair.

I had passed on all of the documents relating to Jacobs' Photographic client file and they were now in Mr Turnbull's possession; from this point onwards I had no access to them. Mr Turnbull had made it quite clear to me that he alone would be handling the account, and all of the documentation relating to it.

It felt like all of a sudden, impenetrable firewalls had risen up like fortresses around Austin. All lines of communication with him had been violently terminated. I had no way of contacting him. For some crazy reason that was completely unknown to me, he had very suddenly, and very dramatically, excommunicated me from his life.

As the morning passed I held on tightly to the hope that this was all a great big misunderstanding. I kept looking towards Mr Turnbull's office in the hope that he'd call me back in to tell me that he had, in fact, got it all wrong, and that it was all a terrible mistake. Every time my phone rang my heart leapt with anticipation as I wished and willed it to be Austin.

By the time the afternoon arrived I was finding it increasingly harder to battle against my tears and fears. The desire to run home and embed myself in the comfort of my duvet was beginning to overwhelm me. Amazingly, I managed to make it to the end of the day in one piece; I even managed to book a couple of appointments with some potential new clients for the end of the week. I don't know where I found the strength, but somehow I held myself together.

Five o'clock finally arrived and I hurried out of the office to my car. This was when my resolve gave up. My stiff upper lip of hope that I had been holding on to with all my might was now quivering with despair.

The floodgates opened and the tears that I'd been holding back burst through. I sobbed uncontrollably like an injured child. This situation that I'd found myself in was too much to bear. The thing that made it worse was the frustrated confusion that accompanied it. Nothing made any sense.

Only twenty-four hours ago I was on top of the world! What was going on? Had my worst fears really come true?

The night that followed was unbearable. The agonising phone silence that filled the air haunted every hour. The phone call that I was desperate to receive never came.

My world had been shot off its axis. Its trajectory had been blasted way off course and it was hurtling blindly towards despair. By the end of the night I was physically and mentally exhausted. My unstoppable tears anaesthetised my senses; my eyes were heavy and swollen and I couldn't even remember falling asleep.

***

As soon as I opened my eyes the next morning the brutal reality of the events of the day before began to batter me again. I scrambled around for my phone ... There were no missed calls.

My eyes were red and still quite swollen. I splashed my face with cold water in a vain attempt to calm them down before going to work. This puffy faced version of me was not a good look. Under normal circumstances I would have spent some time trying to make myself look more presentable, but today I just didn't care.

I was stuck in the office all day and the time passed slowly and uneventfully. By lunchtime my eyes finally returned to normal, and I managed to hold it together again and make it to the end of my working day without letting out so much as a whimper. Every so often I'd try ringing Austin's number and every time I did, the same dead tone greeted me.

As soon as I left the office to go home my resolve broke and I began to sob uncontrollably again. I didn't know what to do with myself. Everything was so confusing and it all felt so wrong.

Stuck in this state of limbo, I spent another night sobbing and hoping against hope that he would call me.

My imagination was out of control and running riot. The optimist in me imagined that he would ring with a wonderfully plausible and simple explanation for all this madness. The pessimist in me imagined events and explanations that were too painful to even consider. Burning questions ignited and tortured my thoughts over the following two days. Trying to analyse all the possible reasons for it all was exhausting me.

Thursday night had arrived; the week was almost over and it felt like I was slowly going insane.

Mr Turnbull had been breathing down my neck and in the midst of the madness I had made one definite decision. At the end of play on Friday I would hand in my resignation. I was in too much of a mess to carry on like this. I needed time out, time to think.

Taking my usual position on my bed, I began my nightly ritual. The first thing on the agenda was to ring my parents. I'd managed to keep our conversations especially brief over the last few nights; I couldn't bring myself to tell them about Austin and what had happened. They were blissfully ignorant of the turmoil I was in, and until I'd worked out what I was going to do, and how I was going to deal with this, I needed to keep it that way.

With the phone call over I nibbled on a piece of toast. My appetite had also taken a turn for the worse.

As I lay back on my bed, a glimmer of dying hope flashed through me.

The doorbell rang. I sat bolt upright, my heart thudding in my chest. The bell's chime ran through me and I began to shake uncontrollably.

It rang again, making me jump and causing my heart to skip.

Could this be him? Could this be Austin?

The bell rang again.

Petrified to the spot, my breathing became erratic and my mouth dried up completely. Slowly stepping forwards, I pressed the intercom.

'Hello?' I said shakily.

The intercom crackled at first then it cleared and the voice at the other end cut through. 'Hi, Rachel, it's Julie. I was passing this way and thought I'd see if you were in. It's been ages since I've seen you.'

A glorious sense of relief washed over me, swiftly followed by an intense feeling of disappointment and despair.

'Julie! Hi! I'll be down in a second.' I ran down the stairs and flung open the front door.

Her friendly, smiling face was a sight for sore eyes. She screamed and hugged me tightly. 'Rachel! It's so good to see you, it's been far too long!'

I wrapped my arms around her, hugged her back and burst into tears.

CHAPTER THIRTY
AUSTIN JACOBS

Relieved and exhausted, I lay back on my warm comfortable bed. I closed my eyes and breathed deeply. Mr Underling had just granted me almost forty-eight hours of free time: no shoots, no back-to-back schedules, no models and, hopefully, no blackouts. I had time to breathe, time to think, time to rest.

The smell of the hotel-supplied, expensive shower gel clung to my skin. I felt more relaxed and at ease than I had done for a long time and I soon drifted off into a deep sleep.

It was 9am the next day when I finally woke up. Dad had already left the hotel to go on another one of his sightseeing trips. Blighty Brian knocked on the door and entered the room.

'Mr Jacobs, would you like me to get you anything?'

'A coffee to start with, I think. Thank you, Brian!'

Brian returned with a cup of freshly-brewed coffee and I sipped it slowly, breathing in its aroma and thinking about the freedom of my day ahead. With a sudden realisation, it dawned on me — why hadn't I thought of this last night? If I acted quickly I would have enough time to fly back to London to see Rachel! My heart began to race at the thought of it. Flights back and fore to the UK were quite regular and with the time delays I was certain that I could be there and back in good time. It wasn't exactly resting, but as far as I was concerned it was medicinal.

I called Brian. He promptly came in through the door.

'Brian, can you check out the times of the flights between London and New York over the next twenty-four hours, please?'

'Yes, sir, certainly.'

He left the room and I paced around thinking about what I was about to do, and what I would have to do to make it all happen. Grabbing a backpack I started to pack a few essentials. Brian returned with a full schedule of the flight times. After quickly studying them I decided which flights I would take and planned my journey.

'Brian, could you book these flights for me?'

'Yes, sir, straight away.'

I would only have a few hours with Rachel before I'd have to return to New York; this was a long way to go to spend such a short time together, but I needed to see her so badly. I would have travelled twice as far just to see her for half the time.

I ran through everything I needed to organise before leaving for the airport. It was one mad rush. I was still checking that I had everything I needed up until the very last moment.

Dad was still out and I had no idea where he was. He hadn't left me a note to tell me where he was going. This time it would be me writing him a note to tell him where I was going. Then I wondered if I should let Mr Underling know that I was going back to London. No – I decided that he didn't need to know. After all, he had given me the time off to rest not fly almost half way across the world. I would ring Rachel from the airport.

Larry, the chauffeur, was waiting for me outside the hotel. He was by far the most entertaining chauffeur I had met; he always had something to say and he talked a lot. He greeted me as he opened the door. His conversation today revolved around the amazing survival story of two water buffalo and a female giraffe.

The detail he relayed was quite impressive and his delivery was very entertaining. As a result the journey to the airport flew by.

We arrived outside JFK and he got out and opened the door for me.

'Enjoy your trip, Mr Jacobs. I'll be here waiting when you return.'

'Thank you Larry – oh! And by the way that was a very interesting story today, thank you.'

He smiled at me. 'Pleasure, Mr Jacobs.'

JFK was a busy airport and the international departures lounge was awash with people. I made my way through the crowds and after twenty minutes of searching I finally managed to find a seat.

I'd just sat down and pulled my phone out of my rucksack to ring Rachel when a familiar voice suddenly spoke to me.

'Austin.'

It was Mr Underling.

'Mr Underling, what are you doing here?'

'I was just about to ask you the same question, Austin.'

I panicked and stuttered, 'W-well I'm flying back to –'

'I know where you're going, Austin, and I can guess why. Larry called me to tell me he was picking you up and bringing you here. Why didn't you ask for the jet? It's much easier and quicker, you won't be so jetlagged when you get back.'

This was not the reaction I had expected.

'Follow me, it's fuelled and waiting for you on a private runway.'

'Mr Underling, I don't know what to say ... thank you!'

I stood up with my phone still clenched in my hand. Rachel – I needed to ring her and let her know I was on my way back.

'Mr Underling, I need to ring Rachel to tell her I'm on my way.'

'No problem, you can ring her from the plane. Come this way.'

We walked through the airport, dodging the crowds, until we reached a doorway that led to a quieter area. A tunnel spanned ahead of us and when we reached the end of it Mr Underling pushed the doors open. Beyond them was a private runway where the private jet was ready and waiting for me.

Mr Underling ushered me towards it.

'Have a good trip Austin. See you when you get back.'

I boarded the jet and took my seat. My phone was still in my hand and as soon as sat down I rang Rachel. The connection was terrible; a loud crackling noise kept interrupting as I shouted down the phone.

'Rachel I'm on my way back to London. I'm on a private jet; we're leaving JFK at 11.45am so I'll be at Heathrow by 9.30pm. I can't wait to see you.'

Before I could say anymore the signal was lost and the call ended. I tried ringing her again but the line was dead. I sat back and hoped upon hope that she'd heard me and that she'd be there to meet me. If not I'd have to ring her from Heathrow. It would mean that I wouldn't have as much time with her but at least I'd get to see her.

We'd been in the air for almost an hour when the weather changed dramatically. One of the stewardesses asked me to put my seat belt on.

As I did, the plane must have hit an air pocket. It dropped fifty feet in a matter of seconds. My stomach flipped and the lights went out. We were plunged into darkness.

***

The next thing I remembered was walking down the steps of the plane at JFK. Mr Underling was standing at the bottom of the stairs, waiting to greet me. As soon as he saw me he asked me if I'd enjoyed my time in London.

What? I'd only boarded the plane an hour ago to go there.

I knew there and then that I had suffered another blackout. What was I going to say to him?

There was no way I was going to tell him that I had no recollection at all of where I'd been, or that the last thing I remembered of my trip was the weather suddenly becoming really bad and the plane hitting an air pocket.

I was not going to divulge this information to Mr Underling, so I smiled politely and said, 'Yes thank you, Mr Underling. I had a great time.'

'Good, Austin, that's very good. I'm glad to hear it.'

Larry was parked about twenty feet away from the plane he was ready and waiting to take me back to the hotel.

As we made our way through New York I sat quietly in the back of the limo. Larry was prattling on about a film he'd watched the night before and I nodded politely every few minutes as if I was listening to his every word.

Of course, I wasn't – how could I concentrate on anything anyone had to say when my mind was somewhere else completely.

This was, without question, the longest and most confusing blackout I had ever experienced.

The flashbacks would begin at some point. As disturbing as they may be, they would at least give me some insight into what had happened. After what Rachel saw in Paris I had reserved myself to the fact that the visions I was seeing were real indications of what was happening to me during these unconscious periods.

This last blackout raised more questions than any other.

Had I actually arrived in London? Had Rachel and I spent any time together at all? Where the heck had I been?

As we neared the hotel there was still no sign of the visions and my frustration was beginning to get the better of me. I needed to speak to Rachel; she was the only person I could talk to honestly about this. I spent the rest of the journey trying to call her. I dialled her number. Her phone rang twice then the connection died. I rang again, and again, but every time the same thing. It would ring twice and then the line would die.

When I arrived back at the hotel I had to put my attempts to contact her on hold.

Dad was waiting for me with open arms, and a broad smile. As his arms wrapped around me I felt the warmth of their security and his unconditional love calm me as it washed over me.

I wanted to tell him about the blackouts, about my fears and my concerns. I wanted to blurt out all of my angst there and then in the security of our embrace, but I couldn't. I knew he'd worry like mad about me; I couldn't have that. He looked so well and so happy, ignorance was bliss and he didn't need to know.

He broke our hug and looked me straight in the eye.

'Austin, tell me all about your trip son!' He lunged forwards and hugged me again. 'I hope you had a good time. How is the lovely Rachel Coast?'

My survival instincts kicked in, and my imagination flew into overdrive. I managed to make up a myriad of fake details about my trip to London, and of Rachel's well-being, all of which seemed to appease and satisfy his concerned curiosity. The conversation continued with persistent questions. I was relieved that the evening shoot was quickly approaching. I had the perfect excuse to leave.

'Dad, please, stop! I'm sorry, I don't mean to be abrupt but I've got to go to work in a little while, I've got lots to do before I leave ... we'll talk more tomorrow.'

I leant forwards and kissed him on the forehead. 'Love you, Dad.'

Half an hour later Dad was getting ready for his afternoon swim, and I was ready to leave for the shoot.

'See you later, Dad I'm off,' I shouted.

'Okay, see you later!'

As I was about to open the door to leave he came rushing out of his room in his swimming trunks.

'Austin! I almost forgot. Chandler's rang this morning to let you know that a Mr Bruce Bellinger will be calling to see you this evening. He's a sales rep in their New York office and he'll be compiling the monthly report for Conik Penster Dewe.'

'Oh! Okay, thanks – see you later! Oh, and enjoy your swim!'

'Oh, I will! I can promise you that, see you later.'

As I walked out of the door I thought about the fact that this was usually Rachel's job. It was going to be strange having someone else prepare the report.

The visions from my blackout still hadn't raised their disturbing heads and my attempts so far to contact Rachel had failed.

All the way to the shoot Larry tried to engage me in banal conversations about animal-related facts and figures that he had acquired from his nights sitting in front of the TV. Fascinating and educating as they were, my mind was still elsewhere.

We finally arrived at the location.

It was a fabulous loft in Manhattan and the models and crew were already there. The shoot was well under way by the time Bruce Bellinger arrived.

He was so much younger than I had expected, he couldn't have been more than about nineteen. His name had somehow conjured up images of a middle-aged man, not a guy a couple of years younger than me.

I walked towards him to greet him. 'Hello, you must be Bruce.'

He nodded towards me with his mouth wide open. He was obviously distracted by the models as they strutted around the room.

I held my hand out to shake his. 'Hello Bruce, Austin Jacobs. Pleased to meet you.'

In a very nervous and quiet voice he finally closed his mouth and answered me. 'Yes, I'm Bruce Bellinger, I'm sorry. Hello, yes, I'm pleased to meet you too.'

I handed him the paperwork he needed. 'Well, Bruce, I understand you're here to prepare the report. Here are all the figures you'll need. Good to meet you. I'm sorry to be so short but I have to carry on with the shoot, we're on a tight schedule today … With regards to the photograph, I'm going to carry on working, you can take the photograph of me whenever you're ready.'

He took the paperwork off me and smiled nervously as his eyes drifted back towards the models. He was obviously spellbound by the flurry of beautiful girls flitting around the room.

'Thank you,' he stammered as he put the paperwork in his bag and pulled out the camera. 'Mr Jacobs, where should I stand? I don't want to get in your way,' he asked politely. 'Is over there ok?' he added, pointing to a corner of the room that was free of anyone or anything.

'Yes, Bruce, that's fine.'

He shuffled awkwardly into the free corner of the room, glancing nervously at the models.

With no more time to waste, my attentions returned to the job in front of me.

After about ten minutes I stopped for a second to adjust my lens. I heard Bruce Bellinger's whispery voice behind me. 'Excuse me, Mr Jacobs, could I take the photograph now, if you've got a second?'

I turned to look at him. His hands were shaking. He looked more nervous than he had when he'd just walked in. The poor guy was suffering. He wasn't coping with this assignment very well and I couldn't help but feel sorry for him.

'Yes, of course.' I stood there and smiled.

He lifted up the camera and *snap!*

The flash from the camera was blinding. I lifted my arm up to cover my eyes and as I did a deep sharp pain hit me in the pit of my stomach. I lost my balance, I could feel the blood draining from my face.

I fell backwards onto the floor.

What the hell had happened? I lay there for a second.

The pain in my stomach had gone. Other than the fact I was lying in a heap on the floor, I felt okay. I shook my head, composed myself and got back up.

'Austin! Are you all right?'

It was Mr Underling. He had just arrived at the shoot.

Brushing myself down as I walked towards him to greet him, I replied, 'Yes, Mr Underling, I'm absolutely fine.'

I couldn't tell him that I didn't know why I'd fallen on the floor. So I made up an excuse.

'I just tripped, Mr Underling. Must have been one of the light cables.'

Bruce Bellinger walked out of his corner. 'Mr Jacobs, thank you,' he said earnestly. 'I've got everything I need. I'll be off now. Goodbye.' He made a quick and sudden exit.

Mr Underling looked at me. His face housed a troubled and serious expression. 'Austin, are you sure you're feeling okay, you look a little pale.'

As he posed the question I felt a pulse begin to tap at the inside of my temple.

'Yes, Mr Underling, honestly I'm absolutely fine.'

He nodded, took a step towards me, and spoke very quietly so that only I could hear. 'Austin, it is of the utmost urgency that I speak with you after you finish your shoot. I will meet you at your hotel later.' The urgency and sobriety in his voice unnerved me.

'Yes, Mr Underling. I should be finished in about an hour or so.'

'Good ... I need to speak with you alone about a very private matter.' His voice quietened even further as he finished his sentence and repeated his last few words once more. 'It is a very private matter. I'll see you in an hour or so.'

He turned tail and nodded his head in acknowledgement towards the models and crew before leaving.

I stared blankly for a moment, bemused by his request. The pulse that had been tapping away had grown louder and it was now hammering away; my head was throbbing. I was still functioning but I felt awful.

What did Mr Underling mean by 'a very private matter'? Trying to figure this out made my head hurt even more.

The following hour passed slowly, but at last the shoot was over and I was back in the limo, making my way back to the hotel.

I headed towards the doors of my suite; they opened just as I approached them. Mr Underling was already there, standing in the doorway.

'Good evening, Austin, I arrived early. Your father let me in before he left to go sightseeing. How are you feeling? Did the shoot go well?'

'Yes I feel okay, and the shoot went very well.'

He closed the door behind us and gestured towards one of the large sofas in the middle of the room. 'Please, take a seat.' He took a seat opposite me.

Blighty Brian suddenly appeared with two cups of fresh coffee. As soon as he left the room Mr Underling turned to me.

'Austin, I need to know how you feel about the conversation we had two days ago. You said that you were thinking of giving everything up for Rachel?' He sat back and crossed his legs before continuing. 'Do you still feel the same, or have you changed your mind?'

I guess I should have expected him to ask me this, but in all of the madness of the last forty-eight hours, I wasn't thinking straight. Mr Underling's question was direct and concise and required a direct and concise answer.

How did I feel?

I knew how I felt about Rachel, and I knew that the last blackout I'd had on the plane was more concerning than any other I'd experienced.

I knew that the repercussions of the answer I was about to give him would be devastating for my career, but I had to respond with the only truth I had. 'Yes, Mr Underling, I'm sorry. I still feel the same. I don't want to let you down and I won't, I'll stay in New York and finish this campaign, but I don't know if I can continue after this.'

He sat forwards and looked me straight in the eyes.

'Well in that case, Austin, you leave me no choice. In view of the fact that you are making a life-changing decision based solely on your relationship with Rachel, I feel bound and obligated to make sure that you are fully informed before making it final.'

He reached inside the breast pocket of his long coat and brought out a brown envelope. He emptied its contents onto the coffee table in front of me.

'Austin, you need to see these.'

A flurry of photographs landed in front of me. I picked one of them up and stared at it in disbelief, I threw it down and picked up another.

My mouth dried and my throat began to close up. My hands began to shake as the impact of the images began to take their effect on me. My whole body began to tremble. My stomach felt like a lead weight had just been dropped into its pit. I wanted to look away, yet my eyes wouldn't let me. They just kept staring at the images in front of me.

'Where did you get these, Mr Underling?'

He sat forwards and put his hands on his knees. 'Before I answer that, I need to explain something ... you have become a very important asset to both me and my company. You have an incredible career ahead of you. I couldn't let you give all of that up without knowing that this Rachel was worthy of the personal sacrifice you were about to make for her. In view of this, I had her followed by a private investigator. He took the photographs.'

At this point I couldn't hold myself together any more. With my stomach heaving and my heart thumping I ran to the bathroom.

These candid photographs of Rachel were now permanent images burnt into the back of my eyes, like indelible stains that could never be removed.

My knees buckled.

I fell to the floor.

My eyes burnt as I bent over the toilet bowl. The images that flashed before me battered my senses with their implications.

I really didn't know her at all!

What sort of woman was she? Why pretend that she was in love with me? Why fool and deceive me like this? She had been lying to me all along. All of those deceitful conversations about how she was alone in her bedsit every night, missing me like crazy.

I heaved into the toilet.

I could feel my heart throbbing faster in my chest with

every convulsion.

A searing heat started to burn me up; I was on fire. The heat began to rise up through me. When it reached my chin I fell to the floor. The pain was intense; I thought I was going to pass out.

I gripped my chest tightly.

Just as I was about to lose consciousness, the photographs of Rachel flashed through my mind again.

A feeling of merciless hatred began to sear its way through every atom in me. My heart suddenly felt as if it had exploded into a million betrayed and broken pieces.

The mere thought of Rachel now conjured nothing but feelings of disgust in me. She made me feel sick.

I lay on the floor, my head and heart drowning in a flood of emotions. I couldn't think straight, I couldn't even think! My head began to throb. I pulled my knees up to my chest and rubbed my forehead in an attempt to dull the pain. It was of no use; the thudding in my head got louder and louder. I pulled my knees up tighter to my chest as the volume intensified, then SNAP! The tsunami of emotions and hurricane of thoughts that had been raging torridly inside of me suddenly calmed.

I breathed deeply and sighed with relief. The beautiful serenity of this stillness was intoxicating; but it didn't last long.

The memories that had been hidden from me by my blackouts suddenly surged through into my consciousness, forging their way through like cold clear water breaking through a damn.

I had always dreaded the moment when I may remember everything that happened during my blackouts. My love for Rachel had made me abhor the mere thought of what their full content may be; but things were very different now!

As the images flooded through my mind and placed themselves into my memory, it became apparent that I had indulged in many a pleasure with a variety of gorgeous creatures and, in view of recent revelations, I was glad that I had.

By the time I composed myself and left the bathroom my perspective had changed significantly. I had changed significantly. My soul felt as if it had been purged ... I felt nothing but banal indifference. A singular desire to have whatever I wanted, whenever I wanted, without a care for anyone else's thoughts, feelings or desires.

Mr Underling's voice called out to me. 'Austin, are you all right? I'm so sorry you had to find out about Rachel like this.'

I straightened myself and walked calmly and determinedly out of the bathroom.

Mr Underling was standing outside waiting for me with a concerned look on his face.

'Mr Underling, there is no need to apologise – in fact, I believe the opposite is true. I am in your debt. You've opened my eyes to the truth. I'm very grateful to you for that. You've saved me from making a terrible mistake. Thank you! I have no intention of giving up anything for anyone, Mr Underling. Send me wherever you want. Keep me here in New York for another six months if you like.'

Mr Underling's faced relaxed and he nodded approvingly.

'In that case, Austin, I suggest that you break all forms of communication or contact with Rachel from this moment on. I will take care of this. You will need a new phone and, of course, Chandler's ... you are still her client. We need to take care of that too.'

'I'll leave the details to you, Mr Underling ... just make sure I never see or hear from that bitch again!'

Chapter Thirty-One
Conik Penster Dewe

Conik Penster Dewe's right arm stretched upwards, his fingertips clinging victoriously to the fifth photograph of Austin.

His voice echoed around the room as he commanded the Cantartis to awaken.

The Cantartis responded immediately.

It began to rock furiously on its plinth before rising into the air and transforming from solid to liquid to gaseous.

It whispered its way in silent pursuit until it reached the clinched photograph, then its enveloping mist span wildly around it, gently snatching and grabbing at it until it had successfully procured it from Conik Penster Dewe's grip.

With the photograph enveloped in its misty vapour it spun upwards into the air, twisting and dancing around the ceiling. Eventually, it slowed into a rhythmical decline and spiralled itself into stillness.

The light within it had grown substantially from the small light that had first appeared in it five months ago.

A congratulatory smile flashed across Conik Penster Dewe's face. Then his brow furrowed. He squinted his eyes in concentration, awaiting any signs of fluctuation.

As the moments passed the light remained stable; it did not flicker at all, not even for a second. He remained quite still, hovering effortlessly in mid-air as he continued his observation.

His stoic expression broke slowly into a broad, self-satisfied smile. He knew his plans to destroy the hold Rachel had on Austin had at last been successful. He had finally broken the barriers, demolished the blockades. The resistance that he had observed during the earlier extractions was no longer in place.

Intoxicated with his victory, he flew at light speed out of the vault. Within seconds he was seated in his grand leather armchair.

'Release your locks.'

The vault doors swung open and the beams from thousands of bright lights darted around the cavernous vault room. He basked in their glory, rubbing his hands together and laughing manically. The light shining from the vault in the middle of the cold steel wall now shone as brightly as the lights that surrounded it.

It was some time before he tired of their incandescence and he sat there lost in their intensity.

Eventually he commanded the doors to close.

With their content locked safely away, he made his way back to his office.

The lift shook and rattled its way back to the hallway of torches. The hooded figures stood silently in front of the gold ornate elevator doors as he made his way past them and the five lit torches.

He entered the elevator at the end of the hallway and ascended to the next floor. Underling was on cue as always and opened the lift doors with succinct timing. Conik Penster Dewe flew out of the elevator, shooting past Underling like a bullet flying through the air. Absolutely accurate in his trajectory, and final in his landing he stopped, stood upright and opened his office doors.

Before entering he turned his head, looked at Underling and gestured to him. Underling rushed down the corridor after him.

'Sire,' he said, as he walked through the large oak doors. 'It is done, sire.' His voice was rushed, breathless.

Conik Penster Dewe was already relaxing in his large leather armchair; his fingers drumming his broad square chin that today boasted a wide, satisfied smile. His deep violet eyes reflected the fire that burnt ferociously in front of him. He stared poignantly at the painting of Catriona above it. A long, deathly silence froze and stilled the air. Eventually a low, deep, satisfied voice boomed around the room. 'Yes, Underling. It is done.'

'Yes, sire, your plan has been most successful. Sending an impostor to meet Rachel at Heathrow worked perfectly, sire. She had no idea that it wasn't really Austin. Her eyes and her heart were totally deceived. As soon as I showed Austin the photographs of her with the impersonator, his resolve was broken instantly.'

Conik Penster Dewe's cruel, callous and terminal plan had been devised, implemented and executed perfectly. He had at last made sure that the force of their love would no longer protect Austin.

He knew that Austin Jacobs would always be his greatest challenge. He was after all the last heir of the Crystal Bloodline; its potency was strong and pure in him. The extraction ritual was never quick or easy at the best of times. The ritual's nature dictated that the bloodline had to be extracted in seven separate parts over a period of seven lunar months.

Conik Penster Dewe had performed thousands of extractions before Austin, and all of his victims had undergone the very same ritual.

Some of the heirs had taken longer to coerce than others, but all of them had eventually succumbed and willingly given up their Crystal Bloodline to him.

It had already taken him decades to get this far. The Crystal Bloodline was a formidable force and he was now on the cusp of achieving his ambitions.

Love had complicated this last extraction. He knew from years of observation that it, too, was a great force. It was unpredictable and powerful with no regard for rules, morals, responsibilities or obligations. Austin's love for Rachel was intense, and up until now it had been very effective in protecting him. Finally, this incredibly infuriating and frustrating situation that opposed his plans was neutralised.

Conik Penster Dewe was visibly bursting with satisfaction and excitement.

Austin had, by his own hand, dismissed and excommunicated Rachel from his life. His love for her had been brutally banished from his heart, from his mind and from his soul. It was now lost forever in the incandescent essence held prisoner in the Cantartis. He was now little more than a shadow of his former self. A poor reflection, a ghost of the man he used to be, unprotected and vulnerable like a veritable lamb to the slaughter.

Austin Jacobs had no idea how dangerous his situation had become.

Chapter Thirty-two
Rachel Coast

As I sobbed into Julie's arms she held me with a grip of concern and care.

'Rachel, sweetheart, what's wrong?'

'Oh, Julie. I don't know where to start.'

She gripped my head gently in her hands and looked at me. 'Well, it's a good job I do. Let's start by getting you and me a nice hot cup of tea.'

We walked up the stairs and into my bedsit. Julie sat me down and put the kettle on.

For two hours she listened to me intently as I blurted and babbled about everything that had happened over the last few months.

'So what do you think?' I sobbed. 'What do you think I should do?'

She leaned forwards and looked straight at me. 'Rachel ... I don't think you really want to know what I think. I can see how much you love this guy and I don't want to upset you.'

'Julie, you're the only person that I've spoken to about this, I need to know what you make of it, and don't pull any punches.'

She took my hand. 'Ok, Rachel, but only if you're absolutely sure.'

I squeezed her hand and smiled at her reassuringly. 'Yes, I'm absolutely sure.'

'Okay ... well from what you've just told me ... bearing in mind that I don't know this Austin guy at all. This is the way I see it.' She took a deep breath, hesitating. 'I don't want to sound mean, Rachel. Honestly I don't, but this guy sounds like he's left you behind for his career and his new jet set life. I honestly think you should start focusing on letting him go and moving on.'

Hearing her verbal confirmation of my worst fears triggered my defence system. I snapped at her. 'No! Julie, that's not it, you don't understand, you've got it all wrong.'

Already in defensive mode and about to enter offensive mode, I pulled myself back. Knowing deep down that she had my best interests at heart, and seeing the hurt look on her face made me stop myself from possibly saying things I'd regret. I had to quickly remind myself that, after all, it was me who had asked her for her opinion. And I had requested that she unleash it with both barrels blazing.

'I'm sorry, Julie, I didn't mean to snap at you. It's just that it hurts so much. I can't bear to even think for one moment that this may be the truth ... I can't allow myself to believe this. The only thing holding me together right now is the glimmer of hope that this is all a big misunderstanding and that he still loves me.'

'I'm so sorry, Rachel. I don't mean to upset you, it's just that this seems like the most obvious answer to everything that's happened.' She sidled up next to me and put her arm around me. 'I really am sorry Rachel. I haven't seen you since graduation, and we kept missing each other's calls. I honestly thought I'd find you deliriously happy and absurdly hectic. To be honest, I thought that you were too busy to socialise with us mere lowly, unemployed art graduates.'

She smiled at me and pulled a face. I knew she was trying to lighten the mood. She leaned into me and leant her short, spiky red hair against my shoulder.

'Rachel, sweetie, I think the world of you, and I'd hate to see you spiral and fall because of this guy. You can either take my advice or tell me to get lost, but I beg you ... please don't let this get the better of you — it'll drive you mad. Cut it loose, forget about him ... move on. Focus on yourself! Focus on the life and times of the one and only Rachel Elizabeth Coast! You're young and beautiful and you have your whole life ahead of you.'

She made me smile; she sounded just like my mum. She had been a good friend and I knew that everything she said made perfect sense to her, but when it came to the way I felt about Austin, perfect sense didn't enter into the equation. I would have changed time, space and everything in between to change things back to the way they were.

We sat chatting for ages, sipping our tea and listening to the traffic as it rushed by. Julie was such good company; I'd forgotten how good it was to spend real, honest heart to heart time with an old friend like this. Since leaving university and meeting Austin, I had pretty much isolated myself. Blissfully locked away in my "Austin and Rachel bubble" that had burst so dramatically. The sudden impact of its demise had left me distraught and lost, bouncing from one desperate emotion to another, trying to hold on to what was left of my fragile hope.

Julie's unexpected visit tonight was like manna from heaven. The evening passed so quickly I was genuinely saddened when it was time for her to leave. Her company had brought a glimmer of sanity to my world of madness.

Time finally ran out on us. We said our goodbyes and promised to not leave it so long before seeing each other again. The emptiness of my loneliness began to fill me up again. I sank into my three quarter bed and cried myself into a dreamless sleep.

CHAPTER THIRTY-THREE
RACHEL COAST

Friday morning arrived and my alarm rang loudly in my ear. Reluctantly, I opened my eyes one at a time. As I peeked through their half opened state, the first thought of the day flooded my senses.

Austin. It was always Austin; he was always my first thought in the morning and my last thought at night. This morning was a little different. I suddenly remembered my evening with Julie, and for a brief moment ... I actually smiled.

I dragged myself out of bed and dressed for work.

I had four appointments booked in, all with potential clients. These appointments were the result of my mundane and enforced day of phone canvassing. I was determined to sign at least one of them before handing in my resignation and leaving Chandler's for good.

The day passed quickly, one appointment ran into another. Before I knew it I was on my way to the last one. The thought at the foremost of my mind, was, 'as soon as this last meeting is over, it will be time to hand in my letter of resignation.'

My earlier appointments had turned out to be nothing more than absolute wastes of time. My last hope of securing a new client before leaving Chandler's for good rested on this last meeting. I had a good feeling about this one, based on the fact that this last appointment wasn't really a cold call like the others.

In between my canvassing calls I'd answered an incoming call from a new business called Fledglings. They had just moved into the area and wanted a representative to visit them with a view to opening an account.

I wanted to win this one. I had to at least try to hold onto the Rachel Coast that would never throw caution to the wind.

The conscientious Rachel Coast who wanted to obtain good references for whatever future lay ahead of her, no matter what was happening in her personal life.

I must have been about two miles away from Fledglings' offices when my car began to slow down. It began to jerk forwards, clanking, chugging and spluttering, until eventually it ground to a smoke-billowing halt.

Just as it seized to a spectacular stop, my phone started ringing. Struggling out of my smoke billowing car I just about managed to answer the call.

'Hello?' my voice was panicked and rushed.

A soft lilting Irish voice spoke. 'Hello, is that Rachel Coast?'

'Yes,' I replied, my voice now even more breathless and frantic as I backed away from the billowing madness in front of me.

'Hello, this is Mrs Lisa Fitzgerald from Fledglings.'

'Oh, hello.' This was not happening to me. Not today!

'I was just ringing to check that you'd be on time for your three o'clock meeting with Mr Gerald Plume, our managing director.'

My car had just ground to a halt, and smoke was swirling all around it. I really didn't need this. I took a deep breath and began explaining my predicament to the very understanding Mrs Fitzgerald. By now I felt completely out of control and totally unprofessional as I stood staring at my car and making my excuses.

She was extraordinarily calm in her response and seemed to totally disregard my concern. She told me not to worry, that she would send a car along shortly to pick me up. She would arrange for someone to take care of my broken car and everything would be just fine.

In what seemed like seconds, a silver limousine pulled up and a suited chauffeur got out and called out to me. 'Rachel Coast?'

'Yes!'

'Good afternoon, Rachel. I'm Celeste, from Fledglings. I've been sent to pick you up and drive you to our offices.'

He looked towards the ball of smoke that was once my car before opening the door for me.

'Don't worry, Miss Coast. I'm sure it will be fine.'

Shaken and panicked by the turn of events this afternoon had taken, I sat back and stared at Celeste. He was incredibly good-looking, with the most perfect skin. Shiny golden locks of his hair peaked out from under his chauffeur's hat and his piercing ice-blue eyes twinkled in the afternoon sun. His broad, enthusiastic smile reminded me of Austin's.

I sat, perplexed, in the backseat, desperately trying to compose myself. After a while we entered a long tunnel and just the other side stood a tall office block. It soon became apparent that this office block was the building that housed Mr Gerald Plume's office. It was at least ten stories high and it looked like it was made entirely of glass. The bottom half was as black as night. Large, dark windows surrounded its sky-scraping stature. Halfway up the building's shaft, the glass changed. It looked as though there were bright lights shining and bouncing off it at different angles. It was quite brilliant and crystal clear.

Celeste opened my door and walked with me up the steps, through the entrance doors and into the foyer. He directed me towards an elevator and told me to press the button for the eighth floor.

When the doors opened a woman in her mid to late thirties with dark brown hair scraped back into a neat bun stood waiting for me. She wore a long, blue skirt that ended just short of her ankles and her white, long-sleeved blouse was buttoned up to her neck.

'Good afternoon, you must be Rachel Coast.'

'Yes,' I replied.

'I'm Lisa Fitzgerald, Mr Plume's secretary. We spoke on the phone, please take a seat in the waiting area ... there's a cup of tea and some biscuits waiting for you.' She smiled sweetly. 'Thought you might need it after your car ordeal. Sit down and relax for five minutes, dear. Mr Plume won't be long.'

I followed her direction, sat down and poured myself a cup of tea from a large white teapot.

She was right, it was exactly what I needed; a strong cup of sweet tea and a digestive malt biscuit, just the thing to calm my nerves. After about five minutes she returned.

'Mr Plume is ready to see you now.'

She led me down a long, brightly lit corridor and into a large, incredibly bright office.

Mr Gerald Plume was sitting behind a very large, very old, highly polished walnut desk; a huge wooden bookcase filled the entire wall behind him. My eyes glanced quickly at the numerous old books and cameras that adorned it. As I panned the shelves I noticed some odd-looking stones in the spaces between them.

Mr Plume stood up to greet me as I walked in. 'Good afternoon, Miss Coast. Please sit down.' He gestured towards the chair in front of his desk.

'Good afternoon, Mr Plume.' I took my seat. His voice was very soft and soothing, and somehow, instantly made me feel incredibly calm and at ease.

As I sat down I studied him quickly and estimated that he must have been nearing fifty. His hair was white and peppered with what was left of his once golden locks. His moustache was really impressive. It truly was a fantastically well-maintained handlebar moustache; it complemented his three-piece suit perfectly, and with the extra addition of a pocket watch made him look like a man out of his time. His kind face and endearing manner made me warm to him straight away.

'Miss Coast, thank you for coming here today. May I call you Rachel?'

'Yes, of course, Mr Plume. I would like to take this opportunity to thank you for considering Chandler's as your supplier. I'm sure we can offer you the best service and prices.' I was in full saleswoman mode and I smiled as broad a smile as I could muster.

'Rachel,' he said in a slow, soothing tone. 'I'm sure Chandler's service and prices are very competitive, and you, my dear, are a fine ambassador for the company.' He paused and sat down in his large office chair. He picked up some paperwork from his desk before continuing. 'Rachel, my dear, I know you believe that you are here to discuss my company setting up an account with Chandler's ...'

I shifted in my chair and sat bolt upright, ready to launch into saleswoman mode once more. 'Yes, Mr Plume,' I responded confidently.

He put the paperwork down and leant towards me, placing his both hands on the edge of the desk.

'Firstly, Rachel, please allow me to apologise for bringing you here under these false pretences. I don't want to unnerve you, but I'm afraid that this is not why you are here ... far from it, my dear. It is you specifically that I needed to meet with and speak to today.'

Okay, now I was really confused. I shifted awkwardly in my seat.

'Rachel, there is so much that needs to be explained to you, and it is difficult to know where to begin, so let me start by telling you this ... Through no fault of your own, you have become embroiled in an acutely disturbing and destructive situation that desperately needs to be resolved. I need your help if I am to be successful in rectifying it.'

His words, though eloquently put, only added to my confusion, and I was beginning to feel a little troubled by the turn of events this meeting had taken. Nothing he had just said made any sense. What acutely disturbing situation? What the hell was he talking about? Why did he need *me* to emend whatever it was?

Still unable to muster any response whatsoever, I looked towards the door that led out of his office; it was just behind me. My fast-growing instinct was to make a run for it, but I didn't. I remained glued to my seat waiting to hear what this decidedly eccentric man was going to say next.

'Rachel, the reason I believe that your help is essential is because of your connection to Austin Jacobs.'

The sound of Austin's name spilling from Mr Plume's mouth hit me so hard I nearly fell off my chair.

'I'm sorry, Mr Plume, what did you say?'

Had I heard him correctly?

'You are here because of your connection to Austin Jacobs,' he repeated.

My palms began to perspire and my heart began to race. Then my stomach began to churn as his words rang through my ears. The reality that I was no longer connected to Austin battered me.

He looked straight at me. 'Rachel, my dear, I am aware

that Austin's actions have upset and hurt you deeply recently, and I realise that you may not feel inclined to say yes to what I am about to ask of you, but you must believe me when I tell you that Austin is not himself. He is in grave danger. If I didn't think your involvement was crucial, I assure you I would not have brought you here like this.'

His tone was sombre and his words resonated loudly and clearly. The words 'Austin is in grave danger' exploded through my every synapse.

All of the pent up hurt, frustration, loneliness and disappointment that had been haunting me over the last few months suddenly surfaced quite spectacularly as I blasted a verbose amount of babbled questions at him.

It seemed this was my breaking point.

Those early, heady days working side by side with Austin, taking every step with him, seemed such a long time ago. For the last few months I'd had to be content with watching him bask in the spotlight of his success. This had slowly but surely made me feel like I was disappearing into the sidelines of obscurity. In the process of becoming lost in his life, I had also abandoned my own ambitions in favour of helping him realise his. My confidence was also at an all-time low. My buried insecurities had slowly exhumed their fiery little corpses and successfully managed to haunt my every reflection.

The truth of the matter was, that by the time Mr Turnbull had delivered the devastating news that Austin no longer wanted me to handle his business I was already half-broken. Now here I was in this weird guy's office, being told that I was here because Austin was in danger. This was just too much.

I snapped — I just couldn't take anymore. My usual temperate nature had been stretched to the limit and both my heart and my head felt like they were about to explode.

It was at this point that Mr Plume reached across the table and touched my hand gently. A calming wave flooded over me and my temper and frustration were suddenly stilled by both his touch and his voice. 'Rachel, please, I need you to be calm and listen to what I have to say.' I remained quiet and still, and he continued. 'Rachel, I'm sure you are aware that a shooting star is not a star.'

WHAT? He could see my frustration intensifying again.

'I'm sorry, Rachel, that analogy was meant to clarify things, not confuse you. Please allow me to explain. You see, a shooting star is not actually a star at all, and is in essence a misleading and inaccurate term. Shooting stars are in fact meteoroids and meteoric dust burning up as they enter the earth's atmosphere. For the past five months, Austin has been undergoing a transformation. The Austin you know will cease to exist in less than eight weeks, but there is so much more than just his welfare at stake. So, just as a shooting star is not a star, the situation that you and Austin have found yourselves in is very different to what either of you believe it to be.'

At this point I thought that either he had stopped speaking English or I had stopped understanding it. I could feel my anxiety rising.

'Transformation? I'm sorry, Mr Plume, what are you talking about?'

'Rachel, please. As I said, I need you to be calm.' His hand touched mine again and I could feel the stillness overwhelming me. 'Rachel, I'm afraid that at this point in time I am unable to tell you everything. You see, the nature of Austin's transformation and this mission are classified ... you will only be privy to this information if you agree to help. Only then will I be in a position to fully brief you ... what I can tell you is, that if you do agree you will be required to undergo a degree of training. This is a necessary requirement. I must make sure that you are fully prepared to face the formidable challenges we will face. There is a real and distinct possibility that you will be put in the face of clear and mortal danger.'

This utter madness that I had descended into was becoming crazier and more unbelievable by the second.

He stood up and started to fiddle with some of the small stones sitting on the large bookcase, then he turned to face me. 'You have less than twenty-four hours to make your decision, Rachel. Celeste will be outside your home at 9am tomorrow morning.' He paused for a moment then smiled kindly at me. 'I do hope you choose to return here, Austin really needs your help.' He stood up and reached out to shake my hand. 'In case you decide not to, I would like to take this opportunity to say that it's been a pleasure meeting you.'

'Yes! You too, Mr Plume.' I tried to sound sincere in the midst of my bemusement.

'Celeste is downstairs waiting for you. He will drive you back to your car ... Oh, and don't worry, it's back in full working order.'

As I walked out of Gerald Plume's office and headed down the brightly lit corridor my shoulders dropped and a sigh of audible relief escaped me.

What the hell was going on?

Nothing Gerald Plume had said made any sense at all. Surely these were the rants of a madman. Was I really supposed to take what he'd said seriously? Was Austin really in danger? And if he was, what could I do? Of course I loved him, but he'd tossed me to one side so cruelly I didn't know how to feel, what to think or what to do.

Either way, I had less than twenty-four hours to decide.

The sane, logical, pragmatic part of me was already screaming 'no!' in a very loud and self-preserving voice. It willed me to run for my life, take Julie's advice, look after number one, don't even think about going back.

The other side of me was screaming, 'Yes! You have to go back. This insanely weird man obviously knows something about Austin.' Whichever way I looked at it, the sad truth was: Mr Plume was my only connection to him.

As Celeste drove me to my car, the battle with myself began.

Should I dive into Mr Plume's crazy world in pursuit of a guy that, to all intents and purposes, didn't want me in his life anymore, or should I put Austin and the last few months of lonely madness behind me and start a new life?

A life without Austin.

EPILOGUE
CONIK PENSTER DEWE,
TWO DAYS EARLIER

Thick, billowy clouds stretched for miles across the dark, starless sky. The long dark tails of Conik Penster Dewe's coat flapped ferociously around his ankles as the wind swirled around him. Stoically poised on the rooftop of a skyscraper, he stared across the skyline watching the tiny lights of the cars below as they snaked their way around the New York streets.

Awash with hubris and self-satisfaction he stood there in perfect silence observing the wonderful madness that spanned in front of him. How he loved to observe and manipulate the chaos and turbulence that mankind embraced so fervently. How ingratiating it was that almost all of the Crystal Bloodline was safely locked away.

With Rachel finally out of the picture, Austin was finally responding fully to the extraction ritual. His plan was finally reaching fruition. Only two more extractions and the Crystal Bloodline line would be his.

This perfect realisation of contented silence was suddenly disturbed by the rushed and troubled voice of his right hand man, Underling.

'Sire, please forgive me for disturbing you.'

In one swift move Conik Penster Dewe pivoted to face Underling, his coat tails rushing around his ankles as they attempted to keep up with his movement.

'What, Underling?' His voice was sharp and curt.

Underling stood shaking uncontrollably in front of him, his head bent over and his eyes facing the ground. He was about to deliver the most devastating news, and he knew that its content would cause Conik Penster Dewe to explode with unbridled fury as soon as he received it.

His voice was full of fear, dread and trepidation as he forced out the words. 'I'm afraid there has been an unexpected development, sire.'

AUTHOR PROFILE

Sarah Barry Williams was born in Llanelli, South Wales. As a young child, she fell in love with Enid Blyton's books; the adventures contained within them spiked her life with an ongoing appetite for adventure that is still as potent as ever.

As an adult Sarah pursued a musical career that took her to London, Germany and Sicily, as well as a few more exotic places like Upper Cwmtwrch and Merthyr Tydfil.

She has achieved a moderate degree of success with her musical career, which includes being signed to a record label when she lived in London, and appearing and performing on BBC Children in Need in 2001. Six years ago, she enjoyed a small flurry of media attention because of a song she wrote, 'She wants to be Mrs Robert Pattinson', inspired by her then 16 year old daughter's celebrity crush.

She still performs once a week as a professional singer, though the rest of her time is spent writing her Crystal Bloodline series and looking after her much loved cats and growing family.

More information can be found at:

www.sarahbarrywilliams.com   www.thecrystalbloodline.com

Publisher Information

Rowanvale Books provides publishing services to independent authors, writers and poets all over the globe. We deliver a personal, honest and efficient service that allows authors to see their work published, while remaining in control of the process and retaining their creativity. By making publishing services available to authors in a cost-effective and ethical way, we at Rowanvale Books hope to ensure that the local, national and international community benefits from a steady stream of good quality literature.

For more information about us, our authors or our publications, please get in touch.

www.rowanvalebooks.com
info@rowanvalebooks.com